Elizabeth has been writing stories since she was very young. She currently lives outside St. Louis where she continues to write any chance she gets.

To Aunt Debbie. Thank you for showing me the movie and then handing me the book. I write because of you.

Elizabeth Speckman

BEAUTIFUL LIAR

Scary Beautiful 2

AUSTIN MACAULEY PUBLISHERS™
LONDON • CAMBRIDGE • NEW YORK • SHARJAH

Ordering Information
Quantity sales: Special discounts are available on quantity purchases by corporations, associations, and others. For details, contact the publisher at the address below.

Publisher's Cataloging-in-Publication data
Speckman, Elizabeth
Beautiful Liar

ISBN 9781638297888 (Paperback)
ISBN 9781638297895 (Hardback)
ISBN 9781638297901 (ePub e-book)

Library of Congress Control Number: 2022921202

www.austinmacauley.com/us

First Published 2023
Austin Macauley Publishers LLC
40 Wall Street,33rd Floor, Suite 3302
New York, NY 10005
USA

mail-usa@austinmacauley.com
+1 (646) 5125767

Thank you to everyone at Austin Macauley who made this second book possible. Thank you to Mom and Dad for their unwavering support. Thank you to Grandma and Grandpa who supported this endeavor. To everyone out there who bought, read, and reviewed *Scary Beautiful*, thank you so, so much! It means the world to me. Last, thank you Remy, even though you can't read.

Chapter 1
Emily

I stood up and glanced around. I had no idea who was screaming my name or why. I walked in a daze the rest of the way to the school. I got in my car and headed for home. My mind was sort of latched on to one thing at the moment and it wasn't whoever wanted my help.

I parked in front of the house when I saw Toby standing out by the curb looking at the house. I got out and stood beside him.

"Whatcha doing?" I asked.

"Thea dropped me off a few minutes ago," he said softly. "I was headed inside, but the front door is…well…" he nodded his head at the door.

You could tell from where we stood that it had been kicked in. There was a boot print right by the lock. It wasn't wide open, but it was open enough.

"Call Drew…and Mason…and Sam. Just call all the guys actually," I stated.

Toby pulled his cell out of his pocket and called Drew. I started to walk up the concrete path to the front porch.

"Drew, you need to get home now," I heard Toby say. "Someone broke in the house…EMILY! DON'T GO IN THERE!" he yelled. "Yes, she is. Hurry up and bring the rest of them with you. EMILY! STOP!"

I didn't pay any attention to him though. I was walking slowly toward the house. I tried to peer in the windows, but the inside of the house was too dark to make anything out.

I heard tires squeal on the road just as I reached the front door. I pushed it open slowly with my foot and peered into the living room. It was destroyed. The couch had been sliced and the stuffing was everywhere. The coffee table was broken in half and the end tables were thrown over. Vases and other glass objects were shattered on the floor.

I felt a hand on my back, but I didn't react to it. I was too shocked. Drew appeared next to me.

"Oh fuck," he breathed. "KATE?" he yelled and took off down the other side of the stairs to where Kate's room was. I knew the rest of the guys were behind me on the porch. I turned and Mason was standing there. "Can you check upstairs?"

He nodded his head and walked past me and headed up the stairs to check things out. Sam was standing beside me. It was his hand on my back.

Drew appeared a moment later. "She's not here. Her car, purse, and keys are still here. Emily, what the hell happened?"

"I...I don't know. My best guess is Talyrians," I muttered. Maybe Lian and Phoenix kidnapped Kate on their way back to the Talyrian stronghold.

"I think those motherfuckers have taken enough from us," he snapped.

"Drew, we can't stay here," I said trying to get his mind off what happened and on to what we needed to do.

"Where can we go, Em?" he asked as Mason made his way back downstairs.

"The upstairs is untouched," he said. "It seems like they came to get Kate was all."

"Toby, go pack some of your things. Drew, you too," I said.

"Where are we going, Emily?" Drew asked.

"The lake house." Both of my brothers looked at me. I think they actually forgot about it.

Toby went upstairs, but the rest of us remained downstairs. "So, we move to the lake house temporarily, what then?" Drew asked.

"You guys need any help?" Sam asked.

"Not right now, Sam. Thanks though," I said.

"I think we should all head home and let our parents know what's happened," Sam said to the other guys. They told us they were sorry and to call them if we needed anything before leaving.

"Emily?" Drew said.

I held my hand up. "One thing at a time. Let's get packed and moved. We'll go from there. Okay?"

Drew let out a huff and went upstairs. I followed behind him. We spent a good hour packing clothes and other valuables into bags and hauling them out to the three cars. I had most of my clothes in a couple of bags and a whole bag filled with just shoes. The rest was school stuff, bathroom stuff, and a few irreplaceable things from my room; one of those things being the picture Toby painted for me.

An hour and a half after I found Toby standing out front and we all got into a car. I was in the Audi, Toby was in Drew's Mercedes, and Drew was in Kate's BMW. Then we hit the road and drove up to the lake house.

I knew my brothers hadn't been there in a few years. I, on the other hand, visited the place quite regularly. That wasn't something I was planning on sharing with my brothers though.

It took us about fifteen minutes to reach the house. I pulled down the long, concrete driveway and slowly drove back to where the house sat. As soon as I saw the house, I remembered what happened last time I was here. It was that weekend that Lian and I had spent together and it ended with me using pulso morsus on him and burning him. Good times!

Toby got out of the car and stretched his back like we'd been on a four-hour road trip, not a fifteen-minute drive. Drew walked up to the house to unlock it.

"Do you really think Talyrians took Kate?" Toby asked me.

"I honestly have no idea. Like I told Drew we need to deal with one thing at a time. We're gonna stress ourselves out if we do too much at once."

Drew came back and we spent the rest of the evening unloading the cars and getting settled in the lake house…our new home for a while.

Drew was in his room which was right across the hall from mine. "Yo, Em!" he yelled to get my attention. We had the same rule here that we had at home: We're not allowed in each other's rooms.

I went over to the door and leaned against the frame. Drew was holding a pair of black boxers by the waistband.

"So, I know for a fact that these aren't mine. And I'm pretty sure they're not Toby's or yours or Camilla's. I'm trying to figure out who these might belong to. Any ideas?" he asked.

I shrugged my shoulders. I knew exactly who they belonged to.

"Alright, let me ask this differently. How many times have you been up here during this semester?"

"I don't know. Three or four times."

"And how many times have you been alone?"

I pursed my lips together. I didn't really want to answer him. Then again, he wasn't Kate, so he wasn't going to ground me or anything. "Zero."

"So, what have you been doing up here? Or rather *who* have you been doing up here?"

I rolled my eyes, but did not answer either of his questions. "Just ask me what you really want to."

"Do these belong to Killian?"

"Yes."

He shook his head like he was disappointed in me. "You know, little sister, I must say that I am impressed. I kind of wish that I had thought to bring girls up here. You're better at sneaking around than Camilla was."

He tossed the boxers in my direction and I just thought the word *ignis*. I did not say it out loud, I only thought it. But a flame rose up in my palm of the hand I was extending to grab Lian's black boxers. A moment later the incinerated remains of the fabric lay at my feet.

I glanced up at Drew who was standing there with his mouth hanging open. "How…did…just…whoosh. How did you do that with saying anything?" he stated once he finally found his words.

I was momentarily surprised myself. "I don't know. I just thought the word and boom. You know, it's kind of sad that these things don't shock me that much anymore. I'll be shocked for a nanosecond and then carry on with my life. Oh, I can throw massive flames out of my hands, better head home and do my schoolwork. I can use my powers without saying anything, mmm I'm hungry."

Drew was shaking his head and laughing at me. "I know that you have found all these powers and things to be kind of a nuisance, but honestly it's really awesome, Emily. You're kind of badass."

"Kind of? Psh, I am full on badass!" I joked as I walked back in my room leaving the pile of charred boxers in the hallway.

A while later we emerged from our rooms. We quickly discovered that there was no food in the house.

Toby and I were sitting on the counters while Drew paced the length of the kitchen, which wasn't that long.

"Okay, so two of us can run to the store…"

"I think something needs to be done before we do anything else," I said.

"What?" Toby asked.

"Someone needs to call Camilla and let her in about what's going on. We should have called her hours ago actually."

"Okay, who wants to do that?" Drew asked.

"I say that honor should go to the eldest sibling here," Toby said.

"I second that," I agreed.

"Dammit!" Drew snapped. He snatched his phone off the counter and walked outside and down to the docks. I sure as hell didn't want to have to make that phone call.

"Hey, Em?" Toby said.

"Hum?"

"Where's Killian? Why didn't he show up today?"

I glanced up at Toby who was sitting on the counter across from me. "Killian had to leave town."

"But I thought you and him were..."

"We were never technically dating," I finished for him.

"Is he coming back?" he asked.

I swallowed down the lump in my throat. I hadn't had time to process everything. My mind was just trying to think of one thing at a time. "Definitely not," I replied.

Drew came back inside. "Camilla's coming home tomorrow. She took it pretty well. Actually, all of us are taking it rather well. I hope that we aren't immune to tragedy in our family."

"It's not a tragedy," I said. "As far as we know she is still alive."

Drew nodded his head. "Okay, I'm heading to the store. Toby, want to come with?"

"Sure," Toby said hopping off the counter. I watched as my brothers walked out to Drew's car and left.

I sat there in the quiet house and that was when everything came rushing back to me. The noise of my brothers was no longer there to distract me. It felt like my chest had been ripped open and someone was stabbing around with a hot poker.

I didn't know what hurt more: the fact that Lian had lied to me about what he really was or that I had told him so much about us Corlissians.

I was completely at fault in this mess. I trusted him entirely too much and look at where that got me. I could already feel that guard inside me rising back up.

I needed to talk to someone and what really sucked was as of late Lian was the person I went to talk through things. He'd give me his opinion and that was that. But seeing as he was the one that was at the center of this cluster-fucked mess I needed to talk to someone else. Someone who knew part of what was going on. And someone who wouldn't want to kill me for my utter stupidity, at least not immediately.

I picked my phone up that had been sitting next to me and scrolled through my contacts. I hit the name I wanted and waited.

"Sup, babe. Sam called and told me what happened. Are you okay? Do you need anything?"

"I'm fine...sort of. There is something I need, Thea. Can we talk?"

Chapter 2

Lian

I sat in the passenger seat of Phoenix's Honda Accord staring out the side window. She had tried to start a conversation with me at least three times since we left Autumn Falls, but I wasn't in a talkative mood. It sort of felt like my whole world just fell apart and I could do nothing but stand back and watch. The truth was I was the reason it crumbled around me.

I was sort of conflicted at the moment. Part of me was so fucking happy to be going home. I was desperate to see my sister and my mom. It had been three years since I left and I would be lying if I said I didn't miss them. I wasn't exactly thrilled to be seeing my father again though. I know he would drill me with questions about why I left and everywhere I went. I would have some serious explaining to do and it would be mostly lies.

The other part of me was devastated. I had found this other life that I was happy with and it was now gone. That was something I could never go back to. Emily always had this light in her eyes and I watched that light go out. I had said the words that extinguished that light. It killed me to say what I did to her, but I did it to protect her. I knew as those words were leaving my lips that it would be the last time I would see her. I tried to memorize her face and the way she looked a few minutes before with that smile on her face and the way she looked at me like I was her everything, but it was all a lie because all I could see was that hurt in her eyes. Kate was right. I did destroy her. I thought I had destroyed her once, but I was such an asshole I had to do it twice. I knew I never deserved to be with her and in doing what I did proved it.

"Are you ever going to talk to me, Killian?" Phoenix asked.

"No," I muttered.

"I need to know what was going on in that town. They're going to ask me just as many questions as they will you. So, what was going on with you and that girl?"

"Why did you come looking for me?" I asked turning my head to where she sat.

She tightened her hand on the steering wheel. "Like I said, there was a bounty on your head for being a traitor. I knew that you weren't a traitor and there was just a misunderstanding. So, I figured if I found you before the guards you would tell me what was going on and we could clear everything up."

"How long were you there before you approached me?"

"Two days. I saw some guy leaving the school and as he walked to his car, he kept making a flame appear on his palm over and over again. I knew then that you were spying on Corlissians. I didn't know how close you got to them until I saw you leaving the school with that girl and I just knew that she was one of them. Did you actually get her to believe you were in love with her?"

"No. She's too smart to fall for someone like me," I replied looking straight out the front window.

"Okay, you have to tell me what was up with her eyes. I thought the Corlissians had blue warrior eyes. Hers were purple!"

"She told me that it's some sort of genetic mutation. If a mutation of the eyes can happen in humans, it can happen in our races too," I said.

I might have known the truth as to why Emily's eyes were purple and she might have hated me right now, but I was not planning on telling anyone what I really knew about her. She had told me that in confidence. I might have been a Talyrian, but that didn't mean that's where my allegiance lied.

"Hold on a sec, are you in love with her?"

I turned my head to look at her. "Do you think I'm really stupid enough to fall in love with a Corlissian, Phoenix?"

She started laughing. "Yeah, yeah, okay. That was an ignorant question on my part. Just thought I'd ask since you were hanging out with her."

"We were just friends," I muttered.

Phoenix drove through the night and into the morning. She blared all sorts of annoying music to help keep herself awake and we even made a few stops at gas stations to pick up coffee that tasted like it was two years old.

Around mid-day we entered the town of Lake Edisto, the town that I was born and raised. The memories I had in this town rushed back to me. I had suppressed the good ones along with the bad ones for nearly three years. Only in my dreams did they haunt me. And now I was back.

The thing was, Phoenix didn't slow down as she drove through the town. She zipped right down the main road and kept on going. She passed the street she lived on and the long drive where my parents' house was and didn't even bat an eye.

"Umm, where are we going?" I asked.

She glanced at me briefly before turning her attention back to the road. "I keep forgetting you've been gone for a while. A short time after you left Aldous made all the Talyrians who lived around the stronghold move into the fortress. He said it was for the best that we lived as one and not separate from one another like the Corlissians."

"But once we're in the stronghold we won't be able to leave," I protested.

Phoenix glanced at me again. This time there was a wrinkle between her brows. "What would you want to leave for?"

"Fresh air," I lied.

"That's what the roof garden is for. You know the stronghold is big enough that you can go days without seeing another person. I'm sure you'll get used to it. Oh, and if and when you see Aldous, we're all required to call him King now." Phoenix rolled her eyes.

"Do we have to bow and kiss his feet too?"

"None of that. Just address him as King Aldous or Royal Highness."

"Why?"

Phoenix shrugged her shoulders. "I don't know if it was his idea or the idea of the council. I was never told the why's of it, just to do it. I know better than to question the decisions of the higher ups. Unlike you, I am not a child of the King's right-hand man."

"It's not as glorious as it sounds," I replied dryly.

We drove on in silence the rest of the way. I knew that the stronghold wasn't that far from Lake Edisto. We had made trips there numerous times when I was growing up. My father had meetings with the leader and random council meetings. He would take me along with him. I never was allowed to sit in on the meetings, so I spent my time wandering around.

I never wandered too far though. The stronghold was a place that one could easily become lost in. I normally kept to a handful of rooms and sometimes I would get brave enough to explore farther. I just had to make sure I was where my father left me when he was done. There would have been hell to pay if I hadn't been.

Phoenix slowed the car down and finally turned onto a gravel road. It sure didn't look like the entrance to the place where all Talyrians lived. A little ways further down the road was a chain link fence that surrounded the entire compound. A guard standing by the gate came to the driver's window as Phoenix slowed to a stop.

Phoenix rolled the window down and the guard folded his forearms on the door as he peered into the car. "Ms. Phoenix, I see you have returned and with..." he paused and stared at me for a moment. "No way! Killian? Is that you?"

I nodded my head. I wasn't quite sure who he was though. Phoenix glanced at me and furrowed her brows.

"You've been gone three years and you don't remember your best friend. It's Tovan!" she stated with a roll of her eyes.

I looked at the guard again. The smile that was on his face faltered a little. "Hey, don't worry about it. It's been a while," he said.

I felt like an ass though. Tovan was my best friend. We had grown up together and known each other since we were three years old. But he had changed so much in three years. His dark brown hair was longer and he had filled out a lot. He was always the scrawny kid and I was the more muscular one. He was a little taller and he had finally lost those chubby cheeks.

"Yeah, but you don't look anything like I remember. We definitely need to catch up," I said.

His smile grew wider and he nodded his head. "I'll come find you after things quiet down for you," Tovan said. He shoved himself up and waved his hand for Phoenix to go on through.

We drove on down the gravel drive. A high brick wall came into view with two tall guard towers on either side of the drive. The wall, like the fence, encircled the stronghold. I could see guards moving in the towers and farther down the wall. Two massive doors formed a gate at the wall. A few guards were opening for us.

I glanced over at Phoenix after we were passed the second line of defense. "I forgot at how long it takes just to get to the stronghold. No wonder people don't leave, it's too time consuming just to get back in."

"Don't worry, just one more to go through," she murmured with a smile just as we rounded the corner to the third, and final, gate.

This was another brick wall, but was twice as high as the other one. Twin towers rose on both sides and guards moved along the top of the wall. This time we were stopped at the gate. A guard with a gray beard and a scowl on his face came to the window.

He bent over slightly with his hands clasped behind his back. "You are to proceed to the main hall. There will be someone there to direct you where to go after that," he said staring at me. He rose back up. He made some hand motion to one of the towers and one side of the gate started to open.

Phoenix hit the gas and sped through. "That guy gives me the creeps," she stated glancing in the rearview mirror and shuddering.

"Please, that guy just gives off the vibe to keep people scared of him. You don't move up in the ranks by being a nice person," I said.

After a few minutes of driving, the trees parted, the gravel drive turned to paved concrete, and the behemoth Talyrian stronghold stood before us. It was an impressive structure. The thing stretched so far in each direction that it was hard to see where it actually started and ended. The place was massive and Phoenix was right, if you didn't want to see anyone for days this was the place to be. The building was eight stories high and the rooftop supposedly had an entire forest up there. So you could go outside, but still be in the building. It was how the immense structure stayed hidden. It just blended it with the surrounding forest. I had never been to the roof, but since this was now going to be my permanent residence, I was sure I would eventually see it.

Phoenix drove the car around a fountain and brought the car to a stop in front of the main doors. I got out of the car and stared at the fountain. To one side was a man with both his hands raised in the air. Water was spewing out of his hands and hitting another figure in the chest. The other figure was falling backward. His hands were facing up and fire was coming out of his hands. Water and fire were the dominant powers held by the Talyrians and Corlissians. At least the Corlissians didn't flaunt their powers in arrogant forms of art.

Phoenix walked up the steps to the front doors and I dutifully followed behind her. She pushed open the massive front doors. It had been so long since I had been in the stronghold, but as soon as I entered the main foyer, did I immediately remember everything about it I had seen and it hadn't changed at all. The same pictures hung on the walls, the same rug stretched out in front of us, and it was probably the same guard standing at attention to the right of the door.

Phoenix walked down the rug that ran from the front door straight down the long hallway that connected directly to the main hall.

The two glass doors were etched in detail with all sorts of scenes, most of them highly gruesome and showing some Corlissian being defeated and killed. I just couldn't help but chuckle to myself. If they only knew that the most powerful person of our races was unconditionally devoted to the Corlissians, it might change their minds about thinking how powerful the Talyrian race was. Emily could face any person in the stronghold and take them down without breaking a sweat.

Phoenix opened one of the doors and walked into the main hall. I had never been in the main hall before, but I had heard that it was a beautiful room. I wouldn't deny that it wasn't beautiful, but the thing was I had seen the room before. I just hadn't realized it at the time.

Emily and I had been sleeping in my bed and she accidentally used pulso metus on me. I had seen my worst fear. It was my little sister, Zoë, lying in a pool of her own blood in this very room. The room looked exactly like it did in my head: floor to ceiling windows on two walls, dark hardwood floors, thick dark blue drapes, mirrors and paintings on the other two walls.

I stood in the spot where I had seen my sister lying in the blood just staring at the floor. How did my brain conjure up a place that I had never been in absolutely perfect detail? It got me thinking that maybe there was more to Emily's powers than she even knew about. Maybe she was showing you your worst fear and maybe she was also showing you what would happen in the future.

I instinctively reached in my back pocket and pulled my cell phone out. I scrolled through my contacts until Emily's name popped up. I glanced up before hitting send to two sets of eyes on me. I had just straight up forgot where I was. And I was pretty sure that the name currently on my phone was the last person on this planet that wanted to speak to me. In fact, I was positive she was plotting my death at this very moment.

"What are you doing?" Phoenix asked.

I quickly got out of my contacts and slid my phone back in my pocket. Let's call the Corlissian girl you're trying to distance yourself from in the Talyrian stronghold. Smart move, dumbass.

"Nothing. What's up?" I asked nonchalantly.

The guy standing next to Phoenix took a step toward me. His head was shaved completely bald and he stared at me with icy blue eyes. He was far shorter than I was, but taller than Phoenix. He was wearing a charcoal gray suit with light blue pinstripes and a matching light blue oxford underneath. His black shoes were shined to perfection.

"Mr. Marlow, I am going to take Phoenix with me first. She will be questioned about her whereabouts and then I will come get you. Please, do not leave this room."

I nodded my head as the unidentified man led Phoenix out of the room through another door. The door closed behind them and echoed in the near empty room. I walked around the room taking in the pictures on the walls. They were all of dead Talyrians who had perished but not before taking out a bunch of Corlissians. It was sad that these people were being glorified for killing people who were not much different than we were.

I walked across the room to where the windows were. Nothing but woods surrounded the entire stronghold, so there wasn't much to look at. I pulled my phone out and checked the time. Only ten minutes had passed and I had no idea how long they were going to be questioning Phoenix or what exactly they were going to be questioning her about.

I leaned up against the windows and slid down until my butt hit the hardwood floor. I stared at the blank screen of my phone before sliding my finger over the surface to turn it on. I went to where the pictures were.

I didn't realize how many pictures were on the thing. I scrolled through pictures of Thea and Emily huddled together grinning on the beach, of Sam and Tyler playing volleyball, and even of Mason and Emily talking. They both had cuts and bruises on their faces and arms, so I knew it was right after they had fought each other.

And then there was a picture I didn't even know was on my phone. It was the night we were all on the beach, before the Nexes attacked. We had been playing volleyball and Emily and I were on opposing teams. We were standing on either side of the net and she kissed me through the net. I sat there just staring at the two of us. We were so happy in that moment that was forever captured.

The door opened and I quickly shut my phone off and stuck it in my back pocket as I rose from my position on the floor. The bald, well-dressed man stood beside the door and beckoned me to go through it.

I walked down a hallway with a dark red rug running down the length. I followed the man down the hall until he stopped by a door, opened it, and motioned for me to go in.

It was a dark room with no windows and the only light came from a lamp that was sitting on the edge of the mahogany desk that took up most of the room. Two chairs faced the desk and in the chair behind the desk sat a man. He smiled at me and nodded toward one of the chairs.

He had dark brown hair with bits of gray poking through at the temples and dark blue eyes. He had a well-trimmed beard and goatee. Half of his mouth turned up in a smile. He was wearing a blood red oxford with a black vest over it. There were two rings on his fingers. On his left ring finger was a simple silver band and on his right pointer finger was a sliver ring with a fat ruby.

I sat down in the chair closest to the door and waited for him to speak to me. He sat up in his chair and picked up a pen that was lying on top of an open notebook.

"Do you know who I am, Killian?" he asked.

"I'm assuming you are the King," I replied.

"Your assumptions would be correct. But I don't wish to be so formal since we are in private. You may call me Aldous."

I knew exactly what he was doing. He was like those few teachers I had that wanted the students to refer to them by their first names. They wanted us to feel like we were all on the same level, but we knew very well that they determined our fate. Sitting here in the office of the King of the Talyrians was no different. He might have seemed like an easygoing guy on the outside, but on the inside, he was a calculating, intelligent man who was going to dissect everything I said to him and decide whether I was lying or being truthful.

"Now, three years ago you left the safety of your father's house. Why did you leave and where was the first place you went?" Aldous asked.

"My father and I have never had the best of relationships," I began. "He always looked at me like I was a disappointment to him. I wanted for him to be proud of me for once in my life. I thought for months about what I could do, but I hadn't started my training yet. I decided that I could try to find Corlissian bases and maybe integrate in with them and learn something by posing as a human. The first town I came across was North Baybridge."

"And what did you do in North Baybridge?"

"I enrolled in the local school and kept my ears and eyes open."

"And did you find anything of use there?"

"Nothing, sir."

"So you kept up with your schooling along your journey?"

"I did."

"Well, I must commend you on that. How long did you stay in each town?"

"About five months. I always stayed for the duration of one semester."

"And in any of the towns did you hear any whisperings of Corlissians being there?"

"None except for the last town."

Aldous looked down at his notebook and scanned the page with his pen. He tapped a spot. "This Autumn Falls?" he asked.

I nodded my head.

"How close did you get with the Corlissians?"

"I got to be good friends with a few of them."

"How did you find out they were Corlissians?"

"I saw one of them murder a Midnight Brother."

Aldous was scribbling something down on the paper. "What was this Corlissians name?"

Emily about rolled off my tongue, but I had no intention of giving her name up so easily. "Camilla Porter," I blurted out.

Aldous' pen stopped moving and he raised his eyes to me without moving his head. "Camilla Porter?" he repeated. He set his pen down and leaned back in his chair. He narrowed his eyes at me. "Killian, this is only going to work if you are completely honest with me. I know that what you were doing was heroic in your mind and you were only searching for your father's approval. That is fine and I have no issue with it. But there was really no reason for you to leave. I have a spy in about ninety percent of Corlissian bases. They have every name of every Corlissian and every power they possess. I just so happen to have a spy in Autumn Falls. I know the girl you speak of is not Camilla Porter, but her younger sister, Emily Porter. And I know exactly how dangerous and lethal she is."

Chapter 3
Emily

I pulled the Audi into a parking spot at Two Pieces Coffee. Thea's car was already there. She lived a hell of a lot closer than I did though. I walked in the café and I was glad to see that there weren't too many people in there.

Thea was already seated with two coffees in front of her. When I sat down, she slid one of the white mugs toward me. I took a sip and let the warm brew filter down my throat and settle in my stomach.

Thea patiently waited for me to begin. I really didn't want to tell anyone about what happened, but someone did need to know. The lives of my family and friends could very well be at stake.

I sat the mug down and fiddled with the handle. I couldn't even look at Thea. She was going to hate me after I told her. She was going to scream at me for being so stupid and yell at me some more for trusting someone I didn't even know.

"How bad is it?" Thea whispered snapping me out of my thoughts.

I raised my head and looked at her. "As bad as it could possibly be."

"Tell me everything, Em."

A few tears streaked down my cheeks and my bottom lip began to tremble. I took a ragged breath. "Lian's a Talyrian."

I watched as Thea shook her head no and brought her hand up to cover her mouth. "No," she breathed. "No. That is not true. You have somehow been misinformed."

"It's true. When the words were spoken, he did not deny them."

"Emily, I need to know what happened."

I took a deep breath. "This afternoon we were walking back to campus from the coffee shop. We were taking the shortcut through the woods. There was this blonde girl standing by the football field waiting for us. She said that she was Lian's girlfriend, but he said that she wasn't. They talked about what the girl was doing here and she said that she was looking for him because there was a bounty on his head for being a traitor. Anyway, the girl said that they're Talyrian and when I asked if she was lying, he said that she wasn't. There were a few unpleasant things spoken and he left with her."

"I still think there is something we're missing."

"His eyes glowed green, Thea. He is a fucking Talyrian!" I snapped.

"And the girl. She was Talyrian too?"

I nodded my head.

"Okay, Killian is a Talyrian." Thea strummed her black fingernails on the table and let her eyes roam across the café. Her eyes snapped back to me. "How much does he know about us?"

"Well he was there that night at the warehouse. I'm pretty sure he knows who all the Corlissians are and what their powers are. And about me and all my lovely powers, well he knows everything. I stupidly told him every power I have and exactly the kind of damage I can do with them. He knows how powerful I am, Thea."

"Emily, if he tells them what you are, they will come looking for you. And I don't know if they would just kidnap you or if they would kill you on the spot. You need to get your powers under control and learn all you can about them. You need to be able to defend yourself when they come for you."

A few more tears ran down my face and dripped off my chin and onto the tabletop. "I guess I'm still holding on to some hope that he won't tell them anything, but then I see that look he gave me. I swear in those eyes there was no humanity left. It made me sick to think that what I was seeing was his true nature. It made me even sicker to think of everything I had said to him and done with him."

"You cannot let him get to you like this. You think he doesn't know that everything that happened between you will be bouncing around in your head and driving you insane. It's what he wants to happen, so stop thinking about him."

"How can I do that? How am I supposed to just stop thinking about him when we spent so much time together?"

Thea shook her head. "I can't help but feel like this is partly my fault. I am the one who insisted that he try and get back together with you at homecoming. If I would have just left it alone then…"

"The damage was already done, Thea. It's no one's fault but my own. I'm the one who stupidly fell in love with him."

"Sweetie…"

"He knew what he was doing the whole time, didn't he? He came here to get information and I handed it to him on a fucking platter."

"Emily, did you ever think that maybe you two were drawn to one another because you're both Talyrian?"

"I AM NOT A FUCKING TALYRIAN!!!"

"Would you keep your voice down? People are looking!" Thea hissed. "You might not be a full-blooded Talyrian, but there is obviously Talyrian in you if you possess the same powers they have."

I let my head fall forward until it smacked the table. "I'm so done with guys. I'm zero for two. Mason was a cheating bastard and Lian is a lying asshole. I'm just going to focus on me using my powers to their fullest extent and that's it."

Thea made a weird noise that brought my head up. "You think just because you're done with guys that they will be done with you? Oh, and now that Killian isn't going to be your bodyguard anymore, you're totally up for grabs."

"Bodyguard?"

"Yes. He might be a lying asshole, but he was still fit. The guys in this school were scared of him. That's why the only one stupid enough to hit on you was Mason…and Sam…and Tyler, but they're Corlissians so that doesn't count. The human males were scared of him. We're getting off topic now. Is anything being done to find out what happened to Kate?"

"At this point? No. Camilla is coming in. I'm just trying to keep what's left of my family together. We're taking things one step at a time."

"Do you think she's still alive?" Thea asked.

I looked my best friend in the eyes. "I'm clinging to the possibility that she is. Maybe Lian and his bitchy accomplice took her and maybe they're going to use her as ransom or something."

"You mean as in they'll trade Kate for you?"

I shrugged my shoulders. "The possibility has crossed my mind."

"And you would do it, wouldn't you? You would just hand yourself over to the Talyrians."

"I'm not answering that because I don't know what I would do. If I did hand myself over to them, I think if they didn't kill me Kate would."

I let my eyes drift around the café. I watched as the people sat there sipping on coffee and laughing without a single fucking care in the world. They had no idea that my world was just completely obliterated by one person. I envied them for their ignorance. They didn't know that a war had been waging on for hundreds of years all around them. They did not know that both of my parents had been murdered keeping watch over this very town. And they certainly didn't know that my aunt had just been kidnapped by the guy who tore my world to pieces.

"Emily?" I let my eyes glide back to my best friend. "How are you feeling?"

No one had asked me that seemingly simple question in a long time. The last time I remember being asked that was by Mom. She never asked us how we were doing; she always asked how we were feeling.

"I feel...I feel like...I feel that..."

Thea reached her hand across the table placed it on top of mine. "It's okay, sweetie. I understand."

That was the thing. She didn't understand. There was no possible way for her to understand. Thea had dated three guys. The first two ended amicably because they just grew apart. Now she was dating my brother. I, on the other hand, was horrible at picking out decent guys apparently. I couldn't really fault Mason for how he acted. He just fell back into his old habits and it just so happened when we were together. That didn't mean that I wasn't still pissed at him for it. Lian, though, was a completely different beast. I could not believe anything he had ever said to me. For all I knew his real name wasn't Killian. It was probably something far less mysterious...like Bob.

"You're going to have to tell them, Em," Thea stated pulling me from my less than pleasant thoughts.

"I know," I whispered. It was something I utterly dreaded. I really had no idea how the others would react. My brothers would no doubt be the most furious with me.

"I've got your back though."

"Thanks, Thea."

We walked out of the coffee shop together, said our goodbyes, and headed for our respective homes. My cell phone rang when I was halfway to the lake house. Drew's name popped up on the screen.

"Yup?"

"Where are you?" he asked.

"Almost home. I needed to talk to Thea."

"Well, Toby and I are in the middle of cooking dinner and Cami just called and said her train is almost to the station. Can you pick her up?"

"I thought she wasn't coming in until tomorrow?"

"You know how she is," Drew sighed.

"Yeah. I do." I ended the call before he could say anything else.

I pulled a U-y in the middle of the road and headed back to town. Camilla was standing out front of the station with two suitcases on either side of her. Some random guy was hitting on her too.

I got out of the car and walked up to her. "Are you coming or do I need to wait for you to fuck this loser?"

"Emily!" Camilla snapped as the guy shot me a dirty look.

"Please, like you haven't slept with most of the guys in this town. Come on. Drew said dinner's almost done." I grabbed one of her suitcases and pulled it toward the Audi.

I could hear her apologizing to the guy for my behavior before the sound of her other suitcase could be heard dragging along behind her. I shoved the case in the trunk and Camilla slid the other one in beside it without a word. We got in the car and I took off.

"When did you get such a filthy mouth on you?" she asked.

"About the same time I found out I've got more powers than anyone else I know," I replied.

"So," she said turning her body to face me. "Anything new with you and that fine ass boy toy of yours?"

I let my head tilt back until it thumped into the headrest. "Yes, but I'm not talking about it right now."

"Oh, come on! I'm your slutty older sister. You can tell me what kind of freaky shit you two did."

I glanced at her before looking back at the road. "There was no freaky shit and if there was, I certainly would not tell you about it. It's something else that happened and I'm not talking about it yet."

Camilla let out a long sigh as she righted herself in her seat. "You are such a buzz kill, Emily," she grunted.

"Buzzes aren't the only things I kill," I murmured.

"Have there been any more attacks?" Camilla asked as I pulled onto the long drive.

"Since the Brother's crashed homecoming? No."

"Yeah, Drew told me about you roasting all those Brothers. I so wish I could have seen that. You're kind of a badass, sis," Camilla said.

"I have to admit that it was rather enjoyable. Well, until the building decided to explode."

"Your homecoming was a whole lot more entertaining than mine was," Camilla said as I parked beside Drew's Mercedes.

We got out of the car and pulled her suitcases behind us and into the lake house. Drew was just finishing up dinner and Toby was setting the table in the dining room.

"Oh joy, Camilla's here," Toby said sarcastically.

"Geeze, Toby, she just walked in the door. Give her a few minutes to settle in and get on our nerves," Drew chimed in.

"Really? I left college because our aunt has been kidnapped and this is how you're treating me?" she snapped.

I ignored their banter and wheeled Camilla's suitcase to her room. When I got back, they were still bitching at one another.

"I swear I'll leave!"

"Fine by me. Not like you can track her or anything. You're a mediocre pyromancer at best," Drew retorted.

"Mediocre? I am so much better than any of you!"

I was standing behind her and cleared my throat. "You really wanna go there?" I asked.

"Okay, Emily is obviously the best, but I'm better than you two are!"

"This conversation is boring. Is dinner done yet?" I asked Drew.

"Almost," he grunted as he turned back to the stove. Camilla took her other suitcase to her room.

I sat down at the table next to Toby. He leaned toward me. "This is going to suck. You know that right? We could hardly stand one another at home and this place is so much smaller."

"We just have to suck it up. We're here for our own safety. Most of our friends don't even know about this place, so the Talyrians definitely won't know about it."

"Do you really think it was the Talyrians who took her?"

I shrugged my shoulders. "Who else would? Midnight Brother or Nexes would have killed her. And for some reason she was the only target. There are houses full of other Corlissians not but a street over. Yet they weren't touched."

Toby shifted in his seat. "Maybe they were after you," he whispered.

That was the second time someone had said that to me in less than an hour. It didn't feel any better coming from my brother. I didn't want to think that Kate was kidnapped instead of me. Maybe whoever did it thought she was me. If that was the case, then it certainly wasn't Lian and his lackey. If Lian had wanted to kidnap me, he would have. Or maybe he knew better than to touch me and decided to take Kate instead. The possibilities were endless for why she was taken.

I went to my room right after dinner was finished. Toby, Drew, and Camilla were cleaning up the kitchen. Three people in that tiny kitchen was bad enough. And I knew that they would start bickering before long. I just didn't want to hear it anymore. I loved my brothers and sister, but sometimes I just needed to get away from them.

I laid down on my bed with my feet propped up on the headboard. I had two pillows stacked on top of one another at the foot of the bed. I was staring at the wall above my headboard. I had put the painting Toby had done for me up there. That painting had always fascinated me. This time I had started staring at it for its artistic beauty, but that drifted into me staring at it for a completely different reason.

Chapter 4

Lian

I was led out of the King's office by the bald man. I followed behind the man in a daze. I could not believe that the King knew all about Emily. He had a spy in Autumn Falls who was feeding him information about all the Corlissians there. As much as I hated that he knew about them, I was glad that he still bought my lie about my reason for leaving my father's house. I wasn't in any kind of trouble, at least not from Aldous.

The bald man opened the door to the main hall and promptly shut it behind me. Then I stumbled backward when someone threw his or her arms around my neck. It took me a moment to realize what was going on. There was a lot of commotion that I was not expecting.

A woman pulled herself off of me and placed her hands on either side of my face. I was looking into eyes that were the exact shade of green as mine. Her long blonde hair was as neat as I always remembered it to be. There were tears in her eyes.

"Mom?" I croaked.

She nodded her head as those tears fell down her cheeks. Black marks were left by her mascara running.

"I have missed you, my son," she whispered.

The door to the main hall burst open and in ran my sister. "KILLIAN!" she screamed when she saw me. She ran to me and dove into my arms. Mom barely moved out of the way in time. She didn't say anything. She just held onto me tightly for the longest time. Mom stood beside us with her hands cupped around her mouth sobbing.

And then my father walked in the open doors of the hall. He looked the same as I remember, just a little older. His head was shaved. He had started going bald when I was about seven and he just decided to shave it all off. His eyes were the same dark brown that I remembered; the only thing was there were crinkles next to his eyes now. He, like all the higher ranked Talyrians, wore a suit.

He nodded his head slightly at me as he walked over to stand next to Mom. I set my sister down carefully on the hardwood floors.

"I have spoken with His Highness. I do believe we have much to discuss. For now, I will let you get some rest. Your mother and sister can show you to your room. We will talk later," Father said. He gave me the smallest of smiles before turning and walking out of the hall.

I don't know what I was expecting from him. I thought maybe he would be overjoyed at seeing me again, but he didn't seem to be. I was hoping that over the three years I was gone that he might have changed. I did at least get a hint of smile from him, which was more than I ever received from him when I was growing up.

Zoë grabbed me by the arm and tugged me toward the door. Mom fell in behind us. Zoë chatted the whole way. But I wasn't paying her very much attention. I was trying to focus on where we were going. The stronghold was a confusing maze of hallways and rooms. If an enemy did make it through the three layers of outer defense and the guards and managed to make it into the building, they could easily become discombobulated and have no idea where they were. It was why the stronghold was so massive. It was just another layer of defense.

We got into an elevator that was near the middle of the building. Zoë hit the 8 button and leaned back against the wall.

"Top floor?" I asked.

"The higher you rank the higher the floor you live on. So, the King and Queen and all the members of the council live up here," Mom said.

The elevator came to an abrupt halt and I felt my stomach do an unpleasant flop. I figured I would be getting a good leg workout living here, because I was going to be taking the stairs. I wasn't the biggest fan of relying on a cable to hold a metal box up in a concrete shaft.

Zoë stepped off first and made a right down the main hall and then took a left, and then another left, then a final right.

She pointed at a door as she walked past. "This is Dad's room." Then she pointed at a second door. "And Mom's room."

She finally stopped outside of one. "And yours. Mine is right there and the King and Queen's room are down there," she indicated with a nod of her head. She pulled a key from her pocket and placed it in my palm.

I stuck the key in the lock, turned it, and pushed the door open. On the drive up here I expected to be living in the house I grew up in. Not the case. Then when I learned I'd be living in the stronghold I expected all the families to be living in apartment style rooms with the family all living together. Not the case. We all lived in separate rooms, even though the families were all grouped together, it was like living on your own. I was so glad for that. I had gotten used to living on my own in the past three years.

Once again, my expectations were thrown off. I was guessing my room would be similar to that of the apartment I lived in just the day before. A bed, small kitchen, couch, and bathroom.

I opened the door to a large living room. The walls were a light gray. A fireplace was against the far wall. Two large windows were on either side of the fireplace and three dark gray couches surrounded the fireplace. Hanging on the wall next to the door was a flat screen TV. A leather couch was facing it with an end table anchoring each side.

There were two doors on one wall. I walked over and opened the first one. It was a bathroom. An all-white bathroom. It reminded me of the Perlinian Hotel in Autumn Falls, which reminded me of Emily.

I shut that door and opened the other one. Bedroom. A king-sized bed was the centerpiece. The room was painted the same light gray as the living room. A dark gray bedspread covered the bed. Two end tables were on either side of the bed. Against the opposite wall the bed was against was the outer wall that was solid windows. Two thick dark gray curtains were hanging on either end.

I walked to the other side of the bed to where the closet doors were. Inside it was full of clothes. I turned around. Mom was leaning against the doorframe.

"I wasn't sure what you liked, so I just kind of picked a variety of things," she said in answer to my unasked question. "Some of them might not fit. I wasn't sure how much you'd grown." Then she started crying.

I walked over to her and wrapped an arm around her shoulders and pulled her to me. "I'm sorry, Mom," I whispered.

"It's not that, Killian." She sniffed. "I'm not upset that you left. There were several explanations for why you did, but I knew the real reason. I'm just upset that I missed out on three years of your life. I didn't know if you were okay, if you were even alive then. And now I see the man you turned into."

"Mom…"

"It's okay. You're here now and that's all that matters to me." She patted my chest and walked into the living room where Zoë was sitting on the leather couch flipping through channels. "Let's go so your brother can get some rest," she said to Zoë. "Your father will send for you when he's ready." With that they exited my room and left me alone.

I went back into my room and dropped face first onto the king-sized bed. I was asleep before I even hit the bed.

I woke up to see that it was dark outside. I crawled off the bed and went to my closet to pick out some clothes before hitting the shower. Luckily, the jeans and button down I chose fit me just fine.

I walked out of my room, locking it behind me, and went down to my sister's room. She opened the door with a smile on her face.

"What's up?"

"Where do we get food from?" I asked.

Zoë shook her head with a smile. "Give me a sec," she said stepping back into her room. She came back a moment later with a different shirt and shoes on. She shut and locked her door and we headed down the hallway.

"Am I going to be your human map for a while around here?" she asked.

"Nah, once I know where my room is and the food is, I'll be fine. I'll explore later and I'm sure I'll get lost several hundred times, but that's how you get to know a place."

"Well, just so you know you can order food from the kitchens and have it brought up to your room. That's what all the higher ups do. But there is a big dining hall that everyone else usually eats in. Or if you want you can come down and get your food and take it to your room. It's pretty much a do-whatever-you-want with the food around here."

"Good to know. So, how have you been?" I asked.

Zoë looked up at me with her big brown eyes. "You want a recap on the past three years? That's going to take a while. I'm a teenager after all, so all things seem important to us."

"I want to hear it all."

Zoë stopped in front of the elevator. "Okay, but you have to tell me everything you did too. It's only fair, Killian!"

"Deal," I muttered. Apparently, my little sister learned about negotiation while I was away.

We got on the elevator and Zoë hit the 3 button. I figured the dining area would be on the bottom floor.

Zoë looked up at me. "Guards live on the bottom two floors, then the dining area and training centers and all that are on the third floor. Fourth, fifth, sixth, and seventh floors are 'normal' Talyrians, and the eighth floors is the council members and the King and Queen. Got it?"

"I didn't even ask."

"No, but I knew you wanted to."

The doors opened and on the other side stood our father. "There you two are," he said with a smile.

"Hey, Dad!" Zoë said stepping off the elevator. "We're going to get dinner."

"Killian, after dinner would you please come to my office?"

"Ugh, sure." It was weird that my father was being nice. He was actually asking me to do something rather than telling me.

"Meet me in front of the main hall since I'm sure you don't know where my office is yet." Ahh, there was that condescending tone I had missed so much!

"All right," I replied as he walked away.

Zoë tugged on my arm to get me moving in the opposite direction. "He got better after you left," she said. "At first, he was worse. He was constantly yelling about everything. Any little thing would set him off. I mean the King's right-hand man's only son ran away and had a kill on sight bounty on his head. I don't know if he was mad about you being a traitor or that your death was imminent. I think one day it dawned on him why you did run away. He just completely eased up. He's been pretty chill since then."

"Well, I hope he doesn't fall back into his old ways now that I'm back," I replied.

"Time will only tell," Zoë said as she walked through two wooden doors that were propped open.

I came to an abrupt stop in the doorway. This room was nearly identical to the room the Corlissians had fought the Midnight Brothers in after homecoming. It was bigger was the only difference. The front part of the room held about eight long wooden tables that were nearly all filled with people eating. There were two pillars toward the back of the room and the kitchen was beyond that. I could see Emily doing a front flip onto one of those tables and running down the length before decapitating a Brother with her daggers.

Zoë nudged my side and snapped me out of it. If I would have stared any longer, I would have seen Emily using her pyromancy like no one else could.

"You know you were weird before you left, but it's gotten worse," Zoë joked as she guided me toward the line where we got our food. It was set up cafeteria style. Get your tray, your plate, and then move on down the line.

We got our food and found a few empty spots to sit. Zoë talked the whole time about what she had been up to since I had left. I listened to everything she said too. I wasn't sure how she managed to eat while talking.

She got through the first year of me being gone when we finished eating. "So when did you move in here?" I asked.

"Almost a year to the day that you left. The King didn't want anyone else sneaking off. Mom took it the worst. She told me that it felt like we were being imprisoned because of you leaving. I think she's gotten used to it now."

"And how old are you now?"

Zoë laughed. "You don't know my age?" She shook her head in mock disappointment. "I'm fourteen."

"I think you're the most mature fourteen-year-old I've ever met."

"You left when you were fifteen."

"Yeah, but that doesn't mean I was mature," I retorted.

Zoë let out a sigh. "Go meet with Dad. I'll come by your room and you can tell me about your first year away. Okay?"

I nodded my head as she got on the elevator. I followed the sign that read "Stairs." I did not want to get on that rickety thing again if I didn't have too.

I walked down the three flights of stairs to the main floor. It took me some time, but I finally managed to find the etched doors of the main hall. I leaned against the wall and waited for my father.

A few minutes later he walked around the corner. "Good, you're here. Come with me," he said.

I shoved off the wall and followed him, not through the main hall, but around it. He took me down the same hall I was in yesterday where I met with the King. Father's office was two doors down from Aldous's.

I sat down in the solitary chair across from his desk as he took the red leather one behind it. He placed his forearms on the desk and leaned forward.

"According to what King Aldous has told me I am to believe the story you told him about why you left Lake Edisto."

"But you don't."

He licked his lips. "I do as my King tells me, Killian. I knew why you left. It took me a while, but it finally clicked. If I was hard on you growing up, it was for your own good. When I die, my position in the Talyrian race will be yours by birthright. I was preparing you for the duty that will eventually come in your life. You will be the right-hand man of the King."

"Why couldn't you have just told me this when I was younger? The whole time I thought you were punishing me. I left because I was scared of you and I couldn't bear to see those disapproving looks you would always give me. I was a kid and you were treating me like an adult. What was I supposed to do?" I said.

He let out a long exhale. "You did the right thing. It made me realize where I went wrong with you and I promised that I would not make the same mistakes with Zoë. But don't you think for a second that I did not worry about you every single day, Killian. I may not have showed it when you were growing up, but I do love you. I thought I had driven my own son to his death. You don't know what that does to someone. I'm glad you're back now."

I nodded my head because I didn't know what to say to that.

"Aldous told me that you were living at a Corlissian base and had become friends with some of them. Is that true?" he asked.

"Yeah. They were no different than we are. They live as normal a life as possible on the outside. The humans they live amongst have no idea that they live next door to some of the most brutal killing machines in the world."

"Ahh, therein lies the difference. We do not live among humans anymore. Talyrians make sure no humans can ever find out what we are. The Corlissians are almost asking to be found out. Aldous also told me that you became very close with a girl who is…shall we say…different from her peers."

That had me shifting nervously in my seat. I didn't know exactly how much the King knew about Emily. I hadn't told him much about her. I played stupid on that part. If the King wanted to know more about her, he wasn't going to find out from me.

"She was very gifted with a dagger in her hand," I replied.

"The King says she has more than one power."

"She never told me about that if she did. She was a Corlissian and in her eyes I was a human. She wasn't about to share any of that with me. I saw her use a dagger and that was it," I lied.

"We heard there was a Midnight Brother raid on what was homecoming night. Were you there for that?"

"I was. I saw the hooded figures enter the building and I left in a rush with the rest of the humans. I don't know where the Corlissians were at that time." Another lie. I remembered that night with perfect clarity. Emily had given me a second chance with her. Then they went to the abandoned warehouse.

"I was told that somehow ten Corlissian teenagers took out a whole regiment of Brothers that night. No one knows exactly how they managed to do that. The King's spy has yet to find that information out."

"I wish I could be of more use, but I really don't know anything. I couldn't even tell you what powers they had. They didn't share any of that information with me."

"Do you think if you had stayed with them longer you may have found out more information?" Father asked.

I shrugged my shoulders. "Probably. They were getting friendlier with me and maybe one of them might have told me what they were and what powers they possessed."

"Is there any way you could go back and integrate in with them?"

I wasn't expecting him to ask me that of all things. I shook my head no. "There was a confrontation in which the girl who apparently has more than one power found out I was Talyrian. Phoenix told her and blew everything. I had to leave at that point."

"That is a shame. I would like to be the one to give this information to His Highness. Oh well. Now, to another matter. You will start your training tomorrow morning. You will start off with weapons training and then you will begin using your aquamancy. I have a feeling that you will be one of the greatest aquamancers of the Talyrians. Your mother and I are both gifted aquamancers and Zoë is catching on very well. I cannot wait to see what you can do!"

I had completely forgot about training. I had skipped town before I even began training. That was probably why I was so fascinated watching Emily and the other Corlissians. The Corlissians started training much earlier than Talyrians. We all accessed our powers around fourteen and that was the same time Talyrians started using weapons. Corlissians were practically born with a dagger in their hands. They were already skilled in wielding nearly every weapon before we even picked one up.

I left Fathers' office and made my way back up to the eighth floor. Those stairs were murder on the legs. When I rounded the hallway where my room was, I saw Zoë leaning against the wall next to my door.

"Are you that excited to hear about my first year away?" I asked.

She nodded her head enthusiastically. I unlocked my door and followed her inside my room.

We stayed up until the early morning hours. She just listened to me ramble on about the places I went. I made it halfway through my second year away before we both decided to go to bed. I needed the sleep since I was going to start training tomorrow. I had a feeling I was going to be exhausted.

Chapter 5
Emily

I woke up to someone pounding on my door. I slithered out of my bed and yanked the door open. Drew was standing on the other side.

"Why aren't you dressed yet? We needed to leave five minutes ago," he thundered at me.

I shut the door in his face and went to my closet. I put on black tights and a long light gray sweater with black heels. I pulled my hair up into a bun and grabbed my bag before heading out the door.

My brothers were waiting for me in Drew's Mercedes. I dropped in the passenger seat and Drew took off without a word.

When we were on the road, Toby leaned forward between the two front seats. "So what is Cami going to do today?" he asked.

"She said she's going to visit the Corlissians and let them know what's going on. Hopefully some of them will offer assistance in tracking Kate," Drew replied.

"How do they plan on tracking her?" I asked.

Drew glanced over at me. He shrugged his shoulders. "I suppose they'll go to the house and see if there are any clues. The only Corlissian tracker I know of in Autumn Falls is Mr. Monroe."

Toby flopped back against the seat. "Ugh, Mason's dad," he groaned. "That's all we need is Bridgette and Mason knowing our family business."

"Toby, the more Corlissians who know what's going on the better chance we have of finding Kate," Drew stated.

Drew pulled into the parking lot and we all got out of the car. My brothers headed into the building, but I leaned against the side of the car and pulled my cell phone out. I scrolled through my contacts and hit send. The phone stopped ringing and I knew he picked up.

"I know you're there and believe me you are the last person I want to talk to. Will you answer me one question as truthfully as you possibly can?"

"Maybe."

"Did you kidnap Kate?" I asked.

I heard him make a snorting sound. "What are you going to do if I did? Are you coming up here to get her back? Are you going to break into the stronghold?"

"Thanks for nothing, asshole." I pulled the phone away from my ear and could hear him on the other end saying, "Emily, wait…" but I ended the call. I didn't want to hear anymore. There is nothing on earth he could say to me to make me forget what he said Friday.

I guess I was just hoping that it was all an act and that he could tell me that he had nothing to do with why Kate was missing. Obviously, it wasn't an act and he really was a Talyrian douchebag.

I headed into the school as the first bell rang. Thea was just closing her locker when I walked up. She leaned against hers as I threw my bag in and pulled a notebook out.

"So, did you tell your brothers yet?" she asked.

"No. I think I'm just going to tell everyone today at practice. That way they can get all their yelling at me done at once."

"If I were you, I think I would leave out some things. Like don't tell them that he knows all about what powers you have. The less they think he knows the better."

I shut my locker and we headed down the hall together. "Sounds like a plan to me," I muttered.

"Just remember I got your back," Thea said as we split up and went to our homerooms. I was glad that I had at least one person on my side. Shit was going to hit the fan during practice today. I was not looking forward to telling the Corlissians anything.

I sat down in homeroom and stared blankly at the empty chair in front of me. The bell rang and Watkins started taking attendance.

"Emily, do you know where Killian is?" Watkins asked.

I shook my head no. The truth would have been a hard one for him to swallow. Why yes, I do happen to know where Killian is. You see, he is of a race that has been in an ongoing war with my race. He got information out of me that I thought I was telling to some lowly human. Just this past Friday it was revealed that he is my enemy and he fled to the north where they all live. Oh, and there is a good chance that he kidnapped my aunt before leaving town with his tail between his legs. Any other questions?

"Emily?"

"No, I don't know where he is. I'm not his fucking keeper," I snapped.

Watkins let out a sigh. "Very well."

The rest of the school day wore on in its normal fashion. I took notes and dodged questions about the whereabouts of Lian. Before the last bell rang, I was pretty sure every student knew that he was gone for good. I didn't tell them; I think they just pieced it together on their own.

Thea and I met at our lockers and headed down to the training center together. She looped her arm through mine as we walked down the hallway where the men's and women's changing rooms used to be.

The others were already sitting around on the blue mat. Hotch was leaning against one of the tables that held some of the weapons we used.

"Emily, I need to talk with you after practice," Hotch said.

"Well, I need to talk with everyone now," I said. Thea let go of my arm and sat down behind everyone else. I stood next to Hotch and took a deep breath. "I know that you're all going to hate me, but you have a right to know what has happened. I found out on Friday that Lian is a Talyrian. He is, I guess, back at the stronghold by now."

It was eerily quiet in the massive room. I was expecting yelling at this point, but they were all just staring at me with their mouths hanging open. I think they were waiting for me to tell them that it was all just a joke.

"Are you fucking serious?" Sam blurted out.

I nodded my head.

"That dickhead!" Tyler yelled.

"I say we head on up to the lovely stronghold and murder that motherfucker!" Micah chimed in.

"No. We are Corlissians. We don't murder people who have betrayed us. We torture the fuck out of them!" Evan stated.

"I say we just chop off that vital organ that all men are attached to. That would teach him not to mess with Corlissians," Bridgette threw in.

While everyone was yelling out unpleasant things to do to Lian Hotch leaned close to me. "How much does he know about us?"

"Not much. He saw me use a dagger on that Midnight Brother mod. I don't think he bought the lie I told him. He knew all along there was something different about us. Friday everything came out. He knew that we were Corlissians and he told me he was Talyrian. I don't know what he found out while he was here."

"Hopefully, he didn't find out anything. It's bad enough if he even knows who in this town is Corlissian. He could take that information back and tell their leader. We need to be on our guard. We could be in for an increase in raids by Brother, Nexes, and Talyrians. Has there been any word about Kate's disappearance?"

"We're assuming she was kidnapped by Talyrians. Camilla is trying to get some of the others to help her. I guess they're going to go by the house and see if they can find anything."

"I'm kind of surprised they took Kate," Hotch said.

"Why does that surprise you?"

"Because it wasn't you. You're the powerful one. You're more powerful than any Corlissian or Talyrian. That makes you one hell of an asset to whomever you side with."

I was getting tired to people telling me that I was the one who should have been kidnapped. Because you have all these amazing powers the Talyrians should be salivating to get their sticky paws on you. Yeah, lovely to hear!

"Is there a doubt in your mind that I would for some reason side with the Talyrians?" I asked.

"I have heard that their leader is very persuasive. He can talk you into doing whatever he wants."

"I already fell for one Talyrian asshat. I'm not about to make that mistake a second time," I muttered.

"…and then we need to attach a rope to both his legs and drag him behind a horse. I heard about it in history. I believed they called it drawing and quartering. We could totally do that!" Evan stated.

"Evan, this is not the Middle Ages. We may not be above torturing our enemies, but we do have better methods. We do not drag our captors around town and then chop them up into four pieces," Hotch said.

"Besides who do we know that owns a horse?" Tyler asked.

"You and Ev own a Mustang Cobra. That counts as a horse, right?" Micah said with a laugh.

"Yeah, and they're gonna let us drag some dude down the road with their car. I don't think so," Drew replied dryly. Ty and Evan weren't protesting it though.

"All right! That's enough!" Hotch hollered. "I want to see you on your feet and using those powers you were all blessed with."

"I was wondering if you have some books on pulso metus and pulso morsus I could read?" I asked Hotch.

"Of course. You're not going to pull another *incendia* stunt, are you?"

"What kind of stunt can I pull with those two powers? They're pretty straight forward," I replied. Which was a damn, dirty lie. Of course I was planning on using them in a more dangerous manner that would cause my trainer to freak out when and if he found out.

I started to walk over to where Sam and Micah were practicing. I enjoyed being around them more so than the pyromancers at practice. But Mason intercepted me on my way.

"Hey!" Mason said.

"Ugh, hi."

"Is there any way you could show me how to do that…" he held his hands out in front of him and made a whooshing noise. "…thing you did at homecoming?" he asked.

"No. There is no way I am showing you that. It was stupid of me to do it."

"Stupid maybe, but you saved our asses, Em."

"MASON!" Hotch yelled. "Why do I not see flames shooting out of your hands?"

Mason rolled his eyes and jogged back over to where the pyromancers were practicing and I finally made it to where Micah and Sam were waiting.

Sam put his arm around me and pulled me to his side. "How you doing, baby girl?" he asked.

"Spectacular!"

Sam looked down at me and gave me a look that said he knew I was lying. Sam had been my friend since kindergarten, so he knew me quite well.

"Okay, that's the beautiful lie you tell everyone else, but how are you really doing?" he asked again.

I smiled up at him. "I feel like shit," I whispered.

He let out a sigh. "What are you doing tonight?" he asked.

"Going home."

"Nope. I'm taking you out to dinner. I'll take you home afterward," he said. I had no choice in the matter.

As was usual with practice anymore, everyone else started to trickle out and I was the last one still practicing. The only difference tonight was Sam was leaning against one of the weapons tables next to Hotch watching me. Good thing I wasn't self-conscience.

"All right, let's call it quits," Hotch said.

I turned around with a flame in each palm. I let the flames lick up my arms and twirl around my fingers as I walked over to the two of them.

"Emily, your powers are not play things," Hotch scolded me.

I looked up at him. "I know they're not. Theses flames are like my babies."

Hotch shook his head. I whispered "*Intereo*" and the flames instantly went out.

"Get out of here you two."

Sam shoved off the table and grabbed my hand as he passed me. He spun me around and pulled me along behind him.

"You in a hurry or something?"

"Nope, I just hate being in the center longer than I have to be," Sam said as we walked down the hall.

"Welcome to my world," I muttered. I hated being there and I always had to stay late. It royally sucked.

We headed over to the only car in the parking lot; Sam's black Audi S5 with black rims and windows so dark that you couldn't see in the car. Everything on that car was black. Sam didn't look like the kind of guy who drove a car that looked like that. He had dark brown dreads that stopped right above his shoulder blades. His bottom lip and tongue were both pierced and he had plugs in his ears. Not to mention the tattoos that were on both his shoulders and biceps.

Sam opened the passenger door for me and I dropped in the seat. He got behind the wheel. "Where you wanna eat?" he asked.

I shrugged my shoulders. "You're treating me, so I don't care."

Sam smiled. "Italian it is."

He drove across town to the only Italian restaurant. It was called Mama Gia's after the little old lady who opened the place. She was ninety-seven and still working in the kitchen. As usual, it was packed on a Monday night. I was pretty sure their parking lot was full every night of the week.

Sam walked in the front door like he owned the damn place. The host was a guy who was a year below us in school. And like everyone else in school he knew Sam. Sam was liked by everyone at school. No one ever had a bad thing to say about him.

"Hey, Sam, Emily," the guy said.

"Jack," Sam said with a nod of his head.

"Just the two of you," Jack said tilting his head to the side to see if anyone else was coming in behind us.

"Yup," Sam replied.

"A table just opened. Come with me," he said grabbing two menus and leading us toward the back of the restaurant. "Your waiter will be with you shortly," he added as we sat down.

"Thanks, man," Sam stated. He leaned back in his chair and eyed me. He didn't open his menu or anything, just stared at me.

"What?"

Sam shook his head. "I just cannot believe that Killian is a Talyrian," he said.

"Believe it. I heard it from his own mouth. Or do you want to drive up to the stronghold and hear him say it himself?"

"I'll pass on that. Still, he gave no hint that he was the enemy. He hung out with us nearly every day, Em. How does someone do that? He never used a power or anything."

"I honestly don't think he has accessed his power yet," I replied.

"I wonder what his power is."

"I don't care. I don't plan on ever seeing that lying sack of shit again."

"He fooled us all, Em. No one blames you. None of us would have dreamed he was a Talyrian. The only person out of us who truly hated him was Mason and that was only because Killian was with you."

Someone stopped beside our table. I didn't immediately look up because I assumed it was our waiter.

"Oh. My. God. First Mason, then Killian, now Sam. How do you get all these guys wrapped around your fingers?"

I glanced up to see not a waiter, but Heather Weston standing there glaring down at me. I had no idea what her problem was.

I leaned forward and placed my elbows on the table. "I fuck them," I said. I glanced at Sam and he was trying to keep the smile off his face, but was failing miserably.

Heather's mouth popped open at how blatant and vulgar I was. She regained her composure. "You are such a slut, Emily!"

I looked over at Sam who was just leaning back watching the show with a grin on his face. "Did this cow just call me a slut?"

Sam licked his lips. "I do believe she did. And if I were her, I would back off now. Don't piss her off, Heather," Sam warned.

"Your whole family are sluts. That's probably what happened to your mom. Was she murdered for sleeping around?"

Sam stood up so fast that his chair flew back and fell on the floor. "Now you're pissing me off," Sam said deeply. Sam towered over Heather. He glared down at her. "I highly suggest you get the fuck out of our faces before you wind up in a dumpster with your throat slit."

Heather blanched. Sam never talked to people like that…ever. Sam was the laid-back guy everyone just adored. Now he was showing that side of him that was a trained killer. Everyone has a breaking point and Heather had breached his.

She still didn't move. I think she was paralyzed by shock. "GO!" Sam yelled. She finally flinched and went back to wherever she came from.

Everyone in the restaurant was staring at us. Sam casually picked his chair up and sat down like he didn't just snap on Heather.

"You okay?" he asked.

I nodded my head then I busted up laughing. Sam was staring at me like I had lost my damn mind. Then he must have finally seen the humor in it. I had never heard Sam yell at anyone before. I just found it hilarious. The bonus was that the first person he ever snapped on was some girl who hated me for reasons I wasn't even sure of.

Chapter 6

Lian

I woke up to the sun's light hitting me in the face. I had forgotten to close my curtains last night before bed and was seriously regretting that memory lapse. It didn't even matter that my windows faced north. I was still getting the full light right in my tired eyes. Awesome!

I threw my covers back and got myself dressed for the day. I made my way downstairs and found the cafeteria with ease. I ate a little for breakfast. I was kind of nervous about starting my training. I was worried that I would be horrible at it and that would just give my father cause to be disappointed in me again.

I was walking down the hall from the cafeteria to the training centers when my cell phone rang. I wasn't even sure why I was still carrying it around. I suppose it was because that little piece of plastic was the only thing I had left Autumn Falls with.

I pulled my cell out of my back pocket and saw the name on the screen. A big ass smile spread onto my face. Emily was actually calling me. Then I remembered that it was Emily and what she was going to say probably wasn't going to be pleasant.

I slid my finger across the screen and held the phone up to my ear. I didn't know what to say and "hello" seemed kind of stupid at this time. I could already hear how moronic I would sound. "Hello. How's it going? Oh, yeah sorry about being a Talyrian and saying the things I did to you right before I left with my ex-girlfriend. So, how've you been?"

I didn't have to think of anything to say because Emily spoke when I was silent for so long.

"I know you're there and believe me you are the last person I want to talk to. Will you answer me one question as truthfully as you possibly can?"

I could tell in her voice that she was absolutely sickened to be talking to me and it was even worse to be asking me a question.

"Maybe," I replied.

"Did you kidnap Kate?" she asked.

I didn't mean to, but I made a snort. I thought she was joking for a second, but then I remembered she hated me and wouldn't be calling me asking that question for no reason. And then I remembered why I said the things I did to her. I wanted her to hate me. I wanted her to forget about me. It was the best thing for both of us.

"What are you going to do if I did? Are you coming up here to get her back? Are you going to break into the stronghold?"

"Thanks for nothing, asshole," she breathed.

It sounded like she was putting all her hope into getting an honest answer from me. She sounded defeated. It was very un-Emily like and it killed me to hear her in that way. Emily was the strongest girl I knew and she was a fighter. This Emily sounded broken and I knew I was the cause of that.

"Emily, wait…" I started but she hung up. I can't say I blamed her. She probably assumed I was going to taunt her more. Even if I would have told her that I had nothing to do with Kate missing I doubt she would have believed me.

I pulled the phone away from my ear and watched the screen go black. I was kind of curious though as to who actually did kidnap Kate. Phoenix and I had left Autumn Falls immediately after everything blew up with Emily. I knew Emily was the vindictive sort and I didn't want to give her the chance to kill the both of us.

I slipped my cell back in my pocket and continued on toward the west side of the third floor where the training centers were. I'm not sure what I was expecting when I arrived at the training center. I had never seen the training center the Corlissians used. I knew it was in the school, but I never actively searched it out. I kind of wondered if it was anything remotely close to what I was looking at.

A glass wall separated the training wing from the rest of the third floor. I walked through the glass door to where a waiting room was. Chairs were set around the room and people were sitting there staring at the new guy who walked in. There was a woman sitting behind the desk. She pointed at the clipboard on the corner of her desk without even looking up. I signed my name and took a seat.

Just behind the woman at the desk was a second glass wall. It looked like a typical gym set up. There were all the machines and weights one would find in a regular gym. And there was a Talyrian using every machine in the massive room. I was guessing that was why there were people sitting around waiting.

The woman at the desk grabbed the clipboard and turned it to face her. Her head shot up and her eyes locked with mine.

"You're Killian Marlow?" she asked. I nodded my head. She stood up. "Come with me," she ordered.

Everyone who had been staring at the people in the gym using the machines like they wished to be doing now turned their eyes toward me for a second time. I stood up and followed the woman through the door that led down a hall that ran next to the gym.

She walked through a second door. The room looked like a dance studio. There were mirrors on three of the walls. The fourth wall looked like the side of a ship. It was metal with rivets running up the side. Even the door that passed into whatever was hiding behind the metal wall was airtight. The woman had to crank the handle and shove all her weight against it just to open the door.

I was a little hesitant to follow her. A myriad of images passed through my head of what was behind that wall. Maybe they had a giant or some super weapon for wiping out the Corlissians. Maybe they had bred a half Talyrian half Corlissian army that had numerous powers like Emily. They had to be hiding something deadly with a wall like that.

The woman passed through the door, but I paused. She stopped and turned around.

"Are you coming, high-born?" she asked in a flirty tone.

"What's the purpose of this wall? What are they afraid will get out?" I asked.

Her face fell. "Are you serious? What's the dominant power that Talyrians possess? Aquamancy. This whole part of the wing is made of these walls even the floors and ceilings. It's watertight. The only thing we're keeping in is a lot of water."

I wanted to smack myself upside the head. I just had a complete moment of stupid. I suppose I'd been hanging out with Corlissians for so long that I got used to the dominant power being fire, not water.

I followed the woman through the door and she quickly shut and locked it behind me. In front of us was a long hall with the same type of doors running along it. She began walking and I once again blindly followed this woman.

She walked almost to the end of the hall where she stopped. She looked puzzled for a moment, like she wasn't sure if this was the correct door or not. She glanced at another door, looked at me, and shrugged her shoulders. Great secretary!

She knocked twice on the door, paused, and knocked three times. She pursed her lips and waited. Then I heard someone inside turning the handle. The door shoved open a moment later. Those doors must have been beasts to open.

Standing inside the room was the bald-headed man who I thought was the King's personal assistant. He must have been an everything man around the palace. He was not in his suit, like I had seen him in the day before, but in shorts and a T-shirt.

"Come, Master Killian. It is time to begin your training," he stated.

I walked through the door and as soon as I was on the other side it was slammed shut behind me. I could hear the handle being turned outside.

"You guys are pretty anal about these doors," I muttered.

The man cleared his throat. "That is because a lot of damage can be done to this place with the amount of water that the aquamancers produced during training. Now that it is the permanent residence of his Majesty and all the Talyrians we go to great lengths to protect its structural integrity."

"Got it. So, what's your name?"

"Corbin. Now that we're done with the small talk we can begin. From what I understand you have had no training. Is this correct?" he asked.

I nodded my head.

"That bit of wanderlust tugged you away before you even held a dagger in your hands."

There was no question, just a factual statement. I nodded my head that he was correct...sort of. It wasn't wanderlust that took me away. It was abhorrence for my father, plain and simple.

"All right, so we will start off with finding out what your power is. After that I will teach you the basics of using weapons. That will probably be enough for one day."

"Okay, how do we find out what my power is?" I had to admit I was kind of excited about it. Everyone I knew had some kind of power or in Emily's case a lot of powers.

Corbin paced the length of the room. "Your mother is an aquamancer?"

"Yes."

"And your father is too?"

"Yes."

"And I know your sister is. I'm guessing you are too. To access your power, you need to use a certain word. We use Latin to summon our powers. So, if you are an aquamancer you need to say *unda*. If nothing happens, then you are not an aquamancer. You might have psychokinesis or pulso metus."

"So, I just say *unda*?"

Corbin nodded his head and stood back.

I took a deep breath to calm my nerves. I was nervous about what might happen. What if I wasn't an aquamancer like everyone else in my family? That would be sure to make my father unhappy.

I held my hands out in front of me with my palms facing the wall. I muttered *unda* and water began to trickle off my palms and fall onto the floor. I was expecting an explosion of water, not a trickle.

Corbin started laughing. "It is not typical for water to spring forth from you on the first try, Killian. It takes time and practice. Most people see an even smaller amount of water than that. Okay, to make it stop you say 'Intereo.'"

I already knew that word. I had heard Emily use it countless times before. I muttered "*Intereo*," and the water stopped trickling from my palms.

Corbin picked up a duffle bag that was on the floor. He pulled two daggers out of it and tossed the bag carelessly back on the floor. It landed right in the water that had come out of my own hands.

"Have you ever held one of these?" he asked. I shook my head no. "Have you ever seen anyone use one of these?"

"Oh yeah!" I stated.

He furrowed his brows at my comment. "Who have you seen?"

"Corlissians."

He straightened up a little. "Were they any good?"

"Yeah, all of them knew exactly what they were doing. They took on a whole company of Brothers one night." Shit! I should not have said that!

"And they defeated them?" he asked in astonishment.

"Yup." I decided to leave out the part about Emily roasting the Brothers and causing the building to explode.

"Impressive," he muttered. "Well, hopefully you picked up few things. Just remember that those kids have been training for a few years. You will not measure up to them for quite a while." I nodded my head that I understood. "Do you have any questions before we begin?"

"Can you teach me how to twirl a dagger between my fingers?" I asked.

Corbin frowned at me. "Killian, no one can do that without tearing their fingers up. Why on earth would you ask that?"

"Because a Corlissian girl I knew did it all the time."

Corbin handed me one of the daggers and he placed the dagger he had between his fingers and attempted to twirl it. The first try it fell and clattered to the floor. His second try he sliced a finger. The third try he sliced two more fingers. He glanced up at me with blood dripping off his fingers and mixing with the water on the floor. "I don't know how she does it without shredding her fingers. Maybe she can show you someday," he stated.

I expected him to laugh, but he didn't. "I don't think I'll ever see her again. She hates me more than anybody at the moment."

"Maybe you shouldn't fall in love with Corlissian girls that you're spying on," he stated.

"I didn't fall in love with her!" I replied indignantly.

Corbin shook his head and rolled his eyes. "That's a flat out lie. I saw the way your eyes had this glazed over, far off look in them when you spoke of her. Only an idiot would believe you!"

"It doesn't matter if I loved her or not, she hates me now. I think if she saw me again, she'd kill me." Actually, I knew that's what Emily would do. There was no question in my mind that she wanted me dead.

"Can you blame her? You pretty much used her to get information about the Corlissians. I'd be pissed if it happened to me. I mean imagine if she used you like that."

By this point I had such a tight grip on the dagger in my hand that my knuckles were white.

"What's her name anyway?" Corbin asked.

"Emily," I hissed between gritted teeth.

"Is Emily pretty?" he asked.

"Yes."

"Mmm, maybe since you fucked up with her, I could have a chance," he smiled.

I surged forward and slammed him against the wall. I had the blade of the dagger shoved up against his throat.

"First rule of training, don't let your opponent know your weaknesses. It took me three sentences to provoke you. Now I know exactly what to say to incite you again," Corbin said shoving me off him. "I must say though that you are quick. I wasn't expecting you to pounce and shove the blade to my throat. I guess you did learn something from those Corlissians."

"I don't recall the Corlissians talking shit to their opponents," I breathed.

Corbin shot me a look. "Do you honestly think if Emily were standing here right now that she wouldn't hit you with some low blows? She would know exactly what to say to make you break."

I didn't respond, but I knew it was the truth. Emily did know enough about me to talk shit to me. Hell, all she had to do was rehash everything I did to her. I was an asshole to her for most of the time I knew her. I didn't deserve the time she gave me.

Corbin must not have taken my silence as a good thing. He cleared his throat. "Well, since your face is red and all your muscles are tense, I think we'll call it a day. I want you here tomorrow at seven in the morning. And make sure your head is clear."

He bent down and picked up the other dagger and handed it to me. "Take care of these," he said walking around me and shoving the door open.

I stepped out into the hall and headed back the way I'd come.

"And no practicing aquamancy in the rest of the stronghold," Corbin called.

I didn't turn around and acknowledge I'd heard him. I wasn't exactly thrilled with him. I thought we were just engaging in small talk. I wouldn't have said a thing about Emily if I had known he was just using the information to piss me off.

I pushed through the main door and locked it behind me. I made my way down the hall by the gym and through the waiting area.

"Have a ni…" the secretary started but stopped when she saw the look on my face and the daggers I was gripping in each hand.

I stalked down the hall to the stairs and ran up them to the eighth floor. I was winded when I reached the top, but I wasn't nearly as mad as I had been.

When I rounded the corner of the hall that my room was on, I saw my sister knocking on my door.

"What's up?" I asked walking up beside her.

She recoiled from me when she saw the nasty look on my face and the twin daggers in my hands. "Put those away! You look like you're about to go postal!" she snapped.

I pulled my keys out of my pocket and walked into my room with Zoë following me.

"Where've you been all morning?" she asked.

I tossed the daggers on one of the end tables. "Training."

"Oooh, who is training you?" she asked flopping down on the leather couch that faced the TV.

"Corbin," I said sitting down next to her.

"Ick. I've heard he's the worst. I don't mean he's a bad trainer, just that he's a hardass."

"Yeah, I've already had a taste of his style this morning," I muttered. "I don't mean to be rude, but what are you doing here?"

"A sister can't spend time with her big brother she hasn't seen in three years?" I just stared at her. I knew Zoë well enough to know that was a load of crap. She sighed. "I want to hear about your other year and a half away."

"Zoë now isn't the best time. Corbin said some things that really pissed me off and I don't want to snap on you for no reason."

"There is no need for you to snap on me. You're just going to tell me what happened after you left West Haven."

Zoë was persistent. She kind of reminded me of Emily.

I tipped my head back so I was staring at the ceiling. "After I left West Haven, I walked around that summer to a lot of different places. I didn't stay in one place longer than a week. I just saw part of the country. Before the fall semester started, I found my next town to stay in. Cambridge. Same as the year before, I made a few friends there and when the semester ended, I moved on to another town."

"For the spring I stopped at Lysteria. I met this guy named Austin who reminded me so much of Tovan. We really hit it off and got to be good friends. I hated to leave. I didn't think I'd find a town I liked better than Lysteria. I had made a promise to myself to keep moving after every semester. So, I took off and wandered around during the summer again. I let my hair get long and my beard grew in. I looked like a hobo. I was actually kind of surprised when I saw myself in a mirror. I usually kept my hair trimmed during the summer. It would still get longish, but last summer I just didn't care. I was walking along this coastal highway. Down below was the ocean and this long beach."

I saw Zoë sit up a little.

"Autumn Falls," I muttered.

"The town with the Corlissians?" Zoë asked.

I nodded my head. "They were all down there that day. I had no idea at the time."

"What made you stop?" Zoë asked.

I turned my head to the side and looked at her. "A girl."

Zoë's mouth parted and then a smile spread across her face. "You're going to have to be more specific."

I sighed. "She was floating in the water away from the rest of her friends. She just looked so carefree out there. I was drawn to her. I went down to the beach and just watched her."

"That's kind of stalkerish, Killian."

"I know, but…" I trailed off. "You had to be there, Zoë. Everyone else had walked out of the water, but she stayed behind and watched the sun set. Once it was beyond the horizon, she joined her friends. She walked right by me and smiled."

"What's her name?" Zoë interrupted.

"Emily."

"What's she look like?"

I pulled my cell phone out of my pocket and went to the pictures. I handed Zoë the phone.

"Oh, she's gorgeous, Killian!"

She handed me back the phone. I nodded my head and stared at the picture until the screen went black.

"So, what next?"

"She left the party and I followed her to the parking lot."

"You're coming off sounding like a real creeper. Staring at her from afar, following her to a parking lot. I'm guessing this ends with you following her home and watching her sleep."

"Don't worry, my creepiness ended there. I asked her in the parking lot where the high school was. She gave me this smart assed remark about it not being open at midnight. She told me where it was though. I found it so strange that she wasn't even scared of this hairy guy approaching her in a dark lot. I later learned why."

"Explain."

"She had a shit ton of weapons in her car. Like I said, I didn't know she was a Corlissian at the time."

"Then what happened?" she asked.

"I stayed the night at a hotel and got cleaned up. I registered for school, bought some clothes, and rented an apartment."

"And then school started."

"Yup. Emily and I had homeroom together. She sat right behind me. She heard the teacher say my name." I laughed a little at the memory. "She asked if Killian was my real name. Then she said she was calling me Lian because Killian was too much of a mouthful."

Zoë had a big goofy grin on her face. "I like Lian. I think Emily and I would get along."

"I think you would too," I said. I knew that would never happen though.

"Then what?"

"She smarted off to the teacher and got sent to the office. But by God did she make a show of it. She had leather pants on. Well, you get the idea."

"When did you find out she was Corlissian?" Zoë asked.

"Later that day. Their trainer had these computer modules that he would have attack them in the town. He made sure there were no humans around, according to Emily. Apparently, it didn't pick me up since I'm a Talyrian. Anyway, a Midnight Brother module attacked us and she just destroyed it. I had never in my life seen anyone do what she had done. She asked if I would forget what I saw, but that wasn't happening. She took me to their family's lake house and I honestly thought she was going to kill me. Instead she told me what she was and about Talyrians, Brothers, Nexes, Avids, and just everything."

Zoë pulled her legs up on the couch and crossed them under her. "You didn't really leave to spy on Corlissians, did you?" she whispered.

I turned my head back so I was staring at the ceiling again. "No."

"Did you leave because of Dad?"

"Yes."

She scooted closer to me. "Why didn't you take me with you?"

"It wasn't planned. Dad dropped me off at school that morning and said some shitty comment like he always did. I just had enough. I went to the bank, emptied my account, and left. Every day that I was gone I kicked myself for leaving you. It was my one regret. Every day I thought about you and I wished I could call you to make sure you were okay. I just…"

"It's all right."

"It's really not." I stood up.

"Finish telling me about Emily," Zoë said.

"Not right now. I can't."

"Killian, please," she begged.

"I just need to be alone."

"Come on, Lian."

I glared down at her. "I love you Zoë, but never call me that again."

Zoë stood up. "Emily only?" she asked.

I nodded my head. I watched as she walked out the door and carefully shut it behind her. I sighed and flopped back down on the couch.

The one person I was trying my damnedest not to think about was the one person who was being brought up. Corbin talking shit, Zoë asking questions, and topping it all off was Emily had actually called me. She was fucking pissed, but it was still her.

I was fooling myself if I honestly thought I could come up here and just forget about her. Every little detail about her was permanently locked in my brain. The way her hair and skin smelled after she showered, and the sound of her voice when she first woke up. How she would snuggle up against my chest in bed and the way she wrapped her legs around my hips when she jumped in my arms. The smoothness of her skin and the way her muscles moved under my touch. The tattoo running down her spine and…

I stood up and slammed my fist in the wall between the door and the TV. I wiped the drywall dust on my jeans and walked into my bedroom. I was doing nothing but torturing myself by thinking about her.

Chapter 7

Emily

I left the lake house before my brothers or sister woke up. It wasn't like I was getting much sleep anymore. I mostly found it impossible to shut my brain off at nights. It was either thinking about different ways to use my powers or everything Lian had said before he left. I was hardly able to process the fact that Kate was missing.

I drove into town slower than usual. Normally, every single one of us, save for Toby, drove at speeds alarmingly over the limit on the road to the lake house.

I stopped by Two Pieces, which never closed, and got a coffee to go. I drove by school and let out a sigh of relief when I saw that there was only one car in the parking lot. I parked the Audi in my usual spot and headed for the doors with my bag draped over one shoulder and my coffee in the other hand.

I was mildly surprised to find the doors unlocked. Not that a simple human lock could keep me out. I'd learned how to pick locks when I was five years old, but I normally just kicked a door in if I needed to. Who has time to bother picking locks when your foot works just as well?

I walked down the main hallway and stopped outside the door that led to the training center. I unlocked it and headed inside.

Hotch was standing by a charred piece of metal when I walked in examining it closely. I could see that his hands were bandaged up with white gauze. I had a feeling someone had attempted to use *incendia* and the results where worse than my first attempt.

"What cha doing?" I asked.

"HOLY SHIT!" Hotch screamed. "You cannot sneak up on people, Emily!" he chastised me.

"Oh, I can. I think you mean I shouldn't," I replied.

He shook his head at me. I've had plenty of people in my life tell me that I was a lot to deal with. I had a feeling my trainer felt the same way as the rest of them.

"What are you doing here at," he glanced at his watch. "Five thirty in the morning?"

"I wanted those books. Did you bring them or do I have to search your house?"

"I brought them. I didn't think you wanted them that bad that you had to get to school at this god-awful hour." He walked to one of the tables and pulled the two books off the shelf that ran below the tables that were always empty.

He handed them to me. "Any word on Kate's whereabouts?" he asked.

I shook my head no. "Camilla didn't say much about it last night. Do you mind if I hang out in here and read?" I asked. Hotch shook his head no.

I was about to walk to the opposite side of the room that he had been using, but paused. "Were you using *incendia*?" I asked.

He glanced down at his bandaged hands. "Maybe," he muttered as a blush rose to his cheeks.

I sat down against the wall and dropped my bag down beside me. I sipped on my coffee as I read the first few chapters of the book on pulso morsus. My cell phone rang right when I was reading about what kind of things Talyr could do with pulso morsus.

I pulled my phone out of my bag and answered it without seeing who was calling.

"Yup?"

"Emily, where the fuck are you?" Drew shouted into the phone.

"School."

"Why?"

"I'm reading."

"Again why?"

"I want to know if there is a word more powerful than *incendia*." I was lying, but my brother of course took me seriously.

"I think *incendia* is bad enough. Remember how messed up your hands were from that. I think anything more powerful would just destroy you," he stated.

"Calm down, you dork. I'm just reading up on my other powers. I want to know all there is to know about them. If I'm going to be stuck with them my whole life, I suppose I should get to know them."

I heard him let out a sigh. "Please, don't leave the house without leaving a note. You scared the shit out of me."

"Sorry."

I could hear him move the phone to his other ear. "You're not planning on using your other powers in extreme ways, are you?" he asked.

"Absolutely not," I replied.

"Don't lie to me, Emily."

"I wouldn't dream of lying to you, Drew. Now leave me alone so I can read." I hung up on him before he could reply. All that he would have said would have been a smart assed remark.

I continued reading about Corliss and Talyr using pulso morsus in its normal fashion. I knew how it worked. I just wanted to know if I could do more with it. Corliss only seemed to use it as it was supposed to be used; Talyr was the one who tried different things.

I got to a part that had me leaning closer to the book. It spoke of Talyr causing pulso morsus to be seen. He could make it look like it was running through his veins under his skin. He could even make it leave his body and still be seen. The bright red glow would circle around him. He even used it on his brother once when Corliss was feet away from him.

I clearly had been so focused on what I was reading that I didn't hear people coming into the training center. I glanced up when I saw a shadow move across the pages. Mason and Micah were standing over me.

"You're here early," Mason said sitting down next to me.

"Well spotted," I muttered. I slammed the book shut and shoved it in my bag.

"I tried to call you last night," he said.

"I had my phone off," I replied putting the book on pulso metus in my bag too.

Micah sat down in front of me. "I think that's girl speak for I had my phone on, but I just ignored your call specifically."

"No, I actually had my phone off." I glanced over at Mason. "Did Camilla talk to your dad?"

He shrugged his shoulders. "Not that I know of. Why?"

"She was going to see if anyone could track Kate. Your dad is the best tracker of us in this town."

"You want me to call him and ask?" he asked eagerly.

"No, don't bother him. Just wondering if he said anything to you."

I heard the door to the training center open and close and more voices carried down the hall. A moment later Sam, Tyler, and Evan came into view.

"Does everyone come here in the mornings?" I asked. I thought it would be quiet in here expect for Hotch.

"Never," Micah said. "We saw your car in the lot and figured you were in here. What are you doing here this early?"

"Nothing," I muttered standing up as the other guys came over to us. I grabbed my bag and empty coffee cup off the floor and headed out of the center.

Sam turned around and walked beside me. "Too good to say hi now?" he joked.

"Sorry. My mind is elsewhere."

"Would elsewhere be Kate and Killian?" he asked as we walked down the hallway to leave the center.

"Maybe."

He glanced at me.

"Yes."

"You know we'll find Kate. That shouldn't be on your mind. And you need to forget about that Talyrian fucker. He's long gone and you never have to hear from him again."

Sam cracked the door open and peeked out to make sure no human students were around. He opened it fully when he saw the hall was empty.

"I called him yesterday," I blurted out. I wanted to take my brain out of my head and smack the shit out if it. Why in the hell did it think that telling Sam about me contacting Lian was a good idea?

"You what?" Sam spat.

"I called Lian and asked if he took Kate when he left town."

"And his response was?"

"Not what I expected. I was hoping for a yes or no answer. Instead I got him taunting me."

"Emily, you cannot call him! I know it's hard that he's gone and I'm sure you miss him, but…"

"I don't miss him! I don't want anything to do with him. I just called to see if he could be honest with me about one thing and now, I know he can't. I won't call him again."

"Promise me," Sam ordered.

"I promise."

"That I won't call Killian ever again."

I let out a sigh. Corlissians were so specific with their promises. No room for reneging. "I promise that I won't call Lian ever again."

"Good. Now, what are you doing tonight?" he asked.

I glanced over at him as we walked back toward the doors that lead to the parking lot. "Umm, training and going home."

"How about dinner tonight?" he asked.

"We just had dinner last night."

"Funny thing about dinner is that you need to eat it every day," he said sarcastically. He shoved open the doors and we walked outside.

"Are you trying to keep my mind off things by feeding me?" I asked.

"Sort of."

"Sort of?"

"I mean that's part of the reason."

"What's the other part?" I asked.

A small smile tugged up half of his mouth. "I'm not telling you."

"Jerk," I muttered.

"Okay, how about no dinner and instead we go get a new tat?"

"So now you're feeding me and buying me tattoos?" He nodded his head with a grin on his face. "Okay, we're totally getting married!"

He laughed and leaned against the side of his car as Thea pulled up in the empty space between my car and Sam's. Sam pulled a pack of cigarettes out of his back pocket, slipped one between his lips, and lit it. Sam only smoked when he was nervous. I didn't know what was rattling his nerves now and I didn't get a chance to ask as Thea bounced up beside me and knocked her hip against mine.

"Why is everyone here early? Why didn't anyone call me? Where's Drew and Toby? Are the other guys in the training center?" Thea blurted out.

"Damn Thea, I think you need to ask us a few more questions," Sam mumbled through the cigarette hanging out of his mouth.

"Seriously, what's going on?" she asked.

"Nothing. I came here early to pick up a few books from Hotch and I decided to start reading one. Micah and Mason showed up, then Sam, Tyler, and Evan. I don't know why they're here early. You'll have to ask."

"Ty, Ev, and I were going to practice this morning. We figured if we got some practice in during the morning, maybe we wouldn't have to stay so late after school."

More cars started pulling in the lot and students started filing into the school. I had no desire to sit through classes today when all I wanted to do was drive out to Culver's and see if I could do what Talyr did. I knew that I had a shot at it working. I had seen blue and red sparks fly out of my hands when we were fighting the Nexes on the beach. That only proved that my idea could work.

"I'm guessing that Ev told Micah and Mason and that's why they showed up early," Sam continued. He tossed the butt on the ground and crushed it with the toe of his boot. "Come along dearies, we need to get learned," he added shoving off the side of his car.

Thea and I followed behind him. We walked inside just as the first bell rang. Thea kept glancing at me as we put things in and took things out of our lockers.

"What?" I murmured.

"I think Sam likes you."

"Of course Sam likes me. We've been friends as long as you and I have. I think you kind of have to like someone to be friends for fourteen years."

"I didn't mean as friends. I think he likes you in the same way Killian liked you and Mason still likes you."

"So he likes me in a cheating, lying, asshole sort of way?"

Thea groaned. "You know what I mean!"

"No, honestly I don't. What makes you think he likes me anymore than as a friend?"

"Toby told me you two had dinner last night."

"Yeah…and? Sam and I have had dinner together before, so have you and I. What does that matter?"

"Emily, you know I love you like a sister, but your biggest flaw is you are horrible at judging people. You can never read them right. I don't have that flaw. I'm telling you; Sam likes you. I was right about Killian after all."

I slammed my locker shut and glared at her. "How long have you been waiting to throw that back in my face?" I snapped.

"Emily…"

"Just drop it, Thea. I don't care if anyone likes me. I'm not dating anyone for a long time. Lian pretty much ruined me. I don't think I'll be able to trust anyone like I did before. I put entirely too much trust in him and it just blew up in my face. It's my own fault."

"You can't let one guy break you like that. If you do that, it means he wins. You're a fighter. You were born and trained to fight. Don't let him win. And besides you and Sam are cute together." With that she split up from me and walked toward her homeroom.

One thing Thea said resonated in my head, "Don't let him win." She was absolutely right. I didn't let Mason break me when he cheated on me and I wasn't about to let Lian destroy me just because he was a Talyrian spying on us. As soon as I learned how to make pulso morsus and pulso metus my bitches I was going to fuck some things up.

I couldn't help it. I knew that if anyone found out they'd lambaste me, but I really didn't care. I pulled my cell phone out and sent Lian a quick text. Sam did make me promise not to call him; he didn't make me promise not to text the bastard.

"Before I set the entire stronghold on fire, I'm going to find you and make you beg for death. See you soon, baby."

I walked into homeroom right behind Watkins. I sat down and he considered asking me a question, but when I threw him a wink he decided not to. Good idea.

He took attendance and the bell for first period rang. I was walking out but he called my name. I hung back while the rest of my classmates walked around me.

"Yes?" I asked.

"Am I taking it that Mr. Marlow is no longer a student here?"

"Why should I know?"

"Weren't you dating him?"

I gave a snort. "No. We were not dating." My cell phone rang and I glanced down to see who was calling me during school hours. I looked up at Watkins. "Wanna ask him yourself?"

Watkins looked down at the name on my screen and glanced up at me. "No. I don't know what's going on, but I have a feeling I'm better off staying out of the way."

I smiled at him and walked out the door. I slid my finger across the screen and pressed it to my ear.

"You must not care about my education if you're calling me during school hours," I stated.

"You texted me first, sweetheart. When can I expect to see your gorgeous face up here?"

I laughed. "Mmm, I think I'm going to just surprise you. You like surprises, right?"

"Honestly, I don't, but if the surprise has you here doing bad things to me then I think I'll deal."

"You don't know half of what I can do," I whispered.

"Then come up here and show me. I'm not scared of you, Emily."

"You should be, Lian."

I hung up on him and slid my cell in my back pocket. I didn't know what sick game we were playing. All we were doing was taunting one another. The thing was, he might have been joking around, but I was dead serious. The thought of torturing a few hundred Talyrians gave me the motivation to keep going.

The final bell for school rang and I met Thea by our lockers. She didn't look happy.

"Mason is driving me insane, Emily. You need to do something about him."

"Umm, he's not my problem," I said pulling my bag out and putting a few notebooks in.

"He keeps asking if now is a good time to try and get back with you since Killian is gone."

"Again, not my problem. He knows damn well I don't want him back."

"I'll deal, I guess. Come on, let's go to practice," she said hooking her arm through mine.

"Actually..."

"Don't make me cover for you. Hotch always knows I'm lying," she pleaded.

"I'm still going to be training. I just need a wide space to do it in."

"So you'll be at Culver's using *incendia*."

"Sure, tell him that."

I slipped my arm out of hers and made my way downstairs and to the parking lot. I slid in my car and drove to the outskirts of town to where Culver's Field was. Half of it was still scorched from the last time I was here. Our fighting ring was untouched by my flames though.

I parked and walked down the small hill and sat down in the center of the circle where Mason and I had beaten the shit out of each other. It was always an exciting time when I came to Culver's Field. Or rather, I always left severely injured.

I just sat there for a few minutes trying to clear my head. I didn't think about Lian or Kate or if Hotch was going to be mad at me for missing practice or if Mason was going to start pestering me or if Sam had a crush on me. I let it all go and didn't think about it.

I took a deep breath and whispered *dolor*. I could feel that power coursing through me. It was under my skin and seeking for my hands to latch on to someone so it could enter them and make them feel pain. I wanted to press my hand into the grass so it would do what it was begging me to do. I didn't though. I focused on what I wanted it to do. I wanted it in my arms only. I could feel it moving up from my legs through my stomach and staying in just my arms.

Then I could see it under my skin. It looked like thin bright red veins. It was moving from my shoulders to the tips of my fingers. My hands were shaking.

"*Dolor*," I said again. It flowed to my fingers and started spilling out. It floated around me still glowing bright red. It engulfed me in a cloud of red. I stuck my hand through it and it followed my hand. It moved out from me making a wider circle around me. I stuck my other hand out and it once again grew wider around me.

I looked just like the guy in Toby's picture. The only difference was I was surrounded by red instead of blue. The blue of pulso metus I would try later.

I was transfixed by what I was able to do. I didn't think it would work so perfectly during my first try.

Then I heard someone scream out in agony.

Chapter 8

Lian

My alarm went off at six thirty in the morning. I squinted my eyes as I searched for the snooze button. I pulled my blankets over my head and turned on my side.

"Where are you?" I heard her ask me.

"I'm right here with you. There is no other place I would rather be," I whispered.

I cracked my eyes open. Emily was kneeling on the side of the bed. She was twirling a dagger in each hand staring down at me. She tossed one up in the air and caught it. She sent it flying down toward me, but it missed and embedded itself into the mattress. She sent the second one soaring and it landed hilt deep in my pillow.

She leaned forward closer to me. "I won't miss next time." She stood up on the bed and stepped over me, hopped down, and walked out the door.

My alarm blared again and had me sitting upright in bed. I glanced down at the mattress to where a moment ago a dagger was. It was untouched. I turned and looked at my pillow. It didn't have a puncture wound. It had all been a dream.

I sighed and shut my alarm off. It was six forty now. I pulled on a pair of basketball shorts and a T-shirt. I slipped my cell in my back pocket and tugged on my shoes as I hopped through the living room. I grabbed the daggers off the end table and my keys and headed down to the third floor.

I didn't have time to eat so I made my way directly to the training wing. I didn't sign in like I did the day before. I nodded my head at the secretary and passed through the waiting room. I passed through the water tight door and closed it behind me. I stopped at the same door as yesterday. Instead of knocking, I shoved it open.

Corbin was leaning against the far wall examining his fingernails. I shut and locked the door behind me.

"At least you have terrific time management skills. Five minutes early."

I didn't respond. I wanted him to know that I still wasn't happy with his dirty trick yesterday. Yeah, I know he was teaching me a lesson, but he didn't have to do it that way. He could have just told me not to let your enemy know your weaknesses.

"Drop the daggers and let's see your aquamancy."

I set the daggers on the floor and lifted my hands up. I shouldn't have had my palms facing me, but I thought I was going to get a trickle like I did yesterday. Note to self: never have your hands facing you when you're about to have water coming out of your hands.

I breathed the word *unda* and water launched out of my hands and hit me in the face. I quickly flipped my hands around and it was hitting the wall so hard it sounded like it was coming out of a fire hose, not my hands.

"*Intereo.*" The water stopped as soon as that word passed my lips.

"Very good, Killian. I have only seen one aquamancer be this successful on their second try."

"Who?" I grunted. I pulled the hem of my T-shirt up and wiped it across my face that had water dripping off it.

"Your father."

Of course. It could have been any other Talyrian aquamancer and I wouldn't have cared. It just had to be the one guy in this entire stronghold I didn't want to be compared to.

"You trained my father?" I asked.

Corbin chuckled. "No. Your father and I are close in age. We trained together when we were younger. He was the best in the class. Our trainer had to train him separately from the rest of us because he picked up things so quickly. He had that water dancing for him in a matter of weeks."

"Then why isn't he training me?"

"Your father is still the best aquamancer in this stronghold. He doesn't want anyone to be better than him, not even his own son. We're just like the Corlissians in that manner, the best like to stay at the top and will do nearly anything to ensure that they do."

I remember Emily telling me that her dad had been the best pyromancer of all the Corlissians. It made me wonder who was the best now. After what I'd seen her do on homecoming, I was guessing she was the best. I couldn't imagine anyone besting her.

"Okay, pick up those daggers," Corbin ordered.

I scooped them up and glanced at him.

"What have you seen done with daggers?" he asked. "Besides the finger twirling."

"I saw the Corlissians toss a dagger in the air, catch it by the tip of the blade, and throw it. Umm, and I saw them hold the daggers like this," I said bringing the daggers up, so one dagger was above my elbow and the other dagger was under the opposite elbow. I pulled the daggers toward one another to demonstrate. "That's how a few Brothers were decapitated."

Corbin furrowed his brows. "These were teenage Corlissians, right?" he asked.

I nodded my head. "Yeah. I never saw their parents fight."

"They are far more skilled than the Talyrians their age. At what age do they start training?" he asked.

I shrugged my shoulders. "From the sound of it they begin training when they enter high school, but there is no way they can be as skilled as they are in two years. I think they begin training when they're toddlers."

"That is not good news at all. If all the Corlissians start their training at such an early age, then if we engage in hand-to-hand combat with them, they will surely beat us. His Majesty cannot have knowledge of this," Corbin muttered.

"I thought the King had spies in most Corlissian bases. I figured he'd know when they start training," I stated.

"Did His Majesty tell you that?"

"Umm…" Maybe I wasn't supposed to say anything about what Aldous and I had discussed on my first day back.

My cell phone chimed in my back pocket indicating that someone had sent me a text. Corbin looked at my ass where the noise came from.

"Do you need to get that?"

I shook my head no.

"Practice is over for today. I need to go speak with His Majesty. If you want to practice your aquamancy a little longer, you can stay. Be here at seven tomorrow morning." With that Corbin left the room and shut me in by myself.

I stood there for a few moments before I shoved my palms out and away from me. "*Unda*," I whispered and watched as the water erupted out of my hands. I squeezed my fingers closed and watched the water form into a different shape. I relaxed my hands and opened my palms wide and the water ran off my fingers in a wide spray. It was pretty damn fascinating.

I said that word that stopped the water from flowing forth from my hands and I picked my daggers up off the floor. I headed out the door and made my way down the hall and pulled my cell phone from my pocket and checked to see who sent me what.

"Before I set the entire stronghold on fire, I'm going to find you and make you beg for death. See you soon, baby." I glanced up at the name on top of the screen. Emily.

A smile tugged at my lips. I hit the call icon that was just below her name on the text screen. I wondered if she would even pick up.

"You must not care about my education if you're calling me during school hours," she answered.

"You texted me first, sweetheart. When can I expect to see your gorgeous face up here?" I asked. I had to fight to keep the smile out of my voice.

She chuckled. "Mmm, I think I'm going to just surprise you. You like surprises, right?"

"Honestly, I don't, but if the surprise has you here doing bad things to me then I think I'll deal." I replied my voice dropping a few octaves.

"You don't know half of what I can do," she whispered so softly I had to press the phone hard against my ear. I walked through the waiting area and the secretary gave me a wave as I passed through. I nodded my head at her.

"Then come up here and show me. I'm not scared of you, Emily."

"You should be, Lian." Then she hung up on me. Of course I was scared of her. How on earth could I not be with all the damage I'd seen her do with her bare hands?

I slid my phone back in my pocket and headed for the cafeteria. I got my food and sat down at a table by myself. A moment later someone slid into the seat in front of me. I glanced up to see Tovan smiling at me.

"Haven't seen you since you got back," he said.

"I've been busy getting settled in and starting training," I muttered.

"Oh, how's that going?" he asked.

"Not too well. Yesterday Corbin ticked me off and I might have put one of my daggers up to his throat. Today he cut practice short because he needed to talk with the King."

"So, I'm taking it you're an aquamancer since everyone else in your family is," he stated.

I nodded my head. "And you?" I asked.

"Pulso metus," he said with a smile on his face.

I gritted my teeth. I'd had that power used on me once before and I sure as hell didn't like what it had conjured up in my brain.

"I mean it's probably the easiest power to use. You grab someone and make their worst fear feel like a reality. It's not like having aquamancy where you can do all sorts of shit with the water."

"Well, I can't do anything really. I was able to get a steady stream of water out of my hands today. So, you're a guard?"

Tovan let out a sigh. "Yeah, it was either that or work in the kitchens. I'm on the first line of defense right now and I will be until the next crop of guards comes up. It's pretty much a stand around job. It's not like the Brothers, Nexes, or Avids attack us at all and the Corlissians sure as hell don't fuck with us."

That instantly made me think of the text Emily had sent me. She said she was going to burn the stronghold to the ground. I might have played it off like she was joking, but I knew that if one person could turn the building, I was currently living in into dust it was her.

"So, you have a girlfriend?" Tovan asked.

That question snapped me back to the present. "Ugh, no."

"Come on. You mean that whole time you were gone you didn't meet even one girl?" he asked in astonishment.

"I met plenty of girls, but I didn't stay in their towns long enough to really date them."

"Not even one made you want to stick around any longer?" he asked wiggling his eyebrows up and down.

"No." Yes. Only one.

Tovan glanced down at his watch. "Well, I need to get back to work. You'll have to tell me about all the places you went during your three-year hiatus."

That wasn't going to happen. Everyone in this stronghold knew that I had been staying in a town with Corlissians and that's all anyone wanted to know about. They didn't care about where I was before Autumn Falls.

Tovan stood up and nodded his head before departing. It was so weird to me that all these people I had known prior to leaving I couldn't connect with anymore. I mean Tovan was my best friend and now he felt like a stranger. Even my own sister was a different person. The only person who didn't feel like a stranger to me was the one person who wanted to torture the hell out of me.

I knew that whatever game we were playing with one another was sick and twisted. We were trying to distance ourselves from one another, yet we still called and texted each other. We were masochist.

I guess what hurt the most was that she seemed perfectly fine without me. It was as if the time we had spent together meant nothing to her. It made me sick when I thought of her being with someone else. I knew we were wrong together and that eventually it would end, but I couldn't imagine being with someone else after her. She really had no idea how much she meant to me and I knew she never would.

I left the cafeteria and was heading upstairs when I ran into my father. I guess crashing in my bed for a few hours was not in my immediate future.

"I'm glad I found you. Come with me," he stated.

He, of course, got into the elevator that I had successfully avoided the past two days. He hit the button for the eighth floor and leaned against the back wall. He glanced at my clothes and his nose wrinkled. There was that look I had missed so much.

He didn't say a word the whole way up or even while we walked down the halls. I wasn't about to try and engage him in small talk. He stopped outside his door and unlocked it and motioned for me to go in. It was one room in the stronghold I never thought I'd be invited into.

His room had the exact same layout as mine. The difference was that his walls were a dark blue in the living room and in the bedroom. Also, there were family pictures on the walls. There was the fake happy family portrait that we had taken a month before I skipped town. On one wall were all of Zoë's school pictures in white frames up until she stopped attending a traditional school. On the other wall were all my school pictures up until I left. I was guessing my mom had put them in here for him.

"I know your mother filled your closet with clothes and I'm assuming they were all jeans and T-shirts," he said startling me. I had been staring at all the picture he had up.

"Umm, yeah," I muttered.

He nodded his head and walked into his bedroom. I stayed rooted to the spot. He came back a few minutes later holding two suits. One was black with thin white pinstripes. It was the jacket, pants, and a vest. The other was a solid black jacket and pants with a dark gray vest.

"I expect that when you are not training for you to be dressed like a highborn male. I'll need to get you more suits, but these will do for now," he said handing them to me.

"Thanks."

"So, is training going well?" he asked.

"It's okay. I just started yesterday."

He nodded his head. "Are you getting around the stronghold alright?"

"Yep." This was probably the most awkward conversation I had ever had in my entire life. "Umm, I'm gonna go. I promised Zoë I'd hang out with her after practice," I lied.

"Okay. Try those on later. If they don't fit right, we can get them tailored."

"Will do," I mumbled. I got the hell out of his room and went directly to my own. I leaned against my door and let out a breath I hadn't realized I was holding in.

It was the same thing with Tovan and Zoë; my own father wasn't the same person I remembered. He was walking this line of his old self that he would sometimes slip into and the new guy he was trying to be. It was just weird. The only person who seemed relatively the same was Mom. She was being a bit more maternal than I remembered, but I guess that will happen when her only son walked out on the family at fifteen.

There was a knock on the door that I was leaning against. It scared the shit out of me too. I dropped the suits on the leather couch and popped the door open to see Zoë standing there with a big smile on her face. She walked past me and into my room.

"Can we pick up where we left off yesterday?" she asked.

"With what?" I asked shutting the door.

"Umm, what was the town…Autumn Falls and Emily!"

"I guess," I muttered.

"What are these?" Zoë asked examining the suits.

"Dad's hand me downs."

Zoë looked up at me. "These will not fit you. Not even the best tailor in the world could make these fit you. You're taller and far more muscular than Dad. The only thing that might fit you is the vest and I'm doubtful it will. These pants are a no go. And if you like jackets with short sleeves you're in luck. You need to buy all new, Killian. I think Dad still sees you as the kid who left three years ago."

"I had a feeling they'd be too small, but I didn't have the heart to tell him." I picked the suits up and took them to my room and dumped them on my bed. I'd deal with them later.

I sat down next to Zoë on the couch. "So, where'd I leave off yesterday?" I asked.

"Umm, I think you stopped with Emily telling you what she was and about Talyrians at her lake house," Zoë stated.

"Right." I had to edit what I told Zoë. I knew during the first week of me knowing Emily did she start finding out about her other powers. That was one thing I was not telling anyone. I didn't care if people in this stronghold knew she had multiple powers, I was playing dumb that I knew anything.

"Nothing really huge happened after I met her. We went to school and she tutored me in history. She did tell me about a fight she and a few other Corlissians had with some Brothers. And we were at a beach party when Nexes attacked. Nothing happened until homecoming."

"What happened at homecoming?" Zoë asked.

"Emily and I were upstairs, umm, talking when her friend called my cell. She was talking to Emily when a company of Brothers rolled into the hotel and ruined homecoming."

"Oh crap! What did the Brothers do?"

"Well, they started looking for the Corlissians. Emily had everyone come up to the room we were in. Emily left to go get her ex-boyfriend who was passed out on another level. On the way back they ran into some of the Brothers and Emily somehow talked them into meeting up at another location so as not to do any damage to the hotel. I don't know how in the hell she did that, but the Brothers agreed."

"Then?" Zoë blurted out excitedly.

"We left the hotel and went to the school. The rest of the Corlissians went inside the school to change clothes. Emily changed in the middle of the parking lot because she just didn't give a damn. She told me she'd call me after they finished with the Brothers. I pretended to go home, but instead I got into the old warehouse they were meeting at. I was hiding in this massive room when the Corlissians all ran in there and the Brothers pretty much followed. Emily came walking in late looking like the most dangerous female in the world. Anyhow, there was a lot of hand-to-hand combat that proved at how deadly the Corlissians were. Umm, after that the pyromancers joined together and roasted the remaining Brothers. We left the warehouse and were about a block away when it exploded. And, that was that."

"And what exactly caused you to come back here?" Zoë asked.

I let out a breath. I hated this part. It killed me a little more every time I remembered what I said to her that day. "Umm, Em and I were walking back to the school from getting coffee and Phoenix was waiting for us by the football field. Phoenix pretty much wasted no time in telling Emily I was Talyrian. I said some things I'm not proud of and Phoenix and I left."

"What did you say to Emily?"

"I'm never repeating what I said to her. I didn't mean it and I only said what I did to hurt her. I wanted her to hate me because at that moment I really hated myself for lying to her the whole time I knew her."

"Killian?" Zoë whispered.

"What?"

"Do you love Emily?"

I looked at my sister and nodded my head.

"Have you had any contact with her since you left?"

I nodded my head again.

"Tell me what was said."

I swallowed down the lump in my throat. "Umm, the first time she called and asked if I had kidnapped her aunt. I never answered her truthfully and I was pretty much an ass to her. I still want her to hate me. And then today she sent me a text that was not pleasant and I called her back. It was pretty much us just taunting one another. It's really fucked up what we're doing, but just hearing her voice makes me want to keep it up. I know it's not right though."

"It's not fucked up. You love her. It's your way of staying connected to her," Zoë stated.

"I'll be right back. I need to use the bathroom," I muttered standing up.

"Let me see your cell. I want to look at the pictures," Zoë said holding out her hand. I pulled my phone out and dropped it in her waiting palm.

When I came back out, Zoë had a big grin on her face. She turned the phone to me so I could see what she was looking at. It was the picture of Emily and me kissing through the net. "Okay, you two are adorable," she giggled.

I snatched the phone back and dropped it on the table beside me. "What are your plans for this evening?" I said tipping my head back.

"Tovan didn't tell you, did he?" she grumbled.

That brought my head back up. "Excuse me?"

Her cheeks turned bright red. "He promised he'd tell you," she whispered.

"Tell me what?" My voice started to rise.

"That he and I have been dating for a year," she mumbled not looking me in the eyes.

"No. He didn't tell me. I think I need to have a word with my old friend."

Chapter 9

Emily

"*Intereo*." The red tendrils of the pulso morsus disappeared instantly. I turned around and saw Sam lying on the ground at the base of the hill. He wasn't moving.

I ran over to him and knelt down beside him. His eyes were open and unblinking. I thought he was dead. I thought I had killed my friend.

I placed my palm on his forehead and whispered "*Sanare*." I felt the healing powers entering his body from mine. He took a deep breath and he blinked. His eyes fixed on me.

"What the fuck happened?" he whispered trying to sit up. I forced him back down with my palm still on his head.

"Just stay down," I ordered. I let more of my power course through him. I didn't know how powerful of a jolt he took.

"What was the red I saw surrounding you?" he asked.

"Pulso morsus. Would you stay down?" I said shoving him back down again.

He looked up at me with furrowed brows. "Emily, that's not how pulso morsus works. How?"

I sat down next to him and pulled my hand off his forehead. He propped himself up on his elbows.

"I won't tell Hotch or anyone else a thing, Em." I looked passed him down the field. "I'm not going to lie or deceive you. I'm not Killian."

I pulled my knees up and wrapped my arms around them. I rested my chin on the tops of my knees.

"I know you're nothing like him, Sam," I whispered.

"But if it was him laying here and you didn't hate him you would be telling him exactly what was happening, wouldn't you?" he asked sitting up fully. I nodded my head slightly. "Then why won't you tell me? I've known you for fourteen years and you knew him what four weeks? That's really not fair, Emily."

"Are you feeling okay?" I asked.

He sighed and stood up. "I feel fine. I can take a more brutal hit than most people since I have pulso morsus too. Are you going to talk to me?"

"This was the first time I've tried it. I'm not totally sure what I'm doing, so I don't have a lot to tell you right now."

"Emily, pulso morsus shouldn't be visible outside your body. It's not normal what you're doing," Sam stated.

I stood up. "Nothing about me is normal, Sam. I shouldn't have four powers. I shouldn't be able to have internal powers visible outside my body. I shouldn't be able to do a lot of things, but I can. If everyone thinks I'm as powerful as I am, then I'm going to prove them right. I'm going to be as deadly as Corliss and Talyr were."

"Sometimes you're really fucking scary."

"Mission accomplished," I muttered.

"Why won't you talk to me about this?" he asked. I started to walk away, but he grabbed my arm and stopped me. "Please, talk to me, Emily. I promise I won't tell a soul," he begged.

"Don't make promises to me."

"Why not. I fully intend to keep my promises."

"Because I have had too many of them broken. I promise I won't leave you. I promise I won't tell anyone what you've told me. I promise I won't cheat on you. I promise I'll be home on Sunday night to tuck you in. I promise I'll read you "Where the Wild Things Are." I promise…"

"Your parents didn't know they weren't coming home."

"It's still a broken promise."

Sam let out a breath. "Please, just tell me what is going on inside that head of yours."

I snapped my arm out of his grip. "I'm having issues trusting people right now. Outside of my family, the only person I totally trust is Thea." I knew he wouldn't like what I said, but he was the one wanting me to be honest with him.

"That really hurts, Em. That really fucking hurts. You have trained and fought alongside Tyler, Evan, Micah, Mason, Bridgette, and me and you're saying you don't trust us?"

"I trust you to have my back, but…"

"But what?"

"I'm just sick of being burned by people who I put trust in. It's my own doing and I'm the one facing the consequences of my decisions. It honestly has nothing to do with you, Sam. It doesn't have anything to do with Tyler, Evan, Micah, Bridgette, or even Mason. It's all on me."

"I know he hurt you, Emily, but you can't treat everyone around you like they're going to do the same."

I tried to form a smile with my lips. It probably came off more as a grimace. "I don't have to worry about being hurt anymore. I can just take what hurts me out of the equation."

"Is that you politely telling me that you are no longer going to date anyone?"

I nodded my head. "Guys are just a distraction and I have enough to deal with at the moment. Anyways, it's not like I'm going to get married or have kids. I'm not passing these powers on."

"Not every guy around you is some idiotic human or a Talyrian posing as a human. There are plenty of Corlissian guys who would do right by you," Sam said.

"I'm sure there are, but I really don't care anymore. I need to get going," I said walking around him. I jogged up the hill and got in my car. I leaned my head back against the headrest and let out a long sigh.

I loved Sam, but he was exhausting. I knew he cared about me and was worried about my mental state, but him hanging around me was only going to cause him more pain…both physical and mental.

I heard Sam's car start up and turn around on the narrow gravel road. I waited until his car was a tiny black dot in my rearview mirror before starting my car up and turning around.

I was driving slowly down the road as usual when my cell phone rang. I didn't used to answer it while driving, but it was becoming a bad habit of mine to do so anymore.

I was concentrating on the road and blindly pulled my cell out of my bag and held it up to my ear.

"Yeah?"

"Umm, is this Emily?" a girl's voice asked.

"Yes. Who's this?"

"You don't know me, but you know my brother."

"And who is your brother?"

"Killian Marlow," she whispered.

I pulled the phone away from my ear and studied the phone number. It was from an area code I was unfamiliar with. I put the phone back up to my ear.

"Are you calling for him?"

"No. He doesn't know I'm calling you. I got your number off his phone without him knowing. He told me about you and I wanted to talk to you."

"Oh, I'm sure he's telling you lovely things about me," I muttered.

"Actually they have been." She let out a breath. "Emily, I hadn't seen my brother in three years. He was never that happy when we were growing up and that was mostly due to our father. There were very few times when I would see his face light up with…with joy. The only time I have seen that same light in his face was when he was talking about you. I know you don't believe it, but he does still love you."

My eyes blurred instantly at her words. A lump in my throat prevented me from saying anything. I was thankful for that since I hadn't a clue what to say. I let out a few mini breaths to compose myself.

"What's your name?" I asked.

"Zoë."

"Zoë, I think you're only trying to help your brother and that's awesome of you, but even if we did still have feelings for each other there is no way we could be together. We're from two races that have been at war with each other for centuries. We're not meant to be together."

"Of course you're not! If you were meant to be together, then you would both be fighting to get back to one another. I have seen no such fight from Killian and I can tell you're not fighting either."

"I'm sorry, but how old are you?" I could not believe at how brass this girl who did not know me at all was being. I kind of liked her for it.

"Fourteen."

I readjusted the phone to my other ear. "So, what all has Lian been telling you about me?" I asked.

She giggled. "You do call him Lian. That is so cute. Oh, he was telling me about when you first met and his first day of school and then he kind of skipped a lot and went right to homecoming. That sounded interesting."

"That was all he told you?"

"I knew he would do a lot of editing. I am his little sister after all. I don't need to hear what he was doing or who he was doing it with."

I started laughing. Lian's little sister was cool as hell. She just spoke her mind. She was missing that mind filter like I was. I felt a kindred spirit in her.

"Hey, umm, I have to go," I said pulling into the driveway of the lake house. "But it was really nice talking to you."

"It was wonderful talking to you too." I heard some commotion on her end of the line. I could hear a male talking to her.

"Tovan is busy right now, so you need to talk to me about what is going on. He's seventeen and you're fourteen and that…who are you talking to?"

"No one," she stated. There was a scratching noise over the phone.

"Hello?" the male said.

"Hi?"

"Emily?" I knew then that it was Lian.

"Sup bitch!"

"Did you steal her number off of my phone?" he asked his sister.

"It's not technically stealing when you willingly handed me your phone," Zoë retorted. Yeah, I really liked his sister.

"What in the hell did you call her for?" he asked. "Seriously, what do you and my…and Emily have to talk about?"

I got out of my car and walked up to the house. All the lights were on and I could see Drew and Toby making dinner. Actually, Toby was making dinner. It looked like Drew and Camilla were at each other's throats…again.

"We were just talking. You'd been talking about her and I kind of wanted to talk to her," Zoë replied.

"Well, this has been a lovely chat, but I have to go," I stated.

"No, I wanna know what you two were talking about?" he said.

"It was nothing of significance. Your sister was telling you the truth. At least someone in your family hasn't lost that trait."

"Emily, I…"

"Don't, Lian." Call ended.

I didn't know what he was about to say, but I just knew I didn't want to hear it. It could have been something bad or it could have been an "I'm sorry." Either way I did not want to hear him say it.

I walked in the door rubbing my eyes. It had been a tiring day and now I was going to have to deal with my siblings. The onslaught started right away too.

"Why weren't you at practice? Thea said you were practicing *incendia* elsewhere. Is that true?" Drew asked.

I stopped and glared at him. "You are not my father, so don't act like you are."

"Emily, I am the oldest male of this family, so for all intents and purposes I am your father. Where were you?"

"I was at Culver's Field practicing."

He walked around the island toward me. "What were you practicing?"

"Does it matter? I was being a good little Corlissian and I was practicing using all my fucking powers at the same fucking time! Does that answer do for you?"

I shoved around him and walked to my bedroom. I wasn't hungry anyway even though I knew Toby was making spaghetti and he always made it the best. I couldn't sit across from my family and pretend like everything was fine when it was far from it.

"Em, wake up," someone whispered.

"No," I mumbled sleepily into my pillow.

"Get up!"

I opened my eyes to see Drew hovering over my bed.

"What the fuck are you doing in here!"

"Shhh. Don't wake Cami and Toby. I got a call from Micah. Him and Mason are tracking ten Brothers. They need back up. Now!"

"Get out of here so I can get dressed," I muttered.

"I'll be in the car," he whispered on his way out.

I shoved the covers back and pulled a pair of jeans on. I strapped my dagger holster to my back and yanked on a T-shirt and a hoodie on over that. I slipped a pair of shoes on and grabbed two daggers before leaving my bedroom. I was strapping them to my back as I walked out of the house and slid in the passenger seat of Drew's Mercedes.

"Where they at?" I asked through a yawn.

"Micah said he'd meet us at school. I guess Mason is tracking them." He drove out onto the main road and nailed the gas. We didn't say a thing to each other the rest of the drive into town.

Just as Drew parked another car pulled in beside us. Tyler, Evan, and Sam hopped out.

Drew turned his head and looked at me. "Seven Corlissians for ten Brothers. Seems a bit excessive," he stated.

I shrugged my shoulders and got out of the car. We barely had time to say "hi" to one another when Micah ran up to us. He bent over at the waist and placed his hands on his knees. He let a few long breaths out before righting himself. He pulled his cell out and held it to his ear.

"Where are you?" he asked. Pause. "We'll be there in five minutes." He slid his phone in his back pocket. "Mase has tracked them to the woods behind Culver's Field. Let's pile in a car and head out."

And we did just that. All six of us squeezed into Tyler and Evan's brand-new Mustang Cobra. It was midnight blue with twin white stripes. Ty and Ev both had separate cars too. Tyler had a matte black Audi R8 and Evan had a lime green Viper. Their parents would by them a new car to share every year. The twins were spoiled.

It was a tight fit. Evan was driving and Tyler was riding shotgun. That left Micah, Sam, and Drew in the small backseat with me sitting on both Sam and Micah's laps. They sure didn't seem to mind, but I was hunched over and uncomfortable. Evan fired up the Cobra and sped out to Culver's.

As we were driving down the gravel road Micah whispered, "Kill the lights."

"How in the fuck am I supposed to see? Where is the moon?" Evan bitched.

"New moon," Sam and I both said at the same time.

Evan grumbled something under his breath and shut off the headlights.

"Oh, and it was nice of you to completely obliterate the field, Em," Micah stated.

"I had to practice *incendia* somewhere, dear," I replied.

"Stop here, Ev," Micah said.

Evan pulled the car to a stop and we all got out. I stretched my back out and so did Sam and Drew. They were both tall and were sitting hunched over too. A tiny bump would cause their heads to whack the roof.

Micah walked down the hill and across the charred field toward the woods on the other side of the field. We followed behind him. It was pitch black out and none of us could see where the hell we were going. I saw Micah's cell light up in front of me.

"We're walking across the field. You still there?" Micah asked. "Okay. And you can see them?" "Well, stay low and light your hand up a few times so we can see you."

A moment later we could see a small light flick on and off several times indicating where Mason was hiding. We headed over and kept quiet as we neared. Mason was hunkered down just outside of the woods. We crept up around him and stayed low.

I could hear Mason whispering to Micah about what was going on. I wasn't listening to them though. I was trying to make out any movement in the woods. It was too dark out see anything. I wasn't even sure Mason knew where the Brothers were.

"How many?" Tyler whispered.

"We tracked the ten in town and followed them here. There are roughly thirty. We're not positive since we can't see them," Mason replied.

"So there could be a thousand?" Sam muttered.

"Ugh, doubtful, but I guess anything is possible," Mason said.

They immediately stopped talking when we finally heard movement. Then a massive bonfire was lit not thirty feet from where we were. The guys hunkered down low and I rose up a bit. I wanted to see exactly what I was up against. There were about fifty black cloaked Brothers milling about around the fire. I took a few cautious steps into the woods.

"Emily," one of the guys hissed.

I felt someone grab the back of my hoodie. I yanked myself out of it and managed to keep out of reach of them.

"Dammit!" someone else muttered.

I crawled in front of a tree and leaned back against it. The Brothers were just talking to one another. I was almost waiting for one of them to pull out a board game and start having a party. It was weird seeing them in this setting. I didn't understand what was going on.

"Take another step closer and I will slit his throat."

That stopped my train of thought. I looked back at where the guys were. Two Brothers were standing there. One had a knife to Drew's throat. All the guys were standing up with daggers in their hands.

"Get over here, pretty little girl," one of them stated.

I stood up and walked over to where the guys were, but I kept inside the woods. All the Brothers who had been around the fire were now staring at us.

"Give us the girl and we'll let the rest of you go," a Brother said.

"Fuck you. You're not touching my sister," Drew muttered.

I knew that I couldn't use *incendia*. They would see and Drew would still end up dead. I had to use pulso morsus. I just hoped it would work as well as it did earlier. The only problem was all the guys would end up on the ground too.

"Come here, girl. You need to pay for killing our brothers."

I whispered *dolor* under my breath and glanced down at my arms. The red was flowing around like it had been this afternoon with it just in my arms. I whispered *dolor* again and it flowed out of my fingers and pooled around my feet. No one could see what I was doing.

I smiled at the Brothers. "If you want me, come get me," I said sweetly.

One of the Brothers walked forward and I raised my arms up toward him. The pulso morsus followed my movement and instantly went up. I heard the two Brothers screams mixed with the guys. I turned my body and spread the pulso morsus out further taking out the Brothers around the fire. The sound of that many screams was both sickening and gratifying.

"*Intereo*." The screams stopped. Everyone was on the ground. Most of the Brothers were lying motionless and a few were twisting around and twitching.

Micah sat up and looked around with a blank expression on his face. He looked lost for a moment. Then he looked up at me. "What in the fuck did you just do?" he asked.

Sam rolled over on his stomach and sat up awkwardly. "That is the second time you've done that to me today, Emily," he muttered. He scrubbed his hands up and down his face and groaned. "Still fucking hurts," he added.

I went over to Drew and placed my hand on his forehead. "*Sanare*," I whispered.

His eyes opened and locked on mine. "You are a deadly creature, Emily Charlotte Porter," he breathed.

"I know," I sighed. I pulled my hand off his head and he remained lying on the ground.

Micah had crawled over to Evan, who was closest to him, and was smacking him on the cheek saying, "Wakie, wakie, Ev-Ev." It actually did work. So, Sam did the same thing to Tyler as I used my healing powers on Mason.

"What was that? It felt like my brain was being ripped from my skull," Mason stated.

"That would be your ex-girlfriends doing," Sam replied getting to his feet. "What are we gonna do with all these guys?"

"I say we roast 'em. We've got three pyromancer here," Micah said.

"I think Emily has done enough. Let Drew and me handle it," Mason replied sitting up.

"But Emily could use *incendia* and it would be done. I wanna go home and sleep off the hit I just took," Evan added.

"I'm sure Emily is tired from using pulso morsus on…let's see…everyone," Tyler said.

While the six guys were standing around arguing over whether or not I should help with torching the unconscious Brothers, I walked around them and went over to where the bonfire was.

"*Ignis.*" A flame popped up in each of my hands. "*Incendia.*" I scorched the bodies that were lying on the ground. "*Sanare.*" I healed myself while the flames were still rolling out of my hands. "*Intereo.*" Done.

I walked around the guys and headed back to the car like I didn't just light fifty Brothers on fire. I heard someone behind me say, "Light those two bastards up and let's go!"

We all piled back in the car, which was even more cramped with Mason added to the mix. He was sitting on the console between the front seats. It was eerily quiet in the car. The only sound was that of the engine of the Cobra growling.

Someone cleared their throat. "So, can you do that with pulso metus too?" Drew asked.

"Probably. I haven't tried it yet," I replied.

"You know, Emily, I'm pretty damn sure that if we got you up to the Talyrian stronghold you could decimate it and all its inhabitants on your own," Mason said.

Chapter 10
Lian

I stormed out of my room and into the hallway. I could not believe what Zoë had just told me. My best friend and my little sister had been dating for a year. I was naïve to think that something like that would never happen. Isn't that how the cliché goes? Your little sister stares longingly at your best friend, then she grows up, he notices her, and the two get together?

I headed downstairs and made it to the main foyer. I was about to the massive front doors when a guard stepped out of a hidden corner and blocked me.

"No one leaves the stronghold!" he grumbled.

"But I just want to go have a word with Tovan. He guards the outer defense," I stated.

"I don't care if you want to go skip around the fountain a few times. No one leaves the stronghold."

"I'll be right back. You can go with me if you want!" I protested.

He glared at me. "I know you are one of the high-borns and you probably think you can get away with anything. That's fine and all, but you are not getting out of these front doors. You make one more move toward them and I will have no choice but to use pulso metus on you. I don't think you want that."

I snorted. "Please, I've had pulso metus used on me before and believe me the girl who used it on me was far more powerful than you are."

His mouth dropped open and before he could ask me any questions that I wasn't going to answer I turned and headed back upstairs. I opened the door to my room to find Zoë chilling on the gray couch.

"Tovan is busy right now, so you need to talk to me about what is going on. He's seventeen and you're fourteen and that…who are you talking to?" I said. I hadn't noticed she was on the phone.

She blushed a little before saying anything. "No one."

I grabbed the phone away from her. "Hello?" I said nastily into the phone.

"Hi?" a cool female voice replied. I glared at my sister. I knew who that voice belonged to.

"Emily?"

"Sup bitch!" she replied. Oh, there was that Emily I had missed.

"Did you steal her number off of my phone?" I asked Zoë. She was sitting on the couch properly looking ashamed of herself.

"It's not technically stealing when you willingly handed me your phone," Zoë replied.

"What in the hell did you call her for? Seriously, what do you and my…and Emily have to talk about?"

"We were just talking. You'd been talking about her and I kind of wanted to talk to her."

"Well, this has been a lovely chat, but I have to go," Emily said. I kind of forgot that she was on the line.

"No, I wanna know what you two were talking about?" I blurted. I sounded like a whiny child.

"It was nothing of significance. Your sister was telling you the truth. At least someone in your family hasn't lost that trait." Ouch. Emily knew right where to throw her punches. She played dirty.

"Emily, I…" I started, but she cut me off.

"Don't, Lian." Then the phone lit up blinking CALL ENDED.

I tossed Zoë's phone on the couch next to her. "Of all the numbers you could have jacked from my phone, you just had to get hers. Zoë, you cannot call her."

"Why not?" she whispered.

"For a lot of reasons. She's a Corlissian. She hates me. I'm trying to distance myself from her. She is probably plotting my death at this very moment. Shall I go on?"

Zoë shook her head no. She looked up at me with puppy dog eyes. "I really like her."

I plopped down on the end of the couch. "Yeah, I do too."

"If you want her back, you need to fight, Killian. Sitting here next to me is not getting you any closer," Zoë stated.

I looked at my sister. "Zoë, the moment I see Emily again she will have a dagger planted hilt deep in my heart."

"I think you are overestimating her hate for you. She wouldn't have talked to you on the phone if she hated you that much. I bet she still has feelings for you."

"You are underestimating how dangerous she is." I let out a breath. "This one day I said the wrong thing to her at the wrong time. She was seriously pissed off. She used…" I stopped. I couldn't tell Zoë that Emily had multiple powers. "She grabbed my forearm and used pyromancy on me." I turned my right arm over so Zoë could see the light pink handprint that was still on my arm. It was barely visible with the tattoos that covered my arms, but you could still make out the light pink mark underneath.

Zoë leaned forward and ran her fingertips over it. "Emily did this?"

"Yup. She is one person you do not want to have on your bad side. This is just a taste of what she can do. Now I think you might have an idea why I can't ever see her again."

Zoë pulled her legs up and turned so she was facing me. "How many Corlissians did you know?" she asked.

I looked up at the ceiling counting them in my head. "Umm, eleven…I think."

"Where they all pyromancers?"

"No. Umm, six of them were. Two had pulso morsus and three had psychokinesis."

"And you got to see them use their powers? I don't mean on you either!"

"Yeah, the night of homecoming. I got to see them all in action." I let out a chuckle. "I pretty much had my eyes glued on Emily though. She comes strutting in that room in all leather twirling that dagger around her fingers like always. She took out two Brothers in a matter of seconds. Then she did this front flip onto a table and decapitated another Brother. She told me one night that she decapitated a Brother with her foot."

Zoë's mouth was gaping open. "I think the Corlissians are deadlier than we are," she whispered.

"There is not a doubt in my mind that they are. I have seen them in action. If we were to meet them in the open, they would decimate us."

"The King knows this, doesn't he? That's why he's got us all in here. It's for our own protection."

"The King told me he has spies in ninety percent of Corlissian bases, so he knows exactly what we're up against."

"Then why aren't we being trained like they are?" Zoë asked.

I shrugged my shoulders. "That's something you'll have to ask His Majesty."

Zoë crinkled her nose. "I'll pass."

I laughed. "Can you promise me one thing?"

"Hum?"

"Will you never call Emily again?"

"I really like talking to her, Killian. She is so nice and it was like talking to a friend." She sighed when she saw the look on my face. "I won't call her again," she pouted.

"Thank you, Zoë."

She rolled her eyes as she picked up her phone and walked out of my room. They could have only talked for ten minutes and Zoë was acting like they were all the sudden best friends. Then again, I had known Emily for a half a day and she made me feel like that. Emily Porter definitely knew how to make you feel like you were her best friend.

That made me remember what Sam had told me about her on my first day of school. "She's not like the rest of these bimbos. She can make you feel like you're the only person in the room with her in a crowd of people, but piss her off and you'll be wishing you'd never met her."

When he'd first told me that I didn't think too much of it. Then again, I had only known her for half a day at that point. Now I knew that what he said was the truest thing anyone had ever understood about Emily.

I didn't know what to do with myself for the rest of the day. My days seemed worthless now. Get up, train, and then do whatever. At least when I was in Autumn Falls my days had a purpose and I was learning.

Being a high-born sucked. The normal citizens all had jobs to occupy their days and us high-borns just sat around like useless lumps.

I went to my bedroom and pulled the suits off their hangers and laid them all out on my bed. Even eyeballing them I knew Zoë was right. They would never fit me. Still, being a good son, I tried them all on.

The two pairs of pants all stopped at mid-thigh. I could get the jackets on, but they were all tight and the sleeves went way up my forearms. The vests fit, but I couldn't button them.

I pulled one of the jackets on over a vest and went down to Mom's room. She opened the door and immediately started laughing.

"Oh, Killian, where did get those?" she asked once she finally stopped.

"Dad," I muttered.

"Your father should know better. You are twice the size he is."

"I think this is his way of showing that we're okay…maybe," I suggested.

"Well, I'll need to buy you some new suits, I guess. Stay here," she said.

Mom's room was the antithesis of Dad's. Whereas his was dark, Mom's was light and airy. She too had family pictures on the walls. She even had drawings Zoë and I had done in school framed.

She came back into the living room with a measuring tape that tailors used. She unrolled the blue tape and said, "Take that jacket off."

"Umm, shouldn't a tailor do this?" I asked. I had been measured when I was younger and I knew that when they took your measurements, they got personal with you. I didn't exactly want my mom anywhere near my business.

She looked at me with an unspoken "pul-ease." "I am your mother. You don't have anything I haven't seen before!"

"Yeah, but you haven't seen it in a long, long time!"

"Killian, stop whining and hold your arms out."

I grumbled under my breath as I took the jacket off and held my arms out. She took all the measurements for the vest and jacket. Then she moved on to the pants.

I have been embarrassed plenty of times in my life. I had peed my pants in kindergarten when I was too shy to tell the teacher I had to go to the bathroom. I had been de-pants on the playground by Tovan when we were in sixth grade. Phoenix punched me in the nose when we were in seventh grade. I later learned this was because she had a crush on me. This was just a small fraction of my embarrassing moments, but having my own mother measure my inseam while I was wearing loose basketball shorts ranked number one on Killian's Most Embarrassing Moments.

"All right. I'll see if I can find some suits that are more you. Do you need ties too? Of course you do. Don't worry about a thing. I'll take care of it."

Then she shooed me out of her room so she could go online and order me suits and ties.

I was walking back to my room when I heard someone calling my name. I turned to see Tovan jogging down the hall toward me.

"Hey! One of the guards said you were looking for me earlier. What's up?" he said with a smile on his face.

As soon as he was close enough to me, I cocked my fist back and jacked him in the nose. He immediately went down on his knees and looked up at me with wide eyes.

We used to tease each other relentlessly and even rough housed plenty of times, but we never, ever got physically violent with one another. This was definitely a first.

"The fuck?" he muttered. He cupped his hands around his mouth and nose when the blood started pouring out.

"You...Zoë..." I said simply.

He stood up on wobbly knees and took a few steps away from me. It was then that Zoë walked around the corner. She stopped momentarily when she saw the scene in front of her. Then she ran toward us and stopped next to Tovan. She fixed her eyes on me.

"What is wrong with you? Now you choose to play the overprotective big brother?" She grabbed Tovan by his elbow and pulled him into her room.

I followed behind at a distance. She dragged him into her bathroom and sat him down on the edge of the bathtub as she wetted a washcloth in the sink. She carefully dabbed it under his nose.

"I don't know if it's broken or not. You should go see one of the healers just to be sure," she said softly to him.

He watched her carefully as she nursed his bloodied nose. Once it finally stopped bleeding, did Zoë come out of the bathroom? The look in her eyes reminded me of Emily when she was pissed off. The only difference was Zoë's eyes weren't glowing.

"Why in the hell did you punch your best friend?" she asked in a rather calm tone.

"You two should not be dating," I muttered low enough that only Zoë could hear me.

She turned where she stood and looked at Tovan. "Why don't you go see the healers and give me and Killian some time to talk? Okay?"

He nodded his head and rose from his spot on the side of the tub. He gave me a wide berth as he walked around me and out the door.

As soon the as the door shut behind him did Zoë start in. "You are the last person on the face of this earth who should be telling me who I can and can't date. You were with a Corlissian, Killian!"

"Yeah, but Emily and I are the same age!" I retorted.

"Age? That's what you're upset about? Our age difference? You are infatuated with a girl from the race that we are supposed to hate and I have not said a thing to you about her. I haven't said that you shouldn't try and get her back and that you should forget her. I've been telling you that the two of you are still a possibility. And here you go beating up your best friend just because he decided he likes me."

"You're my sister, Zoë. I'm going to despise any guy who shows an interest in you. It just makes it all the worse when it turns out the first guy to date you is my best friend. You need to look at things from my point of view too."

"I completely understand you. But you need to see things from my view as well. You can't still be in love with a Corlissian girl and then tell me I can't date a guy because he's three years older than me." She let out a breath. "And besides, Tovan isn't the first guy I dated."

I gritted my teeth together, but kept my mouth closed. I didn't want to know who they were or how many there were before Tovan.

"Just remember, when I left you still thought boys had cooties. It's going to take me some time to realize that you're not the same little girl you were three years ago."

At that Zoë laughed. "Come on. Let's go grab some dinner. I'm starving," she said tugging me out of her room and down the hall.

Chapter 11

Emily

I didn't go back to sleep when Drew and I got back home. I should have been tired from using three of my powers extensively, but I wasn't. I was wide awake. It was mostly due to the fact that I had yet another problem I had to deal with.

As my brothers and sister slept the rest of the morning away, I was on my computer doing research and flipping through books trying to find a solution. The two books that Hotch had let me borrow on pulso morsus and pulso metus didn't offer me a quick fix. Of course. Nothing for me was that easy.

There was a knock on my door. I glanced at the clock to see it was almost time to leave for school. I shoved the research I had in my bag and got dressed. Today was a neon yellow skirt that stopped mid-thigh with a long-sleeved black lace top and six-inch black heels.

I walked out of my room to find Camilla in the kitchen cooking breakfast. This was a sight I had never seen in all my years. Camilla never cooked because Camilla always burnt food. She couldn't even heat up anything in the microwave without burning it. She attempted to make hot tea one time. She left the water in the pot on the stove for so long that she actually burned the water.

"Whatcha doing?" I asked.

"Making you all breakfast before school," she replied.

"Umm, we're usually good with a bowl of cereal," I said.

She looked me up and down. "Damn sis, you're starting to dress like me!" she stated with a smile.

Toby walked out of his room. "Why does it smell like a woodland animal died in this house?" he yelled.

I snorted and backed out of the way. Camilla was about to start whining and Drew was going to come out of his room tearing into her. I walked out to my car and left. I wasn't hungry anyway. My mind was elsewhere at the moment.

I pulled into the school parking lot. The lot was already half full. I saw that Sam's black S5 was there and that was all I cared about.

I parked in between his car and Thea's. Sam was leaning against Mason's red Lexus smoking. Mason was standing beside him, Micah was standing by Mason, and Thea was looking bored. Her face lit up when she saw me.

"Where's Toby? I thought you always drove him?" she asked.

"Drew can drive him," I muttered. "Those two and Cami are constantly at each other's throats. It's annoying."

"There she is," Mason said. "My scary as fuck ex."

I rolled my eyes as I leaned against his car next to Sam. Sam nudged me with his elbow. "You feeling okay?" he asked.

"Yeah."

"I wasn't expecting you to be here today. I thought you'd been sleeping all day."

"I'm actually fine."

The bell rang and everyone headed inside. I was trying to determine whom I wanted to test solutions on. It was probably in my best interest to try them on either Sam or Micah. The hard part was going to be convincing one of them to possibly take multiple hits of pulso morsus until we found what worked.

I sat down in homeroom behind the empty seat that Lian used to occupy. It was weird not having him turn around and talk to me. Then I remembered that he was a Talyrian and I was supposed to hate him. Even so, we had still talked on the phone since he left. We talked twice yesterday alone. His tone seemed to soften each time I talked to him. He was shedding that asshole Talyrian skin that he left town in. Maybe that wasn't who he really was and he was himself around me.

"Emily?" Mr. Watkins called.

I raised my hand in the air. I swear that man had issues. We had been sitting in the same fucking seats since school began. You would think he could glance . across the room and take attendance. It was like he enjoyed lording over us in any way he could.

"Anthony?" he continued.

The bell rang and I headed to my first class. It was the same routine until lunch finally rolled around. Everyone was already at the lunch table when I arrived.

"Sam, I want you after school," I said walking up to the table.

His eyes perked up and a grin appeared on his face. "You have no idea how long I've waited to hear that."

Tyler made a gagging noise and Thea eyed me strangely.

"Oh, you might change your tone when you hear what I want to do with you."

"Emily, there is nothing you can say that can make me not want to do whatever is on your mind," he said dreamily.

"I want you to get symbols tattooed on your body and then I want to use pulso morsus on you to see if they will protect you from it."

His eyes were wide. So were Tyler and Thea's. They were all kind of looking at me like I was crazy.

"You're serious, aren't you?" Sam mumbled. I nodded my head. "I take back what I said. That sounds like the worst possible thing we could do together. I'd be more excited if you wanted to sodomize me with a hot poker."

"Ugh, that's nasty dude. I know Em's pulso morsus packs a punch. She's got a good point. There needs to be some way we can be protected when she does that...thing with it."

"Umm, is someone gonna fill me in?" Thea stated.

"Emily can make her pulso morsus and probably her pulso metus go outside of her body. It's wicked. But when she does that it attacks everyone, not just our enemies. She used it last night and it took us all down."

Thea looked at me. "You can seriously do that?"

"Yup. I would appreciate it if no one told Hotch about what I can do. I don't want another lecture about not using my powers properly...blah blah blah."

"Like I'd ever tattle on you. I don't want to face your wrath," Tyler stated. Thea and Sam nodded their heads agreeing with him.

"Well, Sam if you don't want to do it, I'll ask someone else," I said.

He strummed his fingers on the table and eyed me. "How many tattoos are we talking about here?"

"I've got four protection runes and some Latin words. We just need to try one a day. That way we'll know which one works."

He flicked his tongue ring against the back of his teeth. "Fine. But you own me, Em!"

A huge smile spread onto my face. I sprang up and wrapped my arms around his neck and kissed his cheek. "Thank you," I whispered.

"Anytime, baby," he replied.

The bell ending lunch rang and we all headed out. Thea walked next to me on our way up to our lockers. I knew that she was going to say something. And I was positive that it would be something I would not like.

She spun her lock and I leaned against my locker staring at her. "What!" she snapped.

"I know you want to say something, so spit it out."

"I was just thinking that you've moved on from Killian."

I sighed. "Thea, what have I said to you. I'm not interested in anyone right now. I'm focusing on my powers and protecting others from them. That's all this is."

"Why'd you ask Sam first?"

"Because he's taken two hits from it already. He knows what he's getting into. That's it. That's the only reason I asked him first. If he said no, then I would have asked Micah. Stop reading more into this than is there. We're friends. End of."

She held up her hands. "Fine. I'll stop. But that doesn't mean I don't think he has a crush on you."

"Think whatever you want, just keep it to yourself!" I slammed my locker and headed to science. Another class that reminded me of Lian and that he was no longer around.

I sat through all my classes and paid attention like a good obedient student. I even studied in study hall. Not that I needed to, but I just wanted to keep Watkins off my back. I had enough shit to deal with. I didn't need to threaten him a second time.

When the final bell for the day rang, I went to my locker and dropped some things off. I met Sam in the parking lot leaning against my car. He was smoking again.

"Your habit is getting progressively worse," I said.

"Hanging out with you rattles my damn nerves," he replied.

"You can always stop hanging out with me," I suggested.

"You underestimate your allure, Emily Porter." He dropped the half-burnt cigarette on the ground and stomped on it with his boot. "Show me what you want to tattoo on me."

We walked to where my trunk was. I pulled the four protection runes out of my bag and spread them across the truck. Sam inspected them each carefully. "Tell me about them," he said.

I tapped the first one. "This is a Native American symbol of protection." It was a simple arrow. "And this is a Wicca rune. It's called an Algiz rune." It sort of looked like a bird's footprint. "Umm, this is the Eye of Horus. It's Egyptian and this last one is a Celtic rune." The last one was the most intricate. It was three circles that spun outward and connected to one another.

Sam flicked his tongue ring against his teeth again. "What do you think we should try first?" he asked.

"It's your skin. Whatever you wanna try first I'm cool with."

"Let's go with the Eye of Horus first. I've always been a sucker for Egyptian art. Might as well put it on my body."

I picked up the four prints and shoved them back in my bag. Sam nodded his head and we got in his car. There were four different tattoo parlors around town and everyone had one they liked best. Sam always went to Falls Ink. I preferred Sunken Daggers Tattoos.

He tore out of the schools parking lot and headed straight to Falls Ink. He pulled around the back of the building to where their parking was. He didn't get out of the car immediately. He stared at the brick wall and tapped his steering wheel with his thumb.

"If you're not sure about this, I can ask someone else, Sam," I said.

"The pain of the tattoo is potatoes compared the pain I'm gonna get from you later. You just don't know what it feels like, baby girl. You think you're the unlucky one because you've got all these powers. But it's the rest of us who are unlucky. We get to experience the full brunt of your power's potency."

"Let's just forget about it then. If you don't want to go through it, then let's not worry about it. It was just an idea."

Sam chuckled. "Oh, I'm still gonna do it. This way all of us can fight next to you and not feel anything. It will be worth it in the long run. Let's go before I do lose my nerve." With that he slid out of the car and walked around to the front doors.

As soon as we walked in the guy standing behind the counter said, "Here for another, Sammy?"

"You know it, Paul!"

"What'll it be today?"

"The Eye of Horus. I think I want it in between my shoulder blades," Sam said.

Paul looked at me. "Anything for you, sweetheart?"

"No. I'm good."

"Scared of a little prick?" he asked with a laugh.

I smiled. "Nope." I turned around and through my lace shirt you could clearly see the tattoo running down my spine.

"Damn. Impressive. Where'd you get that done at?" Paul asked.

"Sunken Daggers."

"Huh. Not bad work. All right, let's get you set up, Sam." Sam filled out paper work while Paul drew up the Eye that would be the trace they inked over. About ten minutes went by before Sam was called to get his first protection rune inked on him.

I sat on the leather sofa leafing through their books of tattoos you could get. They were all the standard boring ones that everyone seems to get. There was no originality.

Sam walked out about twenty minutes later with his T-shirt draped over his shoulder. He turned around so I could see the artwork. It was perfect.

"Thanks, Pauly. Hey, we might be in again tomorrow. There's a few more designs I want to get," Sam said.

"I'll be here. And next time you want a tattoo you should come here, princess," Paul said with a wink.

I nodded my head that I had heard him, but I didn't reply. Sam and I walked back to his car. He got in gingerly and made sure not to press his upper back into the leather seat.

"Culver's then?" he asked.

"Yeah, I suppose," I muttered. I wasn't exactly thrilled to go back there having just been there the previous night taking on another company of Brothers. You think they'd get the hint and would leave our town alone. Nope. They were like cockroaches…they just keep coming.

Sam drove out to Culver's Field and parked along the side of the road like we always did. We both hesitantly got out of his car and walked down to the circle we used to fight in.

Sam stood about ten feet away from me. I could see that his hands were trembling. The first two times he didn't know it was coming. This time he knew exactly what was about to hit him. I just hoped that the protection rune would work.

I took a few deep breaths to calm my own nerves. Then I said, "*Dolor*." The power once again contained itself in my arms. It already knew what I wanted it to do. I said *dolor* a second time and it spilled out of my hands and twirled lazily around the lower half of my body.

I looked up at Sam. He gave me a wry smile and nodded his head. I pulled one arm up and faced it toward him. The red mist followed my command and went straight for him. He screamed and went down.

"*Intereo*." I ran over to him and placed my hand on his forehead. His eyes peeled open. They were shiny from unshed tears.

"Guess what?" he whispered hoarsely.

"Hum?"

"The Eye of Horus didn't work." He closed his eyes and took a few deep breaths. "You'd think after the third time it would get easier, but I swear it gets worse." He opened his eyes and looked at me. "I don't know if I can do it again, Emily."

"You don't have to, Sam." I pulled my hand away from his forehead and dropped down onto the grass next to him.

He pulled himself up and draped his arms over the tops of his knees. "Maybe multiple people should get tattooed and you do it all at once. Then we'll know what rune or word works by who doesn't go down," he suggested.

"Sam, you are one of the strongest Corlissians I know. If I could hardly talk you into it, how do you think anyone else would respond? No one likes feeling the effects of pulso morsus in training. They're not going to get hit with it willingly."

I crawled around behind him and saw there was a few pieces of grass stuck to his still healing tattoo. I pulled the pieces out.

"You should probably go home and clean that. You don't need it getting infected." I stood up and walked back to his car. He caught up to me as I was walking up the hill.

"Have you heard anything about Kate?" he asked.

I opened the passenger door and got in. He got in behind the wheel. "Not yet. I know Camilla's been, well I don't really know what she's been doing. I just know in my heart that it's the Talyrians who have her. But since we can't just go strolling into the stronghold it's kind of pointless."

He turned the car around and headed back to town. "Too bad Killian is the only person you know up there."

"Why?"

"Because they could go snoop around and see if they could find her."

I glanced at Sam who was focused on the road in front of him. "That's not a bad idea," I said.

"You are not calling him, Emily. You promised me you wouldn't!" he scolded.

"I wasn't talking about Lian. Geeze, get your panties out of your ass!"

He slammed on his breaks. His eyes were on me before the car came to a complete stop. "I hope that you don't mean you're going up there? That is not what I meant and I swear if you go up there, I will kill you for being that fucking stupid!"

"Wow! Calm down! I know I do a lot of stupid shit, but going up to the stronghold willingly is not on my list of things to do. I think that I may know someone up there who might snoop around for me."

"Who?"

"Oh, that I am not telling you, my dear."

Sam shook his head and drove back toward school. He dropped me off and got out of his car. He lit up another cigarette on his way into school.

I got in my car and left the lot. I drove to the beach and took my cell phone with me. I sat down a ways away from the other people who were enjoying the last of the good days at the beach.

I hit redial on my phone and waited.

"Emily?"

"Hey, Zoë."

"Oh, Killian would be mad if he heard us talking. We got into a big argument last night about it."

"Oh, I'm sorry," I said.

"It wasn't your fault. I called you. So, what's up?"

"Do you think you could do me a huge favor?" I asked.

"Umm, what?"

"I think that my aunt is a prisoner there. Could you sneak around and see if you can find anything out?" I asked.

"Yeah. It's not a problem. I'm a high-born, so I can get away with pretty much anything," she said.

"Oh, okay. Thanks!" I was not expecting my asking her to be that easy.

"Umm, can I ask you something since I have you on the phone?"

"Sure."

"Was Killian ever overprotective of you?"

"Ugh, I can only remember one time he was. Believe me I am very capable of handling myself, but some guy was hitting on me and Lian took it upon himself to kindly ask the guy to leave me alone. And since your brother is not small by any means the guy took off quickly. Why do you ask?"

She sighed. "Yesterday he punched my boyfriend."

"Umm, why?"

"Probably because my boyfriend is his best friend, or was his best friend. I don't know. He doesn't think we should see each other because of our age difference, but he was dating you and you're a Corlissian."

"We never technically dated, Zoë."

"Oh, the way he talked it made it seem like you two were together."

"Whatever our relationship was it was never labeled. Hey, I've gotta go. My ex-boyfriend is headed this way. I'll talk to you soon, okay?"

"Okay! Bye, Emily!"

Mason sat down next to me right as I hung up with Zoë. "Who was that?" he asked.

"My new boy toy," I lied.

"Saying things like that only increases my jealousy, Em."

"What do you want, Mason?" Dealing with him was exasperating sometimes. This was one of those times. I just wanted to be alone for a little while.

"Sam told Micah, Evan, and me what you were up to."

"Umm, which thing?" I had a few different things going on at the moment. I wasn't sure which one Sam had blabbed about.

"The protection runes. I think it's a damn good idea too. Last night was...wow! Well, I certainly would like to never feel that again, but I'm willing to get a tat and see if it works or not," he said.

"You told me that you'd never get inked," I replied.

"I told you a lot of things that became broken promises. What's one more?" He half smiled at me. "But Micah, Tyler, Evan, and I all agreed to go through with it. And Sam said if we did it then he'd do it one more time."

I turned to him with tears in my eyes. "You guys are seriously going to do that?" I whispered.

Mason wrapped his arm around my shoulder and pulled me into his side and chuckled. "Baby, we're doing it mostly to protect ourselves from you."

I sighed and leaned my head against his shoulder. "How'd you know where to find me?" I asked.

"Remember when we'd get in bad arguments over stupid things? You'd always take off just to cool down. You had these spots you'd go to. The beach was always the first place I looked for you. I would normally find you here. You'd be sitting here like you are now watching the sun set. I never approached you. I just needed to know that you were alright."

"Mason…"

"The day you broke up with me I went looking for you. You weren't here or at the coffee shop or tattoo parlor. I didn't know where you were and you weren't answering your phone. I thought something bad had happened and it was all my fault," he said as his grip on me tightened.

I yanked his arm off my shoulder and stood up. "I'm fine though. No worries," I said casually.

He looked up at me with those hazel eyes I fell in love with. "I thought it hurt bad when that realization finally hit me that I was never going to get a second chance with you, but seeing the way you'd look at that Talyrian in a way you never looked at me just killed, Em."

I cleared my throat. "I'm going to remove myself from this situation before either of us say something we don't really mean."

With that I walked away. I didn't need to hear him anymore. He said what he needed to about the protection runes. Mason just always had to push things too far. It was probably why I didn't one hundred percent trust him.

Chapter 12
Lian

I woke up before my alarm went off. Yesterday's dream with Emily throwing daggers at me was enough to scare me awake. I pulled on a long-sleeved T-shirt and a pair of sweatpants. Then I headed down to the training wing for my third day of practice.

When I arrived at our usual room, Corbin was once again already waiting for me. The floor was covered with standing water. I was guessing he got there early to practice himself.

"On time as usual," he stated with a grin.

"Are we going to have an actual practice today?" I asked.

"Yes, of course. I'm sorry about yesterday. There were just some things I needed to discuss with the King regarding the training of us Talyrians."

I figured that's the reason he ended practice early yesterday. I didn't really care about the details though, nor was I sure he would tell me more. I knew that the Corlissians were deadlier than the Talyrians were. Apparently, everyone didn't know that.

"So, let's do some training with the daggers first and then we'll use aquamancy last," Corbin said clapping his hands together.

"Okay," I murmured.

"I need to get you a back holster so you're not carrying those around. Let me guess, all the Corlissians you knew had a back holster for their daggers," he said.

"Yeah, and they had ankle and thigh holsters too."

"And your pretty little Emily? Did she have holsters?" he asked. I knew exactly what he was doing. He was trying to get under my skin in a hurry. He thought bringing up Emily would set me off. I wasn't going to let him get to me using her though.

"Dude, drop the shit with Emily. It's already old."

"You know, I bet she already moved on from you. I would wager that she has another fella. A girl like that doesn't stay single for long. Besides she needed someone to take her mind off you turning out to be a Talyrian spy."

I stood rooted to the spot gripping the handles of the daggers tightly. My teeth were grinding together and all my muscles were clinching and relaxing with each breath I took.

"I wonder which of those Corlissian boys she's with. He's probably got his arms wrapped around her in bed right now. It might very well be a bed you shared with her."

I was trying to tune him out, but being in a confined concrete room it was pretty much impossible to escape what he was saying. Of course what he said was sticking in my head and making me wonder if Emily had already moved on. Who would she be with? Sam, Tyler, Micah, or Evan? Or did she just fall back into the arms of Mason? My stomach grew sicker as that thought expanded in my mind.

"Or maybe she is just so heartbroken over what you did that she is hardly able to even live her life. She's probably curled up in her bed weeping and replaying what you last said to her over and over in her head."

Now I knew that wasn't true. I had talked to her on the phone and she didn't seem the least bit fazed that we weren't together anymore. She didn't even sound mad or upset by it all. If anything, she seemed completely fine about the whole thing. To be honest, that hurt more than imagining her with someone else.

"And there you stand looking at me like you want nothing more than to rip my head off. But you know that this is all your fault. Hurting her and leading her on was your own doing. And why wouldn't she believe the things you said when you were posing as a human? That was your plan all along though, wasn't it? It wasn't so much to spy on the Corlissians, you wanted to make one of them fall in love with you just so you could break their heart and leave them a cold broken shell of what they were."

Two choices were banging around in my head. I could either lunge at him and stick one of the daggers in his throat and the other dagger in his heart or…

I opened my palms and let both daggers fall to the water-soaked ground. "I'm not playing this fucked up game with you. Either you stop what you're doing or I'm going to find another trainer."

"You're giving up like that? If I was your enemy, would you just throw your weapons down?"

"No. You would already have a dagger sticking out of your heart just for mentioning her name. But standing in front of me is just a pathetic Talyrian who sucked as an aquamancer so the only thing he is capable of doing now is training aquamancers the best he can and running around the stronghold because he's the King's monkey," I spat.

I thought I had really pissed him off when I saw the scowl on his face, but then half of his mouth quirked up in a smile. "I didn't think you had it in you, boy. Now, pick up you daggers and come at me."

I picked the daggers up and held one in my hand so it was pointing forward. The second dagger was in my other hand pointing backward. I had seen the Corlissians holding their daggers like that the night of homecoming. I figured I would give it a try.

I took a few hesitant steps toward Corbin. He reached behind his back and pulled two daggers out. I definitely needed a back holster. Emily always had that badass air about her and I knew it was because she was almost always loaded down with weapons. I wanted that feeling too.

Corbin swung out wildly at me. I yanked my head back, but his reach was further than I anticipated and his dagger sliced right through the chest of my shirt. A moment later blood oozed out and started to leak down the front of my shirt and chest.

I took a step back and tossed one dagger up in the air and caught it by the tip if the blade. I quickly sent it soaring toward Corbin. He sidestepped it, but while his eyes were on the one dagger I stepped forward and sliced through his arm. He dropped the dagger that was in that hand. I quickly picked it up and pressed his own dagger against his throat. I had mine placed with the tip against his heart.

He held his hands up in surrender. "Maybe we should send more Talyrians to Corlissian bases just to learn some things. You are very skilled with a dagger for never having held one in your life up until two days ago."

I took a few steps away from him. I flipped his dagger around so the hilt was facing him. He took it back and I picked up my other one. The blade was chipped from slamming into the concrete wall.

"Don't worry, I'll get you a replacement," Corbin said as he returned his daggers to his back holster.

I set mine down on the floor. I looked down at my bloodstained shirt and split the slit open in my shirt so I could see the wound running almost from armpit to armpit across my chest.

"Come on. We need to the get our wounds taken care of. You especially. Your father would have my ass if he saw that."

I followed Corbin out of the room. I expected him to take a left out of the door and go back the usual way, but he took a right. It was then that I realized there were a whole lot of rooms down a whole lot of halls. It was a confusing maze. Luckily there were signs posted at intervals with "YOU ARE HERE" letting you know exactly where you were in the training wing. It was just like being in a mall.

Corbin came to one of the watertight doors and twisted the handle and shoved his weight against it. On the other side was a small white room with a desk in the center. Behind the desk was a man looking all sorts of bored with his feet propped up on the edge of the desk. He perked up when we walked in.

"Feet down, Reggie," Corbin ordered.

Reggie dropped his feet. "What can I help you with?" he asked.

Corbin pointed at me. Reggie took a glance at me and grimaced. "Ouch." He picked up the phone and hit a few numbers. "I need a free healer to the front as soon as possible," he said into the receiver. He placed the phone back in the cradle and looked up at us. "Someone will be with you shortly."

"We'll get fixed up and go finish practice. A flesh wound doesn't cancel training," Corbin said.

"Are you Killian Marlow?" Reggie asked.

I looked down at him staring up me with wide eyes. "Umm, yeah."

"You're the guy who was hanging out with Corlissians when Phoenix found you."

"Okay."

"What? Is that not true?"

"I'm sure a lot of rumors are spreading through this place about what I was doing and I don't really care. I'm not commenting on any of it. Just remember that whatever you hear is probably bullshit."

"Well, if it's not true you should refute it. Just let people know what happened and be done with it," Reggie suggested.

"People would still talk even if I told them the truth. People love to gossip. I don't care what anyone thinks."

Reggie opened his mouth when the door behind him opened and a tall woman with white blonde hair strode into the room. She was wearing a white skirt that showed how long her legs were and a dark blue tank top. Reggie stared at her ass as she passed him.

"Mmm, two patients," she stated looking at my chest and Corbin's arm. "You boys are always roughing each other up."

She went to Corbin first and pulled his sleeve up. She placed her hand just above his cut and whispered, "*Sanare*," I could see the space between his arm and her hand waiver from the power passing through.

She tugged his sleeve back down once she was satisfied with her work. Then she stood in front of me. "Shirt off," she ordered.

Corbin walked over to speak with Reggie at the desk whose eyes were still glued to the healer's ass.

I peeled my shirt carefully off and looked down at the wound. "Corbin did a number on you," she said. She looked up at me when I didn't respond. "What's your name?" she asked.

"Killian."

"Oooh, the Marlow boy who just came back. You're the talk of the stronghold."

"Awesome," I muttered sarcastically. I really didn't give two fucks who was talking about me.

She placed her hand close to my chest and said, "*Sanare*." I had only been healed once before and that was by Emily after she seriously burned my arm. I could vividly see her kneeling down in front of me in my dark apartment not looking at me because she was still pissed at me. Still, she came and healed me because she felt bad about hurting me.

"Do you want to know my name?" she whispered while healing me.

"I don't see what it would matter," I replied kind of rudely.

Her eyes widened momentarily out of shock. I could tell that no one ever blew her off. I'm sure guys would wait for days with bleeding limbs just for her to heal them.

"Do you not find me attractive?" she asked recovering.

"You are very attractive, but I don't see what that matters."

"There must be a girl in your life who you absolutely love," she whispered.

"Something like that."

"So, you love her, but she doesn't feel the same way?"

I felt both of her hands on my chest then. I clamped my hands around her wrists and removed her hands. "I think you're done."

I walked over to where Corbin stood still chatting with Reggie. "All healed? Good, let's go!" I followed him back to the watertight door. The healer stared me down as we walked past her. I was positive no one had ever refused her advances. Yay me for being hopelessly in love with a girl who hated me!!!

Corbin and I practice aquamancy for a quite a while. He taught me a few tricks that were pretty cool. Before I left, he fitted me with a holster and a new dagger to replace the one I busted.

I headed back through the training center. I got a lot of weird stares and I realized that it was because I was wearing a shirt that had a massive hole in it and was covered in blood.

I went up to my room and took a shower and changed clothes. I was heading out to go downstairs to get something to eat when I heard a snippet of conversation Zoë was having with someone on the phone. Her door was partially open, so being the nosy brother I was, I leaned against the wall and listened.

"...doesn't think we should see each other because of our age difference, but he was dating you and you're a Corlissian," Zoë said.

I was pissed off because just yesterday Zoë promised me she wouldn't call Emily ever again, yet here she was on the phone with her talking like they were best friends again.

Zoë paused while Emily said something. "Oh, the way he talked it made it seem like you two were together."

I could only imagine what Emily was saying. "Okay! Bye, Emily!" Zoë said before hanging up.

I ran across the hall to my room and quietly shut the door. I pressed my ear against the door and listened.

I heard Zoë's door quickly close. I barely opened my door just as she whizzed by. I opened the door further to see where she was going. She turned left at the end of the hall and disappeared. I ran out of my room and followed her.

I wanted to know why she was being all sneaky. And what did she and Emily actually have to talk about? They didn't know each other at all. Emily probably didn't even remember I had a sister, and Zoë only knew about Emily because of what I had told her.

I followed in Zoë's wake and managed to catch quick glimpses of her before she would turn a corner and head down another hall. I caught one last sight of her before she went through a door.

I carefully opened the door only to find a stairwell. I went to the railing and could see Zoë jogging down the stairs. I waited at the top to see what floor she exited, but she went clear to the bottom. When I heard a metal door slam, I knew she was out of the stairwell. I ran down them quickly.

I yanked the door open at the bottom. I was not expecting to see the dungeons sprawled out in front of me. The dungeons were like a massive basement to the stronghold. They ran the same length and width. The only difference was the dungeons were not eight stories deep.

A long hall with cells on both sides was in front of me. I could barely make out a tiny light way head of me. I was guessing that was Zoë. What in the hell was she looking for down here?

I walked at the slow pace glancing every so often in the cells at my sides. They were all empty. The floor was wet and there was the occasional drip from above. It was musty down there too. I had a feeling this was the unused part of the dungeons.

The light Zoë was carrying went out. That made me pick up my pace. When I reached where she had been, I realized that she had only turned a corner. I had to hold back because I had caught up to her.

"It's going to take me forever to search down here. I don't even know what she looks like. Maybe she's not down here. Maybe she's not here at all," Zoë muttered to herself.

That really piqued my attention. So, she was looking for a woman. Why? That question nagged at my brain enough that I stepped out. My foot dragged on the ground which caused Zoë to spin around and scream.

"Shut up!" I hissed.

"Killian? What are you doing here?"

"Yeah, I think you should answer that first!"

She sighed and closed the distance between us. "You're gonna be mad at me."

"Don't care. Spill."

"Emily called me a little bit ago and asked if I would snoop around and see if her aunt is up here. I said I would and I figured the first place to look would be the dungeons," Zoë explained.

"Kate," I said.

"What?"

"Emily's aunt's name is Kate. She looks a lot like Emily too. I don't think she'd be in this part of the dungeon. I don't think anyone's ever been in this part of the dungeon actually. If she is down here, they'd have her closer to the central part. Let's head that way."

I started walking and stopped when I realized Zoë hadn't moved. "You coming?"

"You're going to help me?" Zoë asked. I nodded my head. "And you're not mad?"

"I'm not happy that you two are talking on the phone, but I'm not mad."

Zoë let out a sigh of relief and caught up to me.

"So, why does Emily think her aunt is here?" Zoë asked.

"Because she probably is. Emily asked me if I kidnapped her before Phoenix and I left Autumn Falls, but I had nothing to do with it. Kate and I didn't exactly like one another, but I would never kidnap her."

"Why does Emily care so much for her aunt anyways?"

"Both of Emily's parents were murdered by Talyrians. Kate raised Emily and her siblings. She's been their guardian since Emily was pretty young."

"Are you helping me because you think it will put you in good favor with Emily again?"

"I'm helping you because it's the right thing to do."

"And if we do find Kate, it will put you in her good graces too."

I snorted at that. "Kate didn't like me from pretty much the moment she saw me. I don't know why. I was nice to her. I wasn't feeling up Emily in front of her or anything. I overheard her tell Emily one night that I would destroy her."

"Didn't you?"

I let out a breath. "More than once. I keep fucking up with her."

"Maybe next time you'll get it right."

"Zoë, there isn't going to be a next time for us. She gave me a second chance and I burned her. I didn't mean to. I was happy where I was and I would have gladly stayed there forever, but your past has a way of creeping up and biting you in the ass when you least expect it."

"She, umm, she told me that the two of you never technically dated."

"She's not wrong. We didn't ever go on dates. We just spent a lot of time with one another at school, at her lake house, and at my apartment."

"No wonder she doesn't like you. What kind of guy doesn't take a girl he likes out to eat and to see a movie every now and then? Damn, you're a bad boyfriend!"

That made me chuckle a little. "Emily is not the kind of girl you can woo with dinner and movie. She'd prefer to murder some Brothers or Nexes. She's a little twisted actually."

Zoë opened her mouth to say something, but I put my finger to my lips to keep her quiet. I could faintly hear voices up ahead. I didn't know if they belonged to prisoners or to guards.

The dungeons were set up so that all the halls eventually converged right in the center of the stronghold. That was where the guards' offices were and a few of the more high-profile prisoners were kept. A spiral staircase not far from the King's office lead down to the center. The King sometimes liked to conduct one on one interviews with a few lucky, or rather unlucky, prisoners.

We had been walking for some time, so I figured that we were close to the center of the dungeons. We turned one last corner and up ahead were a few guards milling about near the offices. It was well lit in that part of the dungeons with modern florescent lighting. The rest of the dungeons had single bulbs flickering randomly.

One of the guards turned. I shoved Zoë behind me. I was big enough that she couldn't be seen behind me.

"Who are you?" he called. He pulled a flashlight up, but I shielded my face from the light.

"My father sent me here to check on the female prisoner," I stated in a deep tone.

He took a few steps toward us. "There is no female prisoner down here."

"Shit," I breathed. "Zoë, I want you to run back to where we came," I whispered.

I heard her take a few steps back from me and then I heard her feet pounding down the concrete.

"HEY! GET BACK HERE!" the guard yelled.

I turned and took off in my sister's wake. I caught up to her and latched my hand around her forearm and practically dragged her behind me. I could hear a few guards following us.

We ran down several long halls with the guards gaining on us. When I heard water splashing under my feet, I knew we were close. At the end of the hall was the door we had come through. I yanked Zoë in front of me so she could get through the door first. She yanked on the handle and it didn't budge.

"Killian, they lock from the other side. I forgot!"

I turned around when the guards were close. They stopped running and were walking up to us rather casually.

I held my hands up and breathed, "*Unda.*" Water shot out of my hands like I was holding two fire hoses. I felt Zoë lift the back of my shirt up and pull one of my daggers from the holster.

The guards weren't expecting the onslaught of water and went down when it blasted them in the chest. I kept it going until Zoë said, "Got it!"

I whispered, "*Intereo*" and we flew through the door and up the stairs. I don't think I had ever run that fast up eight flights of stairs. I was winded when we reached the top.

We made it my room and we both collapsed on the floor, still breathing heavily.

"If...Dad...hears...about...that...we're...dead," Zoë muttered between breaths.

"I know," I whispered on an exhale. I rolled over on my back. "At least we learned one thing."

"What's that?"

"Kate's not in the dungeons."

Chapter 13
Emily

I woke up to my cell phone ringing. I had gotten so good about shutting it off and the one time I didn't is when someone calls. Of course! I picked it up and squinted my eyes from the brightness of the screen. I couldn't even make out the name, but I answered it anyway.

"What?" I mumbled.

"Why are you calling my sister and having her do potentially dangerous things?"

"What? Who the fuck is this?" I glanced at the clock that was on the shelves that divided my room. 2:49 a.m.

"It's Lian."

"Now, why are you yelling at me at three o'clock in the morning?"

"Because you asked my sister to look for Kate. She's fourteen, Emily. She should not be sneaking into the dungeons. She's impressionable and she likes you. She'd probably jump off the top of the stronghold if you told her to."

I rolled over on my side. "What am I supposed to do, Lian? I'm just trying to locate my aunt."

"You could call me," he suggested.

"Ha! Last time I asked you about Kate you were less than helpful."

"Next time you need something just call me."

"So you can be an asshole and not give me a straight answer? I'll pass."

"Emily…"

"I don't need your help," I spat.

"Fine. You're right. You don't." He let out a frustrated sigh and took a deep breath. Even over the phone I was wearing on him. Go me!

"Where are you?" he asked in a calmer tone.

"The lake house," I whispered.

"You in bed?" he asked.

"Yes. Does that bring back some fond memories of the last time you were in this bed?"

He chuckled. "I think the memories after are more unforgettable. Let's see, you threw my clothes out of the house, used pulso morsus AND pyromancy on me, then left me standing ten miles outside of town in the pouring rain wearing a towel. It was never a dull moment when I was with you."

I didn't like where this was headed, so I changed the subject completely. "So, how's life in that massive prison?" I asked.

"Honestly, it sucks. I haven't felt the sun on my skin since I stepped through those front doors," he said. "Kinda makes me miss the beach."

"What made you decide to come here?" I blurted out.

He paused for a moment. I'm sure that random question threw him off. "You want the Talyrian answer or the Corlissian answer?" he asked.

"Neither. I want the truth from you for once."

"Emily, I did not lie…"

"I think you came into my life to teach me that it's okay to let people go. If they really wanted to stay, they would. That's what you taught me, Lian."

"Emily, I didn't want to…"

Call ended.

I sat up in bed and tossed the phone down on my comforter. I felt the hot sting of tears in my eyes and tried to wipe them away before they spilled down my cheeks. I failed miserably.

My cell rang again. I saw his name pop up on the screen this time. I wasn't raised to be a chicken shit and hide from my enemies. I picked my phone back up and answered it.

"What now?" I asked through gritted teeth. I was not about to sound like he broke me and reduced me to tears with a few words.

"Would you please stop hanging up on me?" he asked nicely.

I didn't respond. The mean bitch in me wanted to tell him I would never stop hanging up on him, but that sweet girl that still resided in part of me wanted to hear every little thing he wanted to say.

"You still there?" he asked.

"Yes."

"Can I just say what I need to once and for all without you hanging up on me?"

"Say it. Just get it over with," I sighed.

"I miss you," he whispered.

I sucked in a breath. That was not what I was expecting. Not even close.

"I miss being with you. I miss just being around you. I miss sleeping in bed with you too, but mostly I miss just hanging out, talking, and even studying history with you. I miss my friend."

I covered my mouth with my hand so he couldn't hear the sob that escaped. Those tears wasted no time in making a return. I hated him for how easily he could turn me into a wreck.

"Emily, please say something?" he begged.

"You cannot say those things to me, you asshole! I'm supposed to hate you. I'm supposed to shove a dagger through your heart. I'm supposed to…"

"I didn't mean…"

"NO! That's why you called, isn't it? Just to prove that you still have some sick power over me? Just to break me down again? Well, congratulations, you win."

"Why can I never get things right with you? Why is it always a battle for us to see eye to eye? I'm trying to, I don't know, I'm trying to show you that the guy you knew in Autumn Falls was the real me. I wasn't pretending with you. Not once was I pretending."

"I can't do this, Lian," I whispered.

"What? What can't you do?"

"Act like I'm okay with what happened. That day you left was the worst day of my life. And this is coming from a person who had someone come to their door and tell them that both of their parents were dead. What you said to me was cruel and I can never forgive you for that."

"I never expected you to forgive me. I said what I did so you would hate me. I didn't mean it, but that's not the point. I said it and I take all the hate from you I deserve for those words."

"I'm sorry I called your sister. I won't do it again. And I would appreciate it if you would never call me again. Goodbye, Lian."

I ended the call and set the phone down on my bedside table. I threw the covers back and got up. I was not going back to sleep after all that. I cracked my door open and the whole house was dark. My brothers and sister were sleeping soundlessly in their rooms.

I crept down the hall and out the front door. I had sweats and a long-sleeved shirt on and still the chill in the air sunk through my skin to my bones. I walked down to the docks. I sat cross-legged on the end of one and stared out across the lake.

It was unnervingly dark out. The only light came from the stars that littered the sky and they didn't light much. They mostly sparkled off the still water of the lake.

I felt dead inside. It seriously felt like that little bit of life I had left in me that had kept me going over the past few days had just been sucked out of me.

I heard footsteps on the dock behind me. I didn't even turn around. It could have been a Brother or a Nexes and I couldn't have cared less. They could have stabbed me in the back, slit my throat, and dumped me in the lake. I had no fight left in me.

A lantern came into view just before Toby sat down beside me. He set the lantern down in front of us and just sat in silence for a while.

"Are you okay?" he asked after a few minutes had passed.

I pulled my knees up and hugged them to my chest. "No," I whispered. I rested my chin on top of my knees.

"You were talking to Killian, weren't you?" I nodded my head slightly. "I heard you on the phone. I didn't hear everything, but I heard enough. I wasn't eavesdropping though. These walls are kind of thin and since our bedrooms share a wall…" he trailed off.

"I don't care that you heard, Toby," I muttered. I wiped my drippy nose on the end of my shirtsleeve. Mom always yelled at me for doing that. It was a habit I had thought I finally broke when I was six.

"You weren't this bad when you broke up with Mason," he said.

I turned my head and laid my cheek on my knee so I could look at my brother. So many people had told us that we could pass as twins. Our hair was the same shade of brown, even though mine had purple streaks through it. Our eyes were both gray, mine were slightly darker though. Our faces were the same shape and both of our noses had that same little slope at the tip. He was a head taller than me, but we both had that same lean muscular build. There was no denying that we were siblings.

"Mason wasn't a Talyrian," I whispered.

"Maybe that's why you were drawn to him in the first place," Toby said.

"I'm not a Talyrian."

"No. I know you're not. You're my sister. But for some reason you have a Talyrian power in you. Maybe that was enough to draw you to one another."

"Have you been talking to Thea?"

Toby chuckled. "A little. She doesn't know what your relationship consisted of. I don't think anyone knows but you and him. Everything she's telling me is purely speculation and theories."

"I'll be alright, Toby. I just need some time."

Toby turned his face toward mine. The light of the lantern was reflecting off his gray eyes making them glow. "That's the thing. I don't think you will be."

That brought my head up. "What's that supposed to mean?" I asked.

"You two seemed to be on another level from the rest of us. And that's not a bad thing. I think with you learning you had all these new powers you needed to find solace in someone who didn't give a fuck about it. You needed to be with someone who wasn't telling you how awesome it was or how wrong it was. I don't blame you for needing that. I probably would have done the same thing. And here's another thing, I really liked Killian. I thought he was good for you. He made you happy and I think in a weird way he helped you deal with having those powers, even though he didn't know about them."

I sucked in a breath at that last part. Everyone knew at this point that Lian knew we were all Corlissians. He had seen us all at homecoming. Everyone was okay with that, I guessed. What they didn't know was that Lian knew about all my powers.

I cleared my throat. "Toby, he knows everything I can do," I whispered.

"You know, I had a gut feeling he did. He would have been a whole lot more freaked out seeing what you could do at the warehouse if he didn't know. I won't say anything to anyone. That's your business. I do appreciate you telling me."

We sat out on that dock for hours just talking about everything. It was nice. I thought I wanted to be alone, but being with my brother was so much better. I hadn't spent this much time with Toby in a long time. We used to be nearly inseparable when we were younger. I forgot how much I missed hanging out with him.

Even as the sun came up, we sat there. I was freezing and Toby was dressed about the same as I was. I was sure he was cold too, but would never say he was. Our heads snapped around when we heard someone coming down the docks.

Drew was carrying a wooden tray with three mugs on it. He laid it down behind Toby and me and sat down himself. Toby and I turned around so we were facing him.

"How long have you guys been up?" he asked through a yawn.

"A few hours," Toby replied picking one of the mugs up and inspecting it. "You made us coffee?"

Drew nodded his head and a sleepy smile tugged at his lips. His black hair was messier than usual. He had his black robe on and black sweatpants on under that. "I had a horrible night's sleep," he muttered.

"Why?" Toby asked after taking a sip of the coffee.

"I was having dreams that some girl was yelling about something. Maybe she was yelling at someone. I dunno," he said with a shrug picking up a mug.

I glanced at Toby out of the corner of my eye and saw he was looking at me with a grin hidden behind his mug. It was probably best to keep some things between just us. Drew wasn't quite as understanding as Toby was. He had a thing for going over the deep end about little things. And this wasn't exactly a little thing.

I picked up a mug and took a sip just as the front door slammed. Camilla came bouncing down the walkway toward us. Drew let out a loud sigh.

"Drew, maybe you should back off her a little," I suggested.

"It's my job as her younger brother to torment her," he replied with a smile.

"Then I should do the same thing to you. You know it's weird how Toby and I look so much alike and you look nothing like us. It's almost like you're adopted," I said.

"Please, I have Mom's black hair and Dad's blue eyes. I definitely have the same parents as you two. It's that one who's the oddball," Drew said just as Camilla sat down next to him.

"Actually, it's that who's the oddball with all her freak powers!" Camilla said nodding in my direction.

"Aww, don't be jealous of her, Cami," Drew said. "And I wouldn't say anything to piss her off either. Our little sister's powers aren't just freaky, they are fucking powerful."

Drew would know. He was the first person I had ever used pulso morsus on even though it was completely accidental. Sam is the only person who'd felt it three times.

"Well kiddies, we should get ready for school," Drew said standing up and downing the rest of his coffee. "And you should do whatever it is you do all day. I'm not sure what that is since you are making zero headway in finding Kate," Drew added glaring down at Camilla.

"I've finally gathered up a few other Corlissians to help with tracking her," Camilla said indignantly.

"Mmm hum," Drew muttered before heading back up to the house. Camilla jumped to her feet and followed him while yelling obscenities to his back that Drew just ignored.

"Well, it's gonna be fun getting ready this morning," Toby groaned. He stood up a stretched his back. He offered me a hand that I gladly accepted. He pulled me to my feet and we followed in our elder siblings bickering wake.

Toby actually rode to school with me. It seemed like it had been a while since he sat shotgun.

"So, I overhead Sam and the other guys talking at the end of practice yesterday. Is it true that they're getting runes tattooed on them to protect them from your powers?" he asked.

"Yeah. We're just trying different runes and words to see if anything works. Yesterday Sam got the Eye of Horus put on him and we tried it out. It didn't work. I guess he told Mason, Micah, Tyler, and Evan about it and they agreed to do it to and Sam said he'd try it a second time."

"I want in."

"Umm…" I didn't know what to say. No one else in the family had any tattoos on them. I was the only one. I couldn't exactly tell him no. I got mine done when I was fifteen. I had a permission slip with Kate's forged signature on it. I kept them both covered until they healed. She wasn't happy the first time she saw them. "I guess, but maybe you should run it by Drew first," I suggested.

"Why? We're all going to get one eventually."

He did have a good point. "All right. Do what you want."

"Sweet!"

"You better hope it works. I've heard it hurts like a bitch."

"I'm a Corlissian, not some sissy human." Yeah, Toby was definitely my brother!

We pulled into the parking lot and Sam had my driver's door practically open before I even had the car stopped.

"Do you have those rune designs with you?"

"Hey, Sam! It's nice to see you too. Oh, I'm doing fine. And yourself? Good to hear." Sam wrinkled his nose at my sarcasm as I dug around in my bag and pulled all the papers out.

"Well, this one works awesomely," he said handing me back the paper with the Eye on it. I slipped it in my bag.

Micah, Evan, Tyler, and Mason walked over then. "All right. Who wants this lovely Native American rune?" Sam asked as he threw his hand around it like it was a prize at a game show.

"I'll do it," Tyler and Evan said in unison. Tyler snatched the paper from Sam and the two of them studied it.

"And who wants this beautiful Wicca rune?"

"Me," Micah said also taking the paper.

"Oh, and last we have this amazing Celtic rune! I think Emily especially likes this one!" Mason snatched the paper from Sam without a word. "Okay, I guess I'll get a word on me. Toby, you getting one too?" Sam asked.

Toby nodded his head enthusiastically. "I get a word too?" he asked looking at me.

"Yeah. I'll get them to you later. You can pick what you want." The bell rang out and people emptied the parking lot and headed into school.

During my first three classes I searched the Latin book I had for the right words. I came up with a substantial list. Toby and Sam would have a lot to choose from.

At lunch, Toby sat with us and I slid the list I created between Sam and my brother. They both studied it carefully. There were several Latin words for protection, cover, and protect.

"I want tego," Toby said choosing one that came from the protect list.

"Hum, I'll go with ara," Sam said picking one from the protection list. "Okay, so we'll go get these done at our parlor of choice and meet up at Culver's field later. Then Emily can turn at least five of us into screaming infants."

"I want in on this," Thea said. She had been sitting there quietly this whole time. I kind of forgot to ask her if she wanted to do it or not. I figured she wouldn't though. Sometimes, even your best friend can surprise you.

She scooted the list that was in front of Sam and Toby so she could see it. She tapped her chin as her eyes roamed the paper. "I choose induco."

Drew walked in the lunchroom a moment later and stood behind Thea looking at the list in front of her. "Put me down for vindico." Then he walked away without another word.

Everyone kind of looked blankly at one another. It looked like every Corlissian except Bridgette and Camilla would be getting a tattoo tonight. Good thing there were four tattoo parlors in town.

As the last bell rang, we all met in the parking lot. Sam and Tyler were going to Falls Ink. Micah and Mason were headed to Pricks & Needles. Thea and Evan went to Leafy Ink and I went with Drew and Toby to Sunken Daggers.

I watched with an amused smirk as both my brothers winced at the pain of the needle. Drew got his on his right bicep and Toby put his on his left shoulder blade.

"I swear only masochist get this done for the hell of it. How in the hell did you not cry like a baby when you got that one on your back?" Drew asked as we walked out to the car. He had the sleeve of his shirt rolled up and was dabbing at it lightly with a paper towel.

"I'm a masochist," I stated.

"You're fucking twisted, Emily!" he said getting in the back seat of the Audi. Toby gingerly got in the passenger seat.

"Don't lean back," I said to him. He nodded his head and leaned way forward. He had the left half of his shirt pulled up so it was far from touching the new ink. I had to laugh at him. He looked up at me and smiled. "Does it hurt?" I asked.

"It doesn't feel pleasant," he muttered.

We drove out to Culver's and Sam and Tyler were standing in the circle. Thea and Evan had just pulled up in front of us. We headed down and joined Sam and Tyler. We waited about ten minutes until Mason's red Lexus could be seen heading down the road.

Once everyone was in the circle, they all stood around me. I was in the middle. "You all ready?" I asked. They all nodded their heads.

I took a deep breath and said, "*Dolor.*" Once again, the red tendrils flowed through my forearms. "*Dolor.*" The red spilled out and hovered around my legs awaiting my command.

"Shit, that's awesome," Toby muttered.

I shoved both my hands out and the red shot all around me and took every Corlissian down...except Sam didn't seem as affected this time. He went down on his knees.

I went to Toby and used the healing power on him. Sam went to Tyler and smacked his face to wake him up. Eventually every Corlissian was awake and sitting on the ground in the circle.

I was sitting in front of Sam. "It still hurt, but it wasn't that bad. It was like I felt like I could withstand it for a bit."

Something just didn't seem right about it. Drew and Toby both had words for protect on them and they went down just as hard as if they had nothing on them. It didn't make sense to me. That should have prevented them from feeling the full effects like it did for Sam. It shouldn't have mattered that he also had pulso morsus.

"What's the matter?" he asked.

"Just thinking," I whispered.

"I'm up to try another one tomorrow if everyone else is," he said. There were a few groans throughout our companions.

"Umm, one person can sit it out since I don't have enough words for everyone," I said.

"Oh hell, I'll do it," Evan said. Eventually everyone agreed to it, but the guys voted Thea out. She really didn't seem to mind much.

Everyone headed up to their cars. Toby, Drew, and I hung back and remained in the circle. Once all I could see were tail lights of their cars, did I say anything? "I want you to both get in the car, okay?"

"You're gonna try pulso metus, aren't you?" Drew asked. I nodded my head. "Then you do not have to tell me twice. Come on, Toby."

Only after my brothers were in the safety of the car did I whisper, "Timor." This time instead of the red tendrils in my forearms it was a bright blue. It stayed in just my forearms like pulso morsus did. I breathed "Timor" a second time and the bright blue wisped around my lower half. It twisted in between my legs and twirled around my hips. I ran my fingers through it and it weaved its way in between my fingers. It was almost like it was alive. It was creepy and awesome at the same time.

I turned around and Drew and Toby both had their faces pushed up against the windows with their mouths hanging open. I shoved one of my arms out and the blue went up with it and wrapped itself around my outstretched arm. It was like it was fiercely protective of me. Eventually it loosened its grip and widened around me. I lifted my other arm up and it formed a massive shield around me.

"*Intereo.*" The blue instantly disappeared. I walked up the hill and got in the car.

"That was the coolest thing I have ever seen a Corlissian do, Emily," Toby said as I turned the car around.

"Thanks," I muttered.

"Mason was right when he said that we could drop you off at the stronghold and you could take care of all the Talyrians for us," Drew said.

"Can you do them at the same time?" Toby asked.

"Haven't tried yet. That was the first time I tried it with pulso metus." I would have to try that tomorrow though.

Chapter 14

Lian

It felt weird that I hadn't talked to Emily yet. I was still kind of mad at her about using my sister to search for Kate though. I was lying in bed staring at the ceiling. I turned and glanced at my clock. 2:47 a.m. I picked up my cell phone that was on my bedside table and called Emily's number.

"What?" she grumbled into the phone. She had clearly been sleeping.

"Why are you calling my sister and having her do potentially dangerous things?" I asked. It was a reasonable question after all. I just might not have said it in a reasonable way.

"What? Who the fuck is this?"

"It's Lian."

"Now, why are you yelling at me at three o'clock in the morning?"

"Because you asked my sister to look for Kate. She's fourteen, Emily. She should not be sneaking into the dungeons. She's impressionable and she likes you. She'd probably jump off the top of the stronghold if you told her to." I knew my voice was getting louder, but I couldn't help it.

"What am I supposed to do, Lian? I'm just trying to locate my aunt." She did have a point.

"You could call me," I recommended.

"Ha! Last time I asked you about Kate you were less than helpful."

"Next time you need something just call me," I replied trying to ignore her previous statement.

"So you can be an asshole and not give me a straight answer? I'll pass."

"Emily…" I said before she cut me off. I swear even over the phone that girl knew how to wear on every single one of my nerves.

"I don't need your help," she growled into the phone.

"Fine. You're right. You don't." I let out a long sigh.

"Where are you?" I asked. I still wanted to talk to her, just about something completely different. I figured her reply to my simple question would be something along the lines of, "Fuck off."

"The lake house."

I was kind of curious about why she was there, but my mind went to other places. "You in bed?" I asked.

"Yes. Does that bring back some fond memories of the last time you were in this bed?" Hell yeah it did, but something else was a little more prominent.

I laughed. "I think the memories after are more unforgettable. Let's see, you threw my clothes out of the house, used pulso morsus AND pyromancy on me, then left me standing ten miles outside of town in the pouring rain wearing a towel. It was never a dull moment when I was with you."

"So, how's life in that massive prison?" she asked. I knew she was changing the subject. I didn't mind. I was just glad she was still talking to me.

"Honestly, it sucks. I haven't felt the sun on my skin since I stepped through those front doors. Kinda makes me miss the beach."

"What made you decide to come here?" That question came from out of nowhere. It took me a moment to process.

"You want the Talyrian answer or the Corlissian answer?" I asked.

"Neither. I want the truth from you for once," she breathed.

"Emily, I did not lie…"

"I think you came into my life to teach me that it's okay to let people go. If they really wanted to stay, they would. That's what you taught me, Lian."

"Emily, I didn't want to…" Then the line went dead. She hung up on me…again.

I was actually getting sick of her hanging up on me. I sat up in bed and redialed her number.

"What now?" she snapped.

"Would you please stop hanging up on me?" I asked in a very calm tone.

She didn't say anything. I was expecting to hear her hang up on me again. It was the kind of thing Emily would do.

"You still there?"

"Yes."

"Can I just say what I need to once and for all without you hanging up on me?"

"Say it. Just get it over with." I could hear the sigh in her voice.

"I miss you," I whispered. I could not believe what popped out of my mouth. That was not what I was intending to say. I'm not saying it wasn't the truth. Now that it was out, I just had to go with it.

I heard her inhale sharply at my words. It was kind of nice to know I still affected her.

"I miss being with you. I miss just being around you. I miss sleeping in bed with you too, but mostly I miss just hanging out, talking, and even studying history with you. I miss my friend."

I could hear a muffled noise on her end. I didn't exactly know what it was, but I think I had made her cry.

"Emily, please say something?" I just needed her to either say something that would break my heart or give me some hope that not all was lost for us and that she felt the same as I did.

"You cannot say those things to me, you asshole! I'm supposed to hate you. I'm supposed to shove a dagger through your heart. I'm supposed to…"

"I didn't mean…"

"NO! That's why you called, isn't it? Just to prove that you still have some sick power over me? Just to break me down again? Well, congratulations, you win."

Fucking hell, this was not going where I wanted it.

"Why can I never get things right with you? Why is it always a battle for us to see eye to eye? I'm trying to, I don't know, I'm trying to show you that the guy you knew in Autumn Falls was the real me. I wasn't pretending with you. Not once was I pretending."

"I can't do this, Lian," she said softly. I knew at this point that she was crying. I could hear it in her voice. It killed me that I made her cry. That was not my intent.

"What? What can't you do?" I asked. I knew my tone held a little bit of panic, but I didn't care. This was my relationship with Emily in danger of completely collapsing.

"Act like I'm okay with what happened. That day you left was the worst day of my life. And this is coming from a person who had someone come to their door and tell them that both of their parents were dead. What you said to me was cruel and I can never forgive you for that."

"I never expected you to forgive me. I said what I did so you would hate me. I didn't mean it, but that's not the point. I said it and I take all the hate from you I deserve for those words."

"I'm sorry I called your sister. I won't do it again. And I would appreciate it if you would never call me again. Goodbye, Lian."

I sat there with the phone still up to my ear even though I knew she had hung up. There was such finality in her words that I knew then all was lost for us. She hated me that much. I had gotten my hopes up. We were talking like old times, like nothing had changed between us. Everything that made us just crumbled around me. I was shell-shocked.

I dropped back and my head hit the pillow. My left arm was dangling partway over the side of the bed. I let my cell slip from my hand and I barely heard it hit the floor.

I lay there and just stared at the ceiling. Even as the sun's first rays poked through my open window I didn't budge. I felt utterly empty. Even though I told Zoë there was no chance for Emily and me in the back of my mind I was still holding on to a sliver of hope that we would end up together. Those two little words just obliterated that hope: Goodbye, Lian.

My alarm went off on the bedside table. I reached my arm back, grabbed hold of it, and gave it a yank. I heard the cord rip out of the wall. Then I threw the damn thing across the room and into a wall. I rolled over on my side and hugged one of the pillows to my chest.

I heard a few knocks on my door, but I didn't move. I lay there replaying in my mind all the times I'd spent with Emily. All the times we sat on the dock of her lake house just talking about her powers. All the times I turned around in my seat in school just to see her. All the times I'd lay in bed with her pressed against me. I would never have any of that ever again.

There was another knock at my door. It became progressively louder and didn't stop. I did a sort of roll and fall out of bed. I caught myself on the doorframe and steadied myself. I stumbled out into the living room and yanked the door open.

Zoë was standing there with her hands on her hips looking all sorts of mad at me. When she saw me, though her mood shifted rather quickly.

"What's wrong? Are you sick? You look sick!"

She ushered me back into my bedroom and pretty much shoved me in bed. I saw her glance at the smashed alarm clock on the floor. She didn't say anything about it though. She did pick up my cell phone and sit on the edge of the bed.

She looked at me for a moment before turning the phone on and scrolling through it. Her eyes landed on me again.

"You talked to Emily twice early this morning," she said.

I didn't say anything. I just flipped over so my back was facing her. I really didn't want to talk to anyone, least of all about Emily and what we had discussed.

"Did something happen?" she asked.

"I don't wanna talk about it," I mumbled. My voice was hoarse and it hardly sounded like me.

"Killian, you cannot stay holed up in your room all day. You already missed practice this morning. Corbin wasn't happy about that when I saw him. That's why I came looking for you. You cannot abandon your training."

"I just don't care about it at the moment."

"What did you two talk about?" Zoë asked.

"Nothing. Would you leave me alone?"

"Fine. I will." I didn't like the sound of that.

I felt the bed shift as she got up and I heard the main door close behind her. I let out a breath and curled deeper into myself. I didn't understand why I couldn't be left alone to be miserable for one day. Just one day.

I heard the door open again and close a lot more softly than Zoë had shut it. I felt the bed sink again from the weight of someone sitting down.

"Turn on your back, sweetheart."

I did as Mom asked. I didn't look at her though. I kept my eyes focused on the ceiling. I felt the palm of her hand pressed against my forehead. I remember her doing that when I was younger. She would sit just like she is now and press her hand against my tiny forehead. "Oh Killian, you are burning up!" she'd always say. Then she'd pile me down with blankets and sweat the sickness out of me.

"You're a little warm, but I don't think you're ill," she said softly.

"That's because I'm not sick," I muttered.

"Then why are you lying in bed looking sick?"

"I can't tell you," I whispered.

"Dear, you can tell me anything. Please. I don't like seeing you in this manner."

I glanced at her. Her eyes were pleading with me to let her in on what was truly bothering me. "You cannot tell Father anything. I mean it. It stays between us."

She nodded her head and pulled her left leg on the bed and bent it underneath herself. She straightened her back and smiled at me. "Not a word will pass my lips concerning what you tell me."

I focused my gaze back on the ceiling and let out a shaky breath. "Okay, when I was in the last town, I met a girl…"

"…and Goodbye Lian was the last thing she said to me this morning."

It took me four hours to recount the story to Mom. She sat there nearly unmoving the whole time and listened to every single thing I told her.

"Killian, our races have hated each other from nearly the moment we came into existence. It is unheard of for a Talyrian and a Corlissian to have any sort of relationship."

I sat up. "Why? Because of some feud that happened thousands of years ago that really has nothing to do with us?"

Mom shook her head. "Darling, I'm not saying it's wrong. I'm saying it's never happened before. Do you know what it would mean if our races were to join together? We could put an end to the Avids, Nexes, and Midnight Brothers for good. We could stop this war that has been waging between us for so long. We could finally leave this place and live among humans again. We could have a normal life."

I knew that at some point my jaw went slack and was dangling open. I could not believe her words. She hated this war and our pointless fighting too. She was actually thinking that if a Talyrian and a Corlissian were together that it would be the catalyst that would bring about the fall of our bitterness toward one another.

Then I remembered the conversation that Emily and I had just had and how we were over.

"Well, you'll have to find someone else to be the undoing of all this. Emily and I are done." I fell back onto my bed again.

"Killian? How many times was Emily angry with you in Autumn Falls?" she asked.

I shrugged my shoulders. "A couple times, but only one that she was really peeved about."

"Then what makes you think she won't forgive you for this?"

"Because the things I did before were forgivable. This is about me being a Talyrian. I can't make that go away."

Mom laughed. "Well, no that you're stuck with. Emily sounds like a very smart girl and I have a feeling that the two of you are not done yet. She needs to be shown that the guy she knew and loved in Autumn Falls is still you."

"And how am I supposed to show her that when I can't leave this confinement? Oh, and I was asked not to call her again, so my only communication to her is gone."

"You know her and I'm confident that you'll think of something." She patted me on the chest and stood up. She stretched her back out. "I have some things to get done, but if you need me for anything I will gladly help. Okay?" I nodded my head. "And getting out of bed and dressing yourself is probably the best start to getting that girl of yours back." She gave me a smile and left my room.

I lay there for a while longer. I didn't feel as bad as I had before. Mom had renewed my hope. I knew in the back of my head that renewed hope could be a bad thing that had the chance of exploding in my face and doing me in for good. Emily actually saying the words that we were done for good would be the catastrophe that would be my end. She thought I had the power over her, but she had more over me.

I did what Mom said I should. I rolled out of bed and took a long hot shower and then dressed myself. I knew that Father said if I was not training that I should be dressed like the son of a high ranking official. I pulled on some dark gray dress pants and a black oxford.

There were a number of pair of shoes in the bottom of my closet. I had only worn the athletic ones that fit me. Mom had bought the same shoes in different sizes since she didn't know how much I had grown since I'd been gone. Only a quarter of the clothes in my closet actually fit and about five pair of shoes. Everything else was too small.

I grabbed the black business shoes out and yanked them on. I remained sitting on the edge of my unmade bed. I was clean and dressed and I still had no idea what to do to get myself back into Emily's good graces.

I heard my door open again and slam shut. I turned my head and saw Zoë carrying a tray of food in her hands. She sat it down on the coffee table and came into my room.

"Hey! You're up and dressed. You look mighty fine, big brother! Quite snazzy."

"Ugh, thanks," I muttered glancing down at my clothes.

"I brought you a mix of breakfast and lunch foods. I didn't know what you'd want."

"I'm really not hungry."

"You need to eat. I need you strong and alert when we search for Kate again today."

"Kate," I breathed. That was it. Kate was my way to get Emily back. All I had to do was locate one woman in this massive stronghold, a nearly impossible feat. But I knew that if I found Kate, I could call Emily and at least tell her that her aunt was here. I didn't know what would happen after that, but finding Kate was my main priority.

I sat down on the couch and inspected the foods that Zoë brought. There was a pile of scrambled eggs, toast, and a couple strips of bacon sitting beside a turkey and bacon sandwich and French fries. I ate a little of everything just to make Zoë happy. I didn't want to be too full though.

"So, where are we starting our search today?" I asked though a mouthful of sandwich.

"Close your mouth when you chew. I'm not sure. I guess I just assumed that if she were here, they'd have her in the dungeons. I'm at a loss on this one."

"Mmm, I think we need to pay a visit to your boyfriend and my probably-not-anymore best friend," I said.

Zoë sighed. "Why? Do you think better when you punch people?"

"That's not what I...NO!" I shook my head. "He's in the guards, Zoë. He might have heard some whisperings about a Corlissian woman being held here." I kindly left the 'duh' off the end.

"Oh...OH! Yeah, that's a good idea. Finish up. I'm excited now." Zoë's leg was bouncing up and down and causing the whole couch to wobble. It doesn't feel pleasant after just eating.

"Well, I'm done. Let's go."

We headed down to the bottom floor. I knew the guards lived on the bottom two floors; I just didn't know which one Tovan lived on.

"All the newer guards live on the bottom floor. If they get promoted, then they move up in rank and in the floor, they live on."

I could always count on Zoë to fill me in on things I didn't even ask a question to. It was kind of nice actually.

I followed Zoë down the maze of halls. I did notice that we were walking away from the main hall and the offices of the King and council's members.

Zoë stopped in the middle of a long hall. She paused and glanced at the door she was standing beside. "I missed a turn. Go back."

"Well, I'm not using you as my walking, talking map ever again!"

Zoë laughed. "I don't care how long you live in this place you can still get lost. I like to think that even His Majesty gets lost from time to time. It makes me giggle thinking of him bumbling around down some hallway looking all confused." She giggled and shook her head as we backtracked and took a right down the hallway we had just passed.

We took a few more turns down various halls until I was good and lost. Finally Zoë stopped and knocked on a door that looked exactly like all the others we had passed. I was half expecting some grumpy old guard to yank the door open and yell, "Stop knocking on my door, you damn whippersnappers!" When the door opened, it was just Tovan, to my utter disappointment.

He smiled when he was Zoë. Then he tried to slam the door when he saw me. I stuck my foot out and prevented him from shutting the door. It fucking hurt too. I kind of wished I had my boots on, not a flimsy pair of preppy shoes.

Tovan kept shoving the door into my foot. I stepped forward and slammed my shoulder into the door. The door flew open and Tovan retreated into his room.

"I'm not going to punch you again. I just had a question." I glanced down to see my pretty shoe was all scuffed up. I'm sure Father would say something about that.

I took a moment to glance around Tovan's room. It was half the size of mine. The living room took up the front part and at the back were two doors. Through one I could see a bed and through the other I could see a shower and sink. This was a place for sleeping and nothing else. I wondered if the other Talyrians places were like this or if it was just the guards that lived in tiny spaces.

There was a couch in the living room with two chairs. There was no TV. Instead there were bookcases along a lot of the walls. They were all filled. I didn't know if it was by choice Tovan didn't have a TV or if it was just a distraction that he didn't need.

"Ask him," Zoë whispered.

I turned my attention back to Tovan who was standing behind his couch. I guess he was assuming that if I wanted to beat the hell out of him that I couldn't just jump over the couch. They were tricky things to navigate, those couches!

"He's not going to answer me. Look! He's scared of me," I replied.

"Well, yeah. The last time you saw each other you did punch him."

"For good reason."

"Not for good reason. We've discussed this already. Drop it!"

It was just my sister and me arguing with one another like Tovan wasn't standing across from us. It was at that moment, right then, that it hit me. I had really missed my sister. I felt like an ass for leaving. Not because I didn't take her with me or anything like that. I just missed her growing up. The thing was, she didn't care. She was just glad I was back. And here we were bickering like siblings. It felt like old times. Like I never left for three years.

I smiled down at her. A wrinkle formed between her eyebrows. She probably thought I was going slightly insane. I turned my attention back to Tovan who hadn't moved at all.

"Have you heard anything about a Corlissian woman being in the stronghold?" I asked.

"No one can break into the stronghold," Tovan answered automatically.

I snorted at that comment. I knew one person who would have no problem breaking into this place and then setting the whole damn thing up in flames with one word.

"I didn't ask if someone broke in. I'm asking if she's being held here as a prisoner."

"The prisoners are all held in the dungeons."

I rubbed my hands up and down my face and groaned. I looked at Zoë. "Can you deal with this? I'm getting nowhere."

"Tovan, sweetie…" I made a very audible groan at that. "Can you please let us know if a Corlissian woman is being held in the stronghold somewhere other than the dungeons?" Tovan seemed to relax when Zoë was talking to him.

"Umm, I haven't heard about it, but I am one of the lowest ranked guards. I can keep my ears open though. I'll let you know if I hear anything. What's this about anyways?" he asked.

Zoë looked up at me and I just arched an eyebrow. "Just a favor we're doing for a friend."

"Why can't you just ask your dad?"

I snorted, shook my head, and walked out his door. I leaned against the wall next to his door and waited for Zoë. She came out a moment later. She glared at me then walked down the hall.

"Don't give me that look. I wasn't getting anywhere with him!"

She stopped. "That's why you can't punch anyone you please, Killian. If people are scared of you, they aren't going to answer simple questions you have for them."

"Well, I'm sorry I'm not as nice and sweet as you are!" I said that a little more snidely than I intended.

"You've changed."

"That's what happens when you see the real ugliness in this world," I said.

"So, being holed up in here is a good thing? Not interacting with those crazy humans or experiencing things? You don't know how lucky you are, do you? No one in here had the experience you did, Killian. You got to meet people and do things that some of us couldn't even dream of. You got to live. We won't get that."

"I guess I never thought of that," I muttered. I hadn't. I never thought of everything that happened to me while I was gone as an experience. I was just moving along and hoping that no one would catch up to me.

"You should probably change clothes and go practice. You missed it this morning, but you should still do it every day," Zoë said.

"Zoë..."

She looked up at me. "She ended it, didn't she? She took that little bit of hope that you had left and she squelched it, didn't she?" I nodded my head. "I didn't have to see your cell phone to know exactly what happened. That light that you had in you was gone. I know it's a paltry substitute, but maybe you and Phoenix can get back together."

"Once you've been in the presence of Emily Porter no one else will do." I turned and walked down the hall to presumably get lost on the first floor of the stronghold.

I wasn't any closer to finding Kate and I had no idea where or even if she was in this building. I felt hopeless.

Chapter 15
Emily

I lay there staring at the ceiling for hours. Several thoughts were bouncing around my head all at once. There was no way I was going to get any sleep.

Thought Number One: Kate was lost for good. The only hope I had of finding her had vanished instantly. Even if she was at the stronghold and even if I did manage to get in the place was entirely too large to locate her. I hated to give up on her, but our only option was to attack the stronghold. That itself was a suicide mission and there was no way the council would okay a Talyrian attack for one Corlissian. Even if it was our family that had taken a massive loss at the hands of Talyrians already.

Thought Number Two: There was something that was causing the protection runes to start working on Sam. They weren't working on anyone else though. I didn't know if it was because Sam had taken more hits of the pulso morsus than anyone else. That seemed ridiculous though. You didn't get used to pulso morsus. I was missing something that was probably really fucking simple.

Thought Number Three: Lian. I guess in way I hoped he hadn't taken what I said too seriously and that he would call me again. I was just mad at the whole fucked up situation we were in. He was the one person I could keep pushing away from me and with one final shove he went. I always put-up walls when people had wronged me. With him I put that final wall up and he sure as hell didn't try and climb over it. I knew then that we were done. Now we weren't fighting for each other, we were fighting against one another.

There was a light knock on my door that made all those thoughts disappear instantly. "Come in," I said. The door cracked open and I could see a mess of dark brown hair followed by the rest of my brother.

"You awake, Em?" he whispered.

"Yeah. What's up?"

He slipped inside my room and quietly closed the door behind him. He walked around the shelves. I scooted over and he laid down next to me. When we were little, he would always come into my room when he was scared. Dad would tell him to man up, Drew told him to stop being a wimp, and Camilla would call him a perv. I was the one who would comfort my brother by just letting him sleep next to me.

"I've been thinking about the runes and words," he said.

"And?"

"Well, I have one tiny theory. I think that since Sam has pulso morsus himself that he can take that hit better than the rest of us can."

"I'm busting your theory. Micah has pulso morsus too. He went down just as hard as the rest of you."

"Damn."

"Maybe it's because he has two protection runes and the rest of us only have one."

That had me sitting up. Of course! It was something stupidly simple like I thought it would be. Sam had two tattoos on him. He said that he felt like he could withstand the pain for a little longer. The more runes and words one had the more protection they had.

I looked down at my brother who was staring at me like I had lost my damn mind. "I need you to get like four tats tomorrow. You down?"

A smiled spread onto his face. "Hell yeah. Especially if it will protect me from feeling that awful pain tear through every fiber of my body again."

"I sure hope it works. If this isn't the key, then I'm at a loss and all of you are screwed."

Toby sat up. I figured he was going back to bed, but he paused. "How are you doing, Emily?" he asked.

"Umm, fantastic."

"No. I mean with the whole Killian thing."

"Oh, well there is no Lian thing. I'm over it. In my mind he is just another Talyrian."

Toby stood up and stopped by the shelves. "Do you really think you could kill him if it came down to it?"

"I'm a Corlissian, Toby. It's my fucking job to murder those bastards. I think it will be easier to kill him since he's given me plenty to be pissed at him for."

"Hum," Toby muttered before walking out the door.

I rolled over and pulled the covers tighter around me. I had dreams about all the ways I wanted to torture Lian the next time I saw him. I even thought about how easy it would be for me to kill him. But Toby's question struck another chord in me. I wasn't so sure I could anymore. Talking to him on the phone was one thing. Seeing him in person would be different. I was just hoping that I would never see him again and therefore eliminate that possibility.

I smacked my alarm to shut it up, not that I needed it to wake me up. I hadn't gotten any sleep. As soon as Toby left those thoughts, he had made go away quickly returned to attack my brain again. At least the protection one didn't bug me, just the other two: Lian and Kate.

I threw my covers back and took a shower. I picked out my clothes for the day: black tights, black booties, a white linen top, and my fitted black leather jacket. And, as always, my twin daggers holstered to my back.

I grabbed my bag and walked out my door and nearly collided with Toby. "Hey, I was just coming to see if you were up. Ready?" he asked.

I nodded my head and we left the lake house before we could hear our elder siblings bickering with one another. I swung by McDonald's since Toby begged me to stop since I pulled out of the driveway.

"But I'll starve if we don't stop. I can't eat the food at school. It's alive. I swear I saw a pile of "meat" crawl off Kyle Sims plate. I'll buy you a coffee if you want. I'd have to wait until lunch and by then my stomach would sound like a dying whale in every class. I don't what to be known as the kid with the grumbly stomach." After that I got the pout and caved in.

Toby ate with gusto in the passenger seat while I drove with one hand while sipping on the crappy coffee. No amount of sugar in the world could make it taste good.

When I pulled in the parking lot, everyone was standing around Sam's and Mason's cars. They all surged forward once I pulled to a stop in the space next to Sam's car.

"Can we see the list of words to choose from?" Micah asked excitedly. I got out of the car and pulled the slip of paper from my bag and handed it over to the salivating masses.

I looked at Toby as he got out of the car and gave him a smile. I was going to tell Drew to get a number of tattoos as well. I wanted my brothers to be the only two standing in the circle not flinching from the pulso morsus floating around them attacking everyone else.

The guys were arguing over who was going to get what words on them and where. I had already made the list of words and runes my brothers would be getting this afternoon, so I left the guys standing there with that paper.

Sam caught up to me as I walked toward the school. "Don't you want to write down who chooses what word?" he asked.

"I think you all learned how to write the same time I did. You're big boys. You don't need my help."

Sam grabbed my arm to pulled me to a stop. "What's up with you?" he asked. Oh, wouldn't I love to tell him what was up with me. The list seemed endless these days. But that list of what was really bothering me had nothing to do with what was nagging at me on this day.

It was a little insignificant thing that no one else but me would realize. The rest of them didn't remember that it had been a week to the day since Kate was kidnapped and Lian left. Only a week had passed since my little happy world crashed and burned around me. It felt like it had been so much longer than that. And yet, not even my brothers remembered that their aunt was missing. I didn't expect anyone to remember it as the day that Lian revealed he was a Talyrian.

"I didn't get any sleep last night. I'm just tired," I lied.

He let go of my arm and let me walk into the school. I could feel his eyes on my back. I didn't have to turn around to see it. Thea ran up to me and laced her arm through mine and drove any weird thoughts from my head.

"So, it's Friday!"

"Well spotted."

"And I think that we should have a beach party. Let the guys build a massive fire and just have one more bash before it is too cold," Thea said.

"It's already too cold."

"That's why they'll need to build the biggest bon fire of all times. I'm talking Guinness Book of World Records big."

"It's fine with me, but you might want to run it by the guys first. We are doing a pulso morsus test after school, so I don't know if they'll be up for it or not."

"Oh crap! I forgot about that. How long will it take?"

"Probably not much longer than yesterday."

"They'll have plenty of time to recover." She dropped my arm and turned around. "Hey! Micah? You up for a party tonight?" she yelled.

"Hells to the yeah!" he hollered. They rest of the guys chimed in and then the news spread around the school like fire from me using *incendia*.

As the day progressed it sounded like every student would be at the beach for one last party. In all honesty, I didn't give a fuck about going to another party. Most of my time at that school was deciding whose party we were going to on this night and that night. I had other things to worry about. Partying was the farthest thing from my priorities. But I knew that Thea would literally drag my ass there, so I would show my face for a while just to make her happy. I didn't need my best friend hunting me down.

The day went by as usual with the teacher's trying to convince us that what we were learning would be the foundation for our growing knowledge base when we went to college. I would have agreed with them if I was a human, but I wasn't. I learned everything I truly needed to before I was even in school. Learning who the fifteenth president was did not help me learn to throw a dagger straight and true. Learning the square root of pi did not help me decapitate a Brother. And dissecting Romeo and Juliet did not help to train me in using pyromancy.

School was merely a distraction for me. What I was taught behind these walls only filled a void. And that was only because I wasn't old enough to be a warrior yet. I couldn't go on scouting missions and I couldn't help in raids. I couldn't take out a troop of Brother's or Nexes all because I was still in school and my age prevented it.

I knew damn well that I had taken out more of our enemies than any Corlissian in this town. I roasted fifty Brothers in an instant without batting an eye. But until I was eighteen, I couldn't become a fighter. We were considered liabilities to take into the field until we were adults.

If only the council knew what we had done with the enemies that decided to unwisely come into our town, then they might rethink their policy. The thing was, the council would punish us if they found out we were fighting. That why our parents and guardians allowed it and kept mum about it.

I couldn't wait until our generation shoved those old councilmen out of the way and replaced them. I could see Mason as one of them. He'd make the changes that were right for our race. I hoped.

The final bell rang and we all headed out to our cars and drove to whichever tattoo parlor we wanted. Everyone knew what to do, so we didn't need to discuss it. I handed my brothers the list of what I wanted them to get.

Drew's list: the Native American rune, a word for protection (fides), a word for cover (obvolvo), and a word for protect (contego).

Toby's list: the Celtic rune, a word for protection (tutela), a word for cover (induco), and a word for protect (defend).

My poor brothers were going to be hurting. But then again, the pain from their tattoos would be nearly painless compared to what pulso morsus felt like. It would be worth it and they knew that.

I waited on the well-worn leather couch as my brothers got a lot of new ink. I sat there and played on my cell phone since I had nothing else to do. I heard a few cuss words from Drew and a couple of groans from Toby. There were also a few "I hate you, Emily!"

Two and a half hours later we left and headed out to Culver's Field. Everyone was already there. They were not happy either, but I really didn't give a fuck. I didn't have to do this. It was for their own good, not mine.

I walked to the circle with my brothers flanking me. They took their spots and I stood in the center. Sam was standing on Drew's right and Toby was on Drew's left, so I could see what affect it would have on all three of them. Not that I didn't care about the rest of them.

"*Dolor*," I said. Once I saw the red flowing in my forearms, I said it again so it spilled out of me. I locked eyes with my youngest brother. He gave me a nod. I shoved my arms out. I heard the screams of Tyler, Micah, Evan, and Mason. Sam was standing, but was bent over. Drew and Toby were standing there. The pulso morsus wasn't touching them.

"*Intereo*." I stood there staring at my brothers who were staring right back. I let out a really girly giggle and ran toward them. Drew picked me up and spun me around.

"I cannot believe that fucking worked!" he said. He set me back down on my feet.

I grabbed Toby's face in my hands and looked in his eyes. "Tell me you didn't feel a thing?"

"I didn't feel a thing," he replied with a huge smile on his face. "We guessed right, Em," he whispered.

Sam had woken up Tyler and Evan. He was working on Micah. I placed my hand on Mason's forehead. He cracked his eyes open. "It didn't work," he breathed.

I leaned in close to his ear. "Yes, it did."

"But..."

"I tried something else with Toby and Drew. They didn't feel a thing."

He sat up and I leaned back. "I knew you'd figure it out. You're so smart, Emily."

"Actually, Toby thought of the idea," I said standing up and walking over to my brothers. If I lingered any longer, he would start saying crap that I didn't want to hear. He had a knack for doing that.

"...and that's all. A few extra tats and you don't feel a thing!" Drew was telling the other guys.

Sam caught my eye and nodded his head. I walked a little distance away from the others with him. He turned and made sure we were out of earshot.

"Why didn't you tell me this new theory you had?"

"Because it wasn't my theory. It was just an idea Toby came up with and we decided to try it out."

"You should have told me, Emily. We've been working together on this from the beginning. It should have worked on me first, not your brothers who just started yesterday. It should have been me."

"Sam!" I didn't know what to say. I had known Sam for most of my life and he had never said anything so selfish. This was something we were doing for the good of our race, not for individual benefit. I just didn't understand where this was coming from.

"Just...never mind. I'm glad you figured out what would work." He walked past the guys and got in his car. I stood there confused as hell. This was not the Sam I knew.

The others got in their cars and headed out too. They had a party to get to after all. I could think of a thousand places I would rather be than on the beach surrounded by people I had spent the last week around.

"Em! You wanna test out pulso metus before we leave?" Drew hollered.

"You up for it?" I asked walking back toward them.

"I am now that I'm pretty damn confident that it won't hurt," Drew replied.

"Toby?" He nodded his head enthusiastically.

They stood an arms-length apart. I whispered, "Timor," and those bright blue tendrils appeared in my arms. I said the word again and the blue once again twisted around my arms and kept close to my body. It was like a vicious guard dog daring someone to get close enough for it to bite.

I raised my arms up and the blue shot out toward my brothers. They remained standing. It didn't affect them. I sighed with relief. Then an idea popped in my head. "*Dolor*." The red flowed through my arms with the blue still floating around outside. "*Dolor*," I said a second time. It spilled out and mixed with the blue creating a beautiful violet shade.

I saw that my brother's eyes were wide with fear and that was not from the pulso metus. They were worried that their protection runes wouldn't protect them from both the powers at the same time. I was more confident than they were.

That violet surged toward them and I saw them both clamp their eyes closed and prepare for the onslaught, but it never came. They remained standing. There was no whimpering or crying and asking for their mommy. They were fine and unharmed.

"*Intereo*." The violet disappeared instantly. There were worried sighs and then nervous laughter from the both of them. Then they both lunged at me and embraced me in a tight hug.

"You are scary talented, Emily," Toby said. "I'm so glad you're on our side."

I laughed. "How about we go to the party of all parties to celebrate you two not having massive brain damage?"

"That is the best idea I've heard in a long time," Drew said.

Chapter 16

Lian

"Well, look who decided to show up for practice today," Corbin said sarcastically as I entered the room.

"Sorry, something came up and…never mind. There's no point in giving you excuses."

"Could it be girl trouble?" Corbin asked.

I sighed. "Not anymore."

"All right, let's get started. Today I'm going to show you some other things you can do with aquamancy. Aquamancy works similarly to pyromancy. There are a few key things you can do with it, but for the most part it is a straightforward power. Now, if you squeeze your hand into a tight fist, it makes the water spray. Likewise, if you hold your palm flat out you get a direct flow of water."

I did the two things he said, even though I had already done them already. It was pretty basic stuff.

"You're a natural like your father," Corbin stated. I did not reply. I wasn't here to be compared to my father. I just wanted to do my training and get out of here.

"This is something that a lot of aquamancers cannot do. Hold your hands palm up and say *unda*."

I did as he told me to do and the water instantly started pouring over my hand and onto the floor.

"Now cup your hands," he said reaching into his back pocket.

I furrowed my brows, but did as he asked.

He pulled a lighter out and flicked it so the flame was on. He brought it forward so the flame was hovering just above the water that was running off my hand. "Okay, when I tell you I want you to say *intereo*."

I nodded my head. I didn't know what I was going along with, but it seemed like it might be a cool trick.

"Now!" he shouted.

"*Intereo.*"

Just as the flow of water was stopping, he shoved the flame down into my palm. I thought the crazy fucker was trying to burn me. Instead something amazing happened. It looked like stars and galaxies in my palms. I swear I was looking at the universe. I was transfixed by what was happening in my hand.

"What is it?" I mumbled.

"It's a trick of the water and the flame. Only a few aquamancers can do it. Some think it's because a few of us have residual powers in us from our descendants having other powers."

"That sounds like a load of crap."

"It probably is, but that's the rumor."

"Could my father do this?"

I peeled my eyes away from the stars in my hand to look at Corbin. There was a smile on his face. I knew what his answer was before he even said anything.

"No. It was the one thing that he couldn't do. I was so damn happy when he failed and I succeeded."

I found it kind of strange that something so simple could make him so happy. Then again, I knew my father. I was sure that he flaunted his power rather arrogantly in front of the other students who were training with him. So I could understand being joyous that even one of them could do something he could not.

"And how do I get it to stop?" I asked. Not that I really wanted to. I rather enjoyed watching the universe spin lazily in my hand.

"Just close your hand," Corbin stated.

I slowly brought my fingers forward. When I opened them again, it was gone. I was kind of excited to try it again later.

"Now that we covered that, it's time to train with the daggers again. And how about we try not to cut one another this time. I would like to not visit the hospital wing again."

We trained with those daggers for two hours until sweat was pouring off the both of us. We managed to only deliver small cuts and scrapes to one another, nothing that required a visit to the healers.

I was walking back to my room with a hand towel draped over my head while sucking back a bottle of water when Tovan came sprinting up to me. I waited patiently as he bent over trying to catch his breath.

He straightened up after a minute. "I've been looking for you half the morning."

"I was training," I said.

"Yeah, that makes sense. Anyhow, I have word about that Corlissian woman you were asking about."

That perked me up. I wasn't expecting Tovan to hear anything about Kate or any Corlissian. I thought it was a lost cause at this point.

"I overheard some of the higher ranked guards talking about having a Corlissian woman in the stronghold. One of them said she would be transferred to the dungeons once she recovers."

"Recovers? What the hell does that mean?"

Tovan shrugged his shoulders. "No idea. They didn't say much more about her after that."

"They could have her in any room recovering," I muttered.

"Yeah, that was my first thought too, but don't you think the best place to recover would be the hospital wing? Maybe she was injured and they are healing her. Just a theory. They could have her in some random room though. But I hope this helps in your search."

He started to walk away. "Thanks, Tovan," I called after him.

He turned part way around. "No problem."

I jogged upstairs and hopped in the shower. I came out with a towel wrapped around my hips. I just opened my closet to find something to wear when there was a knock on my door.

I sighed and went to see who it was. Of course it was Zoë and Mom standing there holding several boxes and bags in their hands.

Mom looked down at me. "Killian, honestly! It's not like you don't have any clothes to wear!"

"I just got out of the shower!"

"Well, we bring you plenty of fancy clothes," Zoë said laying her burden on the coffee table and floor. Mom laid the boxes she was carrying down next to Zoë's.

Mom sat down on the couch and Zoë flopped down beside her. They started opening boxes and bags. They pulled out a large array of items: a number of black suits, some with pin strips and some without, dark gray suits, light gray suits, blue suits, vests of different colors and styles, undershirts in solid colors and stripes and checks, ties with all sorts of patterns and colors, gloves, hats, and shoes, jeans and sweaters and even a pair of sunglasses. It was all really too much. And I was positive it cost a fortune, not that my family couldn't afford it.

"Is this enough?" Mom asked looking up at me.

"No, definitely not. I think you missed some things!" I muttered sarcastically. Mom rolled her eyes and stood up shaking her head. She started to walk to the door, but I stopped her. "Thanks, Mom."

She smiled. "No problem. But seriously, if you need anything else let me know." Then she left.

"You can go too," I said to Zoë who was still sitting on the couch.

"Nope. I'm picking your first snazzy outfit for you!"

"You really don't…"

She gave me a glare that made me clamp my mouth shut. I went to my room and shut the door and pulled on some boxers, a T-shirt, and socks. When I came back out, Zoë had picked out a plain black jacket and pants, with a light gray vest, a white oxford, and a black and white striped tie.

I had to admit that my little sister had an eye for choosing a nice outfit. I would never tell her that or else she'd pick out my clothes every day.

I took the clothes into my room and pulled everything on. When I came out, Zoë assaulted my ears with a high-pitched whistle. I shook my head at her.

She leaned against the back of the couch. "So, where are we off to look for the lovely Kate today?" she asked.

"The hospital wing."

She furrowed her brows. "Why?"

"Because that's where your boyfriend thinks she is."

"Wait? He told you that?"

"Yup. He overheard some guys saying they were going to move a Corlissian woman to the dungeons once she recovers. He figured that's where she was and that's where we're going."

I walked out the door with Zoë behind me. "But Killian, the hospital wing is not small," she groaned.

"Yeah, but it's a lot smaller than searching through the entire stronghold," I remarked.

"You do have a point there." Zoë hit the down button the elevator and once we were in, she hit the 3 button and down we went.

Zoë had lived in the stronghold a whole lot longer than I had. I was glad she was with me since she knew the ways to get to places. The only way I knew how to get to the hospital wing was through the training center and down a lot of halls. I really didn't relish the thought of going that way again.

After going down an assortment of halls, did we finally come to a set of double doors that swung both ways, much like doors in a real hospital, not one set up inside a palace.

I figured there would be an all-white room we'd come to with someone looking like Reggie. But there was nothing but a long hall stretched out in front of us with doors on either side. Unlike the rest of the stronghold, these doors had numbers outside them.

"Well, I think they'd have her deeper in the wing, not right beside the exit," Zoë whispered.

Still, we poked our heads in the rooms to see if Kate was in one. No one was even in any of the rooms. We kept our eyes and ears open to make sure no healers were sneaking up on us.

We made our way deeper into the wing. A few halls branched out that we followed, but we never saw anyone, healers nor patients.

"They may have her close to the center, where the healers' station is," Zoë suggested.

"Probably, but how are we going to get passed the healers?" I asked.

"Well, Kate doesn't know me, so I could create some diversion and that would allow you to talk to her for a moment at least."

"And what if they have the door guarded?"

"Then we're fucked."

I certainly couldn't argue that. The thing was I would know that Kate was in there, but I wanted to see her before I let Emily know that Kate was definitely here. I didn't want to give her false information. It could have been a different Corlissian woman. Who knew how many Corlissians they had kidnapped.

Eventually, we did start to see patients in their rooms and a few healers scurrying down the hall who didn't pay us any attention. I'm sure, like a normal hospital, this one too had visitors roaming around.

Up ahead I could see the massive octagonal desk of what I was assuming was the healers' station. There were ladies wearing the pastel-colored scrubs that typical nurses wore standing around chatting to other healers.

"You go that way, I'll go this way," Zoë muttered. I nodded my head that I heard her and we both walked around the desk and peeked in the doors that were there. I was grateful that there weren't any guards standing around at least.

There were two doors at the back of the circle and Zoë had just peeked in the one and I was heading in the other.

"Can I help you?" I stopped and turned around. There was a lady glaring at me in all her pink pastel glory. She was a wide woman with dirty blonde hair with her hands on her hips. I saw Zoë peek her head out of the door beside the one I was wanting to go in. She snickered at me.

"I was, ugh, looking for, umm, my sister," I stuttered like a fool.

I did a quick glance in the room I wanted to check out. And there she was. Dark brown hair spread across her white pillow and her tanned skin covered in scratches and bruises.

"Well, she certainly wouldn't be here. What's her name?" the healer asked.

I caught Zoë's eye and nodded my head as nonchalantly as I could to the door I was standing in front of. Zoë nodded her head and ducked into the room. A moment later she ran out screaming with one dagger sticking out of her arm and another in her shoulder.

My first instinct was to go to her. But she shot me a look that said, "Get your ass in that room now!"

The healer who was grilling me got to Zoë first and I slipped into the room Kate was in and shut the door behind me.

I went to her bedside. Her eyes were closed and there were all sorts of tubes and machines hooked up to her. There was a deep cut along her forehead that no one had bothered to heal and both of her eyes were black and blue. There was even a bruise around her throat. I imagined there were more injuries that I couldn't see.

"Kate?" I whispered. She didn't stir.

"Kate." I said a little louder while giving her a shove. She made a noise, but she didn't wake.

I said her name again and shoved her hard. Her eyes wobbled under their lids and she took a deep breath. Then she stilled.

I said her name, shoved her, and then smacked her across the face. That brought me a little bit of satisfaction. She didn't like me for unknown reasons and basically called me a bad influence. I think Emily was a lot worse of an influence on me.

Her eyes flew open. It took them a moment to focus, but they eventually landed on me. Then they narrowed when recognition hit her.

"You!" she hissed.

"I did not bring you here."

"Oh, I know you didn't, but you're still one of them."

It's funny that our races hated one another when really we were the same. The only real difference we had were that some of us were descended from Talyr and the others were descended from Corliss. That was it.

"I only came to find you because Emily called and asked my sister to look for you. I'm doing this for her, not for you."

Kate struggled to pull herself up into a sitting position. "Emily? Is she here?"

"No. She was convinced you were here and as usual, she was right. So, I'm just going to let her know you're here and wash my hands of you."

"Don't you dare call her. You know she'll come here and I don't want her near this place. They will take my sweet girl and use her against her own people." Tears streamed down her face.

I knew that Emily would come here, but I doubted Emily would ever turn against the other Corlissians. She was born and raised to hate Talyrians. It was in her blood to hate my kind. It would take something damn powerful to change her mind.

"I knew you were bad for her the moment I saw you. I knew you would hurt her. I knew you would do something that would just break her. I was right. Look at you, standing over me so proud of yourself. Oh, but I bet the moment she found out what you were you fled with your tail between your legs. You were too scared to even fight her, weren't you?"

"Well, Kate, this has been a nice chat. I'm glad to see that my people are taking wonderful care of you. Bye."

"You're not even man enough to stand up to me! I knew you never cared for Emily."

"No, it's just that I have nothing to say to you. I get it that you don't like me. That's fine. I don't like you either. But don't even act like you knew what

Emily and I had. I cared for your niece more than you or she will ever know. Good. Bye."

I walked away from her. I peeked out of the door and saw that Zoë and the commotion she brought were gone. I cracked the door open just enough for me to squeeze out, then I turned around and carefully closed the door behind me. I straightened up and turned around only to have two people standing there right in front of me.

One was big momma in the pastel pink and the other was the blonde healer who I blew off only a few days ago. Both of them were glaring at me.

"Have a nice little discussion," Pink Pastels asked.

"No. She wouldn't wake up," I lied.

"What were you doing?" Blondie asked.

"Well, she had a massive cougar crush on me when I lived in Autumn Falls and I was wondering if she still did. I guess I'll never know!"

"Oh, is she the one who stole your heart? Is she the reason you wanted nothing to do with me?" Blondie asked.

"Nah, her niece is the one I'm madly in love with." I started to walk around them, but Blondie put her hand on my chest and stopped me.

"Oooh, someone's been working out. And may I say how fine you look out of those workout clothes. You clean up rather nicely," she crooned leaning closer to me.

"Could you get your skanky hand off my brother?" Zoë had appeared from nowhere and was glaring at Blondie.

"I am not a skank!" Blondie said taking her hand off my chest and turning toward my sister.

"Oh, sure you're not. Because that's what kind of name you get when most of the males who live here haven't slept with you!"

"I have not..."

"Don't care, slut. The rumors have been swirling around about you for years."

"But they're just rumors. They're not..."

Before she could finish, Zoë grabbed my arm and pulled me along. She walked at a brisk pace away from the center of the wing. Once we got to the part of the hall where no one was, did Zoë slow her pace.

"So, did you talk to her?"

"Sort of. That woman is a bitch. Even after I told her I was looking for her for Emily, she still chewed me out."

"Well, I wouldn't be too happy if the Corlissians kidnapped me either," Zoë muttered.

"Trust me, her attitude has nothing to do with who kidnapped her and where she is. That woman just hates me. Hey, gimme your cell."

"Why?"

"So I can call Emily."

"Use your own phone!"

"She won't pick up if she sees my name pop up. Trust me, she won't."

Zoë let out a sigh and dropped her hot pink covered cell in my hand. There were some dangly metal pieces attached to it. I couldn't believe that someone would buy all this crap for a phone. I just shook my head.

"Are you calling her now? Is she out of school?"

I slid my finger across the screen and saw it was just after six o'clock. I looked up at Zoë and about made a smart-ass comment, but then I remembered that she wouldn't know if it was light or dark out now. We were standing in a hallway with no windows around.

"Yeah. She should pick up." I hoped she would at least.

"Well, I'll let you talk. Just swing by my room and drop that off for me."

I nodded my head and when she was a good distance away, I scrolled through the names on Zoë's contact list, and hit SEND when I found Emily's name.

She picked up on the third ring. "What's up, kiddo!"

I could hear a lot of people in the background and I thought I could hear water sloshing. They were probably having one last beach party.

"I just wanted to let you know we found Kate," I said in a deep voice.

"Lian? Hey, hang on a sec I can hardly hear you." I heard her say, "Don't lay in the sand, Toby. You'll get sand on it and that could make it useless." I could hear the voices drift away and I could really hear the waves crashing on the beach once the human noise was gone.

"I'm sorry, what did you say?"

"I said we found Kate."

I heard her suck in a sharp breath. "Really? She's there? Is she okay? Did you talk to her?"

I wanted to laugh, but I was trying to sound as indifferent as possible. "She's in the hospital wing because she's pretty banged up. I talked to her briefly."

"What did she say?" Emily sounded so damn excited.

"Umm, pretty much all she said was that she hates me and she didn't want me to call you."

"What? Why not?"

"Because she knows you'll come here to get her back and she wants you nowhere near this place."

Emily was quiet. "Nowhere near the stronghold or nowhere near you?"

I cleared my throat. "Ugh, probably both, but more so the stronghold."

"Thanks for calling me, Lian."

"I promise I won't call you again." Then I hung up. I smiled down at the phone feeling a brief moment of gratification for being the one to hang up on her for a change. That was quickly replaced by me feeling like a dumbass. She could have been in a chatty mood and wanted to talk and here I just stupidly made that go away with the push of a button. Sometimes I didn't use my brain wisely.

Chapter 17
Emily

Drew and Camilla left the house before Toby was ready. I sat on the kitchen counter as he primped in the bathroom because he had to "look" good for Thea. I opened a bottle of pop and sipped on it while waiting.

He came strutting, yes strutting, down the hallway a good half hour after Drew and Cami left.

"Oww, oww, watch out there is one sexy beast coming through ladies and gentlemen!" I hollered from my perch.

"Fuck off!" Toby snapped.

"Fuck you!" I snapped back.

"I don't even want to go to this stupid party," he grumbled as we walked out to the Audi.

"Aww, I fink someone needs a wittle nap because he's a wittle grump," I mocked in a baby voice.

"Sometime, I really don't like you. This is one of those times," he groaned before dropping into the passenger seat.

"Cheer up! You'll get to see Thea in fifteen minutes. What's got your panties in a wad anyways?"

"This damn tattoo is itching like crazy and I can't scratch it!"

I said, "Timor," under my breath twice until those bright blue tendrils were floating around inside the car.

"What the fuck are you doing!" Toby yelled.

"This is why you need to stop complaining about a little itching. It will go away."

Toby let out a sigh. "You're right. It is kind of nice to be able to sit next to you and not be in pain or see my worst fear."

"*Intereo.*" The blue light in the car was gone and was replaced by the darkness that surrounded us. There were no streetlights along the road expect for the one that was near our driveway. It didn't shine on our driveway, but it was about a quarter mile away. We didn't want anyone sneaking up on our house in the middle of the night.

"So," Toby cleared his throat. "What's up with you and Sam?"

"I swear I'm going to choke Thea! There is nothing going on with us. We're friends. That's it. I'm tired of having to explain that Sam is one of my best friends and we do hang out sometimes!"

"Yeah, but it was after Lian left that you started hanging out more," Toby said.

"He was just trying to cheer me up. That's all."

"Have you talked with Lian since the other night?"

"No and I don't want to talk about him either." I was grateful once we finally reached town. I knew the beach was a few minutes away.

I pulled in the packed parking lot and found a spot near the end. Even from up here you could see how massive the bon fire was. I was surprised no cranky citizen had called the fire department yet.

Toby hopped out of the car and made a dash for the beach. I got out, locked the car, and strolled down there. I was in no hurry to be around people. I swear I was turning into a grouchy old person already.

It looked like the entire school had showed up for this party. I was kind of impressed by how quickly my best friend could turn an idea for a party into a massive party in less than twelve hours just by word of mouth. Thea had a gift.

I saw that she had her arms around Toby's neck and I wanted to be nowhere near that, so I walked around the other side of the fire only to run into Mason. I would have rather had a front row view of my best friend making out with my brother.

"Hey!" he slurred. He wrapped his arms around my waist and picked me up. "I didn't think you were coming!"

"Could you put me down?" I asked rather nicely.

"Oh, sorry," he said breathing his beer drenched breath in my face. He set me carefully back down on the sand. "What are you drinking?"

"Nothing. One of you fools has to stay sober."

Mason laughed. "Man I love you."

"All right. Well, I'll talk to you later," I said just to blow him off.

I walked around making small talk with my fellow students. Some wanted to talk about homework we had or papers that were due, and others wanted to talk about the mysterious disappearance of Lian. That was one topic I played completely dumb about. It really wasn't their business anyways. They were just being nosy.

I was talking to Molly Green about an upcoming paper due for English when I felt an arm on my shoulder. I looked up to see Evan standing there. His eyes were glazed over and bloodshot and there was this dazed look to his whole face.

"Did you know she's a wizard?" he said leaning in close to Molly. "She can make colors shoot from her fingers," he added standing upright and waving his free hand across the sky.

"I think she'd be a witch. Males are wizards," Molly stated.

"Yeah, I don't think Evan is going to remember the difference," I said with a smile.

"And she can make fire appear in her hands. She could melt your face off right now if she so chose to."

"Well, I hope she doesn't," Molly said with a laugh. I loved that humans were naïve enough to think that it was all make believe. It made it easier to play it off as a drunken man's ramblings.

"Oh, I wouldn't," I said with a wink. "Ev, where is your brother?"

"My twin and I are one. Where he is I am."

"Where is Tyler at in his physical form?" I asked again.

"Dunno."

"How about we go find him, okay?"

"Okay! Bye Mol...Mole...Molt...Malt...Oh can we get milkshakes? You're so nice, Emily."

"What the hell did you take?" I asked as I guided him around the fire searching for Tyler.

"Some pill then I smoked some, umm, what's that stuff called that you smoke and it makes you say funny things?"

"Pot?"

"No. The other stuff."

"Marijuana? Cannabis? Reefer?" I said using the different names for the same substance.

"Yeah, that's the one! You're smart, Emily. And because of you, we got awesomer tattoos that protect us from your sorcery."

"Evan, I love you, I really do, but if you don't quit running your mouth in front of these humans about my powers, I'm going to cut out your fucking tongue."

"Damn girl! No need to get nasty!"

"Oh, then how about I talk about how you can heal things with your hands and make things move with your mind?"

"Shh, Emily! Are you trying to get us founded out?"

I rolled my eyes. I saw Tyler talking to Sam up ahead.

"Hey, when are we getting milkshakes?" Evan asked.

"Umm, in a little bit. Tyler said he'd take you and Oh look, there's Tyler now!"

"TYLER!" Evan said letting go of me and crashing into his twin.

Tyler looked at me like, "What the hell did you do to my brother?"

"Yeah, he wants a milkshake," I said before walking away.

I heard Evan say, "Oh yeah, I want a milkshake and Emily said you're taking me to get one."

Sam jogged up beside me. "What's with him?" he said jabbing his thumb in the direction we had just come from.

"He's had a variety of drugs. None of which I provided."

"You not drinking tonight?" Sam asked before taking a swig of his beer.

"Nope. You know me, I don't like for my mind to be bogged down."

Sam smiled and pulled his cigarettes from his back pocket. I took his beer from him while he lit it and put the lighter and pack in his pocket. He took the beer back from me.

"It's been a long week, eh?"

"Yes, it has."

"Hey? You heard anything about Kate yet?"

"Ugh no. Cami's supposedly gathering a party to go track her or something, but I don't see that happening."

"I bet you could get Mason to do some tracking. He's not as good as his dad, but he's not bad," Sam suggested.

"Sam, he is the last person I want to owe a favor to and that would be a massive favor."

Sam chuckled. "Well, then I suggest you hope for one hell of a miracle."

"I don't believe in miracles. They are for desperate humans, not for someone like me."

"Someone like you?"

"Someone who has had every adult in their life ripped away from them by Talyrian assholes. It's a miracle that I haven't driven up there and set their pretty stronghold on fire."

"Why are you so sure it's Talyrians who took her?"

"Because it's always Talyrians who take things from me."

Toby was being given a piggyback ride by Drew. But Mason saw them goofing off and dove at Drew which caused a massive pile up on the sand. Sam just shook his head as the three of them lay on the ground laughing like maniacs.

"Boys," Sam muttered.

My cell vibrated against my butt. I saw Zoë's name pop up on the screen. "What's up, kiddo!"

I could hear someone talking and it sounded like a male. It was too loud for me to hear what they were saying though.

"Lian? Hey, hang on a sec I can hardly hear you." I glanced at Sam who was shaking his head and glaring at me. I stepped over Mason, and Drew, and finally Toby. "Don't lay in the sand, Toby. You'll get sand on it and that could make it useless."

Toby sat up and nodded his head that he heard me. He dusted the sand off his back and so did Drew and Mason.

I walked a good distance down the beach until the voices and music were a low hum and the bon fire was nearly a tiny dot.

I took a quick breath before putting the phone up against my ear. "I'm sorry, what did you say?" I asked.

"I said we found Kate," he replied in a deep tone.

I was not expecting that. I felt this sudden rush enter my body. One I hadn't felt in a week. "Really? She's there? Is she okay? Did you talk to her?"

"She's in the hospital wing because she's pretty banged up. I talked to her briefly."

"What did she say?" I could not keep the excitement out of my voice and I really didn't care. I was glad to hear that at this point my aunt was alive and I knew where she was.

"Umm, pretty much all she said was that she hates me and she didn't want me to call you." Yeah, that sounded like Kate all right. She had no love for Lian. Even though he did find her she was still going off on him. Though I couldn't blame her. She was probably beat up and lying in the Talyrian stronghold. I'd be pissed too.

"What? Why not?"

"Because she knows you'll come here to get her back and she wants you nowhere near this place." That was my plan.

I held the phone for a second. "Nowhere near the stronghold or nowhere near you?"

"Ugh, probably both, but more so the stronghold."

"Thanks for calling me, Lian."

"I promise I won't call you again." The line went dead after that. I was shocked. He never hung up on me. That was my thing! I guess our last conversation must have stuck with him. He was really done with me.

He might have wanted nothing to do with me anymore, but he still sought out Kate and let me know that she was alive and sort of well. He didn't have to do that. I honestly didn't think he would. Maybe he still did have feelings for me and just didn't want to sound like he did. Maybe that was his grand gesture to me; finding Kate.

I walked slowly down the beach and could see the bon fire grow larger and the sound of people's voices and the music grow louder. I didn't relish going back there to hear drunken and stoned people laugh at stupid things. I really didn't want to hear Corlissians talking about our powers around humans. Yeah, the humans thought it was a joke, but what we could do was nothing to be joked about.

I sat down on the sand and took my shoes off. I was close enough to the shore that the tide was barely touching my toes. It was cold, but I didn't mind. It was actually kind of refreshing.

I could hear someone walking toward me. It was hard to be sneaky when the sand crunched under your feet. I knew it was someone from the party and not one of my enemies. I always knew when Brothers or Nexes where near. It was those shifty Talyrians and devious Avids that you had to watch out for.

I instinctually slipped my hands underneath my shirt and palmed both my daggers. Thea plopped down next to me and gave me a funny look.

"You gonna knife me?" she asked.

I let go of my grip on the blades. "No."

"What are you doing over here by yourself?"

"Umm, I got a phone call and I couldn't hear with all that noise."

"Ooooh, who was it?" she asked nudging me with her elbow and wiggling her eyebrows up and down.

"I don't think you want me to answer that, but let's just say that I know where Kate is."

Thea's eyes popped open. "Really? Where?"

"The stronghold. As I expected."

"Hold up! That means it was Lian who called you, wasn't it?" I nodded my head. "Emily, he could be lying to you. It's not like he hasn't done that before. He knew you were looking for Kate and of course he told you she was there. He wants you to come up there. I can imagine the reward he'd get for handing you over to their leader."

"Thea..."

"No. Don't tell me that he wouldn't do that. HE. IS. A. TALYRIAN. He is a ruthless bastard. Don't think he won't use you for his own personal gain. You may think you knew him, but that was all a lie. And you know it was. Oh, and over my dead body are you going up to the stronghold!"

"Excuse me?"

"Emily, as far as we know they don't know anything about you. You are a one of a kind with more powers than anyone has ever had. I don't even want to think what they would do once they got their hands on you. They could find a way to duplicate your powers and then we'd all be goners."

"No, you wouldn't."

Thea's face scrunched up for a moment before realization hit her. "The tattoos worked, didn't they?"

"Yeah, it wasn't a particular tattoo, it's all about how many you get. They stop pulso morsus, pulso metus, and a combination of the two. Toby and Drew were unaffected."

"Well, it looks like tomorrow morning I will be visiting Leafy Ink and getting some words and runes on me. Sounds like a perfect way to start a Saturday! So, does everyone know about it?"

"Yeah, all the guys know to get more tats and I'm guessing Mason told Bridgette."

"Have you told Hotch?"

"I haven't seen Hotch in days. I was kind of expecting a call from him about skipping practice."

"I talked to him yesterday. I didn't tell him what you all were doing, but he knew something was up. He's gotten kind of laid back lately," Thea said.

I stood up and dusted my butt off and Thea stood up too. "I mean what I said, Emily. Don't even think about going to the stronghold."

I held my hands up in surrender. "I won't!" I already knew that was an enormous lie. It was practically the only thing rotating around my brain. I needed to figure out how I was going to leave without anyone following me. Monday was my best chance. That would give me the weekend to do some planning.

Thea and I walked back to join the party. I think Thea, Sam, and I were the only ones who weren't drunk or high. I had all sorts of people coming up to me and talking straight gibberish. Then they would laugh and run off.

Sam walked up to me. "It looks like we get to be dd's tonight."

"I'm making sure my brothers and sister get home. I don't care about the rest of these people!"

"Looks like that leaves me on Ty, Ev, and Micah duty. And Thea can take Bridge and Mase home. That way at least all us lovely Corlissians will be safe." He paused for a moment looking around at all our classmates acting like complete fools. "What did Lian have to say?" he asked. His voice dropped to a deeper tone. He used that tone when he was ticked off.

"That he found Kate," I replied not looking at him.

"Well, that has to be bullshit." He walked around so he was standing in front of me. "Tell me you are not even toying with the idea of going up there?"

"I'm not even toying with the idea of going up there," I repeated in a dry tone.

"Dammit, Emily! I will chain your ass to a chair if I have to. You are not going anywhere near that place."

"I'm pretty confident I could burn through those chains."

Sam rolled his eyes and stalked off. It amazed me at how easily I could piss people off nowadays. It used to take me a little more taunting and sarcasm. Now in three sentences or less BOOM! Pissed off. Go me!

Chapter 18

Lian

I was woken up early by the sound of thunder rumbling outside. The sky was a dark gray and every now and then a streak of lightening would rip across that gray sky and light up the whole area. I knew it was far earlier than I needed to get up, but since I didn't have an alarm to wake me, I went ahead and crawled out of bed.

I pulled on a pair of sweats, a T-shirt, and my shoes. It was becoming my usual morning outfit. The afternoons were for dressing like a high-born preppy guy.

I strapped my daggers to my back and headed downstairs to grab something to eat. It was rare for me to be up this early, so it was kind of nice to get to eat before practice. I was almost to the dining hall when the King strode out of the open doors. I stopped and did a small bow toward him.

"Oh, there is no need for that kind of formality in the halls. And anyways, you are from a high-ranking family," he said pausing in front of me. "I am glad to run into you though. I was informed that you were in the hospital wing yesterday and you visited a certain Corlissian woman who is in there. Is this true?"

"Umm, yeah." There was no point in lying to him. He already knew the truth.

"May I ask why you went to see her?" He leaned against the wall and crossed his arms over his chest.

"One of the Corlissians I knew in Autumn Falls called me and said that his aunt had been kidnapped and he was convinced she was here. I decided to go look and see if I could find her and I did." That was partially true.

"And did you let him know she's here?"

"No."

"Who is this Corlissian?" he asked.

"Drew Porter."

I saw his eyebrows pop up. "Isn't he Emily's, umm" – he snapped his fingers – "older brother?"

"Yes. He is." It kind of bothered me at how much he knew about the Corlissians in Autumn Falls. It bothered me further because he knew a hell of a lot about Emily's family in particular.

"You're surprised at my knowledge, aren't you? Well, when you have someone as powerful as Emily you get to know all you can about them. That includes their family. I know about her parents and their untimely deaths, and her aunt, and her sister, and her brothers. I know so much about them that it would scare you," he said as a devious smile spread across his face.

He stood up and straightened his suit jacket. "I do have a feeling that we will be seeing one of the Porter children very soon. As for me, I hope it's Emily." He patted me on the shoulder and walked down the hall.

I stood rooted to the spot for a while. I was just staring at the floor. I had made a huge fucking mistake.

I bypassed the dining hall and headed straight for the training center. I had a lot of rage that was about to boil over inside of me. I walked through the waiting room where the secretary smiled at me and I only glared at her. I stalked right down the hall, through the water tight doors, and into my usual room.

As soon as that door was closed, I whipped a dagger off my back and threw it across the room. I somehow threw that bitch with enough force for it to embed itself in the concrete wall. I threw the second one and it bounced off the wall and came back at me. I ducked out of the way. Then I opened up my palms and unloaded water all over that damn room until I was soaking wet and standing in a knee-deep flood. After that I proceeded to punch the concrete walls until my knuckles were a bloody mess. Then I kept punching.

I heard the door open and felt the water quickly drain out. "What the hell?" Corbin barked at the mass of water that flowed out and probably soaked him.

"Fucking hell, Killian! STOP!" he said grabbing my wrists and yanking me away from the wall that was covered in my blood.

I saw him, with a tight grip on my wrists, take a look around the room. His eyes landed on my dagger that was in the wall. He looked at me with wide eyes. "Letting off a bit of steam, are you?"

"Something like that," I grumbled.

"You mind telling me what this is all about?"

"I'd rather not," I said stiffly.

"Killian, as your trainer it is my duty…"

"To train me. End of. My personal life is of no concern to you," I said cutting him off.

Corbin let go of my wrists. "This is about Emily, isn't it?"

"Not everything is about her!" I snapped.

"But this is."

"OF COURSE THIS IS!!!" I yelled. I grabbed my one dagger off the floor and using some unknown strength I ripped the other dagger out of the wall leaving a nice chunk of concrete missing.

Corbin stepped out of my way and let me go. "I highly suggest you visit the roof. It helps clear the mind," he called as I walked down the hall.

I noticed that people walking past me in the halls were giving me funny looks and it didn't click why that was until later. I was soaking wet, holding a dagger in each hand, my knuckles were a bloody mess, and I was emitting a low growl. I must have looked like a madman.

Corbin's suggestion obviously stuck in my head because as I jogged up the stairs I kept going until I punched through the door at the top that read ROOF. The back of my mind was like, "Look at how pretty it is up here. There is grass and flowers, and potted trees! Look at how lovely and green it is." But the front of my mind was just a constant scream that blocked out everything else.

It was still pouring down rain. I didn't notice it much since I was already wet from using my aquamancy earlier. I walked down the stone pathway until I was about in the middle of the stronghold. I walked off the path and ducked under a leafy tree and a bush. A few more steps and there was the edge of the stronghold. I leaned forward slightly and glanced down. Looking down nine stories made my stomach tighten. I didn't like heights at all.

I sat down and leaned my back against the small wall that was the edge of the building. I didn't know what to do at this point. I had fucked up so bad. The reason Kate was kidnapped was because they wanted Emily to come up here. And here I went and did all the dirty work for them. I knew Emily well enough to know that she would come here. I felt sick that I had unknowingly played into their plan.

I had to call Emily and beg her not to come here. I doubted she would listen to me, but it was worth a shot. If she told me to piss off, then I would have to call one of the other Corlissians and ask them to stop her. That was going to be the issue though. None of the other Corlissians would pick up if they saw it was me calling. I still had to do everything in my power to keep Emily far away from here.

Sitting up here and pouting about it wasn't doing me any good. I hauled myself up and went downstairs. I walked in my room to find clothes laid out on my bed. A dark blue suit, a baby blue oxford, and a dark gray tie.

I let out a sigh and walked across the hall and pounded on my sister's door. I left a bloody fist print when I did too. She opened the door with a bright smile on her face. "Hey, Killian!"

"How'd you get in my room?"

"Ugh, what happened to you? Did you do that to my door? Gross!" She walked into her room and came back with a wet wash cloth and wiped the blood off her door. "I know how to pick locks. I figured you'd be tired from training and I wanted to pick something out for you. I was just being a nice sister."

"Stay out of my room, Zoë." I turned to walk back to my room when she grabbed my arm and yanked me back. She was so much like Emily. They were both petite and strong as hell.

"Why are you dripping blood and water everywhere?" she asked.

"Because I was training and I punched a wall and I went on the roof."

"Umm, why did you punch a wall?"

"I need to take a shower. Can we talk about this later?"

"Sure."

I went back to my room and took a burning hot shower. I was mildly surprised when it didn't melt all my skin off my body. I did a quick shave and then I put on the clothes that Zoë laid out for me.

Finally, I sat down on the dark gray couch with my cell phone in my hand. I called Emily's number.

"You're a liar," she stated.

"Umm, what did I lie about now?"

"I believe just last night you said and I quote, 'I promise I won't call you again.'"

"Yeah, well this is important." I heard water splash. "Are you at the beach?"

"Nope. I'm at the lake house. What's so important?"

"Emily, you cannot come up here to get Kate."

"Okay."

I held the phone for a moment. I was expecting her to yell obscenities at me. I was expecting her to say something along the lines of, "Don't tell me what to do." Instead, I get an okay.

"That's it? Okay?"

She let out a sigh. "See Thea and Sam already threatened me and said if I try to leave town then they will chain me or something. So, as far as you or anyone else is concerned I'm staying here."

I swear I could hear the lie in her voice. I knew Emily well enough to know that she probably already had a very detailed plan about how to get up to the stronghold and the best way to get into the stronghold. She wasn't the kind of girl who would sit back and let things play out as they may, she was the one who caused all the action.

"Are you lying to me?" I asked.

She snorted. "You're one to talk to me about lying. I'm talking to the King of Liars right now."

"Please, just stay far away from here. I'm only telling you this because I don't want to see you get hurt."

She cleared her throat. I could even imagine the look on her face too. It was probably a very serious look. That one where she kind of narrowed her eyes and her lips pursed and her nose wrinkled ever so slightly. "Lian, I think that if I do come up there, I am not the one who needs to worry about getting hurt. You, on the other hand, are still at the very top of my hit list."

"Even after finding Kate for you? What do I have to do to get on your good side?"

"Not be a Talyrian."

"Something that I can control."

"Get Kate out of the stronghold and I have no reason to come there."

"This place is impossible to get out of."

"Well then, I guess I'll be seeing you soon. Bye, baby!"

"Bye, Em," I said grumpily before she hung up.

Well, that did not go how I planned. I guess it started to and then she revealed that she was lying to me. I wished I could take back calling her last night. I was doing it for my own selfish reasons and look where that got me.

I should have been happy that Emily was coming here, but she wasn't coming here to see me. She was coming for her aunt and to probably torture me. That was it.

I knew calling any of the other Corlissians was pointless. They already knew that at some point she would be trying to leave town. I was sure they had her under a very watchful eye…or eyes.

I needed another plan. Calling Emily did no good and the other Corlissians were not going to do any good either. I paced back and forth across the length of the living room racking my brain. I had nothing.

There was a knock on my door and I yelled, "Come in!"

Zoë opened the door and looked at me funny. Of course she did. I was pacing around like a crazy person.

"Whatcha doin'?" she asked rocking back and forth on her heels.

"Trying to think of a way to stop Emily from coming up here to get her aunt."

"Umm, isn't that what you wanted? Isn't that what we scoured the dungeons and the hospital wing for? Isn't that why I stabbed myself as a distraction?"

"Yeah, well it's also what the King wants?"

"What?"

"The King wants Emily to come here."

"Why?"

"Emily is very, very powerful, Zoë."

"Yeah, we're Talyrians and Corlissians. We're all very powerful," she stated.

"See…damn I promised her I would never tell anybody this. You cannot let what I say to you leave this room. Am I understood?"

Zoë nodded her head up and down real slowly. Her eyes were wide. "I won't say a thing to anyone. I promise."

"Emily has four powers."

"No, she doesn't. We only have one, well unless you have psychokinesis then you're a healer too, but no. There is no way she has four powers."

"I have had all four of her powers used on me. Believe me, she does."

"What does she have?"

"Pyromancy, pulso morsus, pulso metus, and she's a healer."

"Why does she have a Talyrian power if she's a full blooded Corlissian?"

I shrugged my shoulders. "She never figured that out."

"So, the King wants to get his hands on her because she is probably the deadliest person in both of our races. He wants her on his side."

"Exactly! I need to somehow stop her."

"Go to Autumn Falls," Zoë said like it was no big deal.

"I...I can't just walk out the front door of the stronghold. How in the hell am I supposed to just go to Autumn Falls?"

"Let's go visit Tovan," she said with a smile.

"Dude, I can get anyone out of the stronghold. The only problem is I'll need until late Sunday night to get everything set up. Will that be a problem?" Tovan asked.

I looked at Zoë who was sitting there with a smug look on her face. Of course she knew that Tovan could get people in and out of the stronghold. Hell, he probably had some side business raking in extra cash doing it.

"Umm, no it's not a problem. What do you need me to do?" I asked.

"Be ready when I come and get you."

"That's it?"

"That's it!" He grabbed a yellow legal pad and started taking down notes. "How long will you be gone?"

"Umm, I'll probably be back Tuesday, Wednesday at the latest."

"And what kind of car would you prefer?"

"I'm not picky, but everyone in Autumn Falls does drive expensive, luxury cars."

"A Lexus will do then." He scribbled something down.

"And will it be just you returning or will you have someone with you?"

"Just me."

"Good. That makes things easier. Less explaining to do. Okay, I'll provide your exit on Sunday night, your car for the duration you're away, and your entrance back into the stronghold on probably Wednesday. Sound all right?"

"Yeah! Wow! Thanks man!"

"No problem. I guess I'll see you Sunday then."

I stood up and shook his hand. "And I am really sorry for the whole," I pointed my finger at my nose.

"Eh, no biggie. You can't even tell it happened. You're still my best friend, Killian. Anyhow, it's good having someone on your side who can punch like you do," Tovan said with a grin.

Zoë and I headed to the dining hall to grab some dinner. "So, what are you going to do once you get to Autumn Falls?" she asked.

"I have no idea, but I do have a long drive to think of something."

Chapter 19

Emily

"EM, COME ON!" Drew yelled through my door.

"I just got up and I need a shower. Can you take Toby and I'll drive myself?" I asked.

"Yes. And make sure you scrub up good, I can smell your stank through the door," Drew said before laughing at himself and walking down the hallway.

I got in the shower and dressed. Though I was not wearing school appropriate clothing. I was wearing my fighting leathers. I shoved some other clothes in a bag along with plenty of daggers and throwing stars to stash on myself later. I still had the twins that were almost always on my back.

I was about to walk out the door when I heard Camilla's high heels clonking down the hallway. "Hey Em, I'm going to run some errands. You need anything?" she asked.

"No, I'm good."

"Okay, bye sweetie!"

"Bye!"

I stood with my ear pressed against the door. She took her sweet ass time too. She walked back to her room and was in there for about twenty minutes, and then she walked back to the kitchen, back to her room, back to the kitchen. It was no wonder she never got anything done. She spent half her day walking around the house. It took an hour before she finally left.

I sighed with relief when I poked my head out and saw her car driving away. I walked out into the kitchen and waited there for a few minutes. Knowing Camilla's morning routine, she would be coming back to the house another four times.

I leaned against the kitchen counter and made myself a cup of coffee. There really was no rush for me to leave. It would be lunch before my brothers would realize I was not at school. By then I'd be a long way ahead of them.

I heard a car coming down the drive. I figured it was Camilla, but it was a black Audi S5 with tinted windows and black rims. Sam got out and walked up to the house. He walked right in like he lived here.

He took one look at me and shook his head. "I make good on my promises, Emily. I will go get a long length of chain and strap you down to something."

"And I will still burn through it," I said before taking a sip of my coffee.

"Emily," he said with a sigh. "I know you want to get Kate back, but going there by yourself is not the thing to do. Take a few Corlissians with you. I can't sit by and let you do something this stupid by yourself."

"I don't want anyone going with me and getting injured. It's better off for everyone else if they just stay down here."

"Better for who exactly? And don't you think Drew and Toby would want to help rescue their own aunt?"

"I don't want any more of my family members up there. One is enough. I'm not having Talyrians take my brothers from me too," I spat.

"Emily…"

"I have no reason to stay here, Sam. Kate was the glue that was barely holding this family together. She kept us strong through all the shit we've been through. I owe it to her to get her away from those bastards."

"And that's fine. I understand that. But don't say you have no reason to stay. You have more reasons than anyone. Everyone here loves you and adores you."

I snorted at that. "I think there are plenty of people who can't stand me."

"I'm not one of them," he stated. He took a step closer to me. "Are you really going up there just to get Kate or are you going to see Killian too?"

"This has nothing to do with Lian."

"But wasn't he the one calling you and telling you that Kate's there? I can't believe you still talk to him on the phone like nothing bad happened between th̄ ̄f you. Didn't he break your heart? How can you trust someone like ̄d never hurt you like he did."

 ̄'re not dating, sooo…"

"We should though. You know that we would be prefect together. We know so much about each other. Hell, we've been best friends since we were four!"

Fucking hell, Thea was right. I really kind of hated Thea right now. I swear that girl could read people like no one else could. I should have known she'd be right about this.

"Sam, I just don't think we'd work out," I said. "And I don't want to ruin our friendship."

"Is there something wrong with me? What? You don't like my dreads? I can cut them. I can change the clothes I wear and I can be more, I don't know like a mix of Mason and Killian. Is that what you want?"

"No. I don't want you to change for me. I really need to get going. I promise we can talk about this when I get back."

"We're talking about it now!" he said firmly. "Actually, I think there are a lot of things we need to talk about before you go prancing out that door." He folded his arms across his chest and almost dared me to try and get by him.

"Fine. Besides there ever being an us, what else do we need to discuss?"

"Can we go sit in the living room and get comfortable?" he asked gesturing with his hand.

I nodded my head and set the half-drunk cup of coffee on the counter behind me. It was lukewarm anyways. I sat down on one end of the couch and Sam took the other. He was closer to the door and would make my escape a lot harder if I chose to bolt for the door. I don't know why, but I had a feeling Sam and I were going to fight. And I didn't mean fight as in an argument.

"I know you like me too, Emily," Sam said.

"No, I..." I started but Sam held his hand up to stop me from going any further than that.

"I've seen the way you look at me sometimes and the way you flirt with me like you never do with any of the other guys. But I know there is something holding you back. It took me a little while, but I finally figured out what it is. You still love that Talyrian. He still has his claws in you; still holds sway over your heart, doesn't he? I just can't break that pull he has over you."

I knew my mouth was hanging open. Sam had really lost his damn mind. I honestly did not know who this guy sitting beside me was, this guy who I had spent countless nights on rooftops and goofing off around town with.

"Who the hell are you?" I whispered.

"Yeah, I guess that brings up the other thing I wanted to discuss with you. See, I've sort of lied to everyone for a long time about who I am."

"You mean you have a different name or something?" I asked softly.

He chuckled. "No, my name has always been Samuel Aleksander. The thing is, I'm not a Corlissian."

I busted up laughing. It was the most ludicrous thing I had heard in a long time. I think I needed a good laugh too. "Yeah, good one, Sam! Now, if you're done making shit up, I need to go."

I stood up to go, but Sam stood up too and blocked my way. "Emily, I'm an Avid." I wanted to laugh again, but there was this look in his eyes that I had never seen before. I knew deep down that he was telling me the truth, but a bigger part of me didn't believe him.

"No, you're not. You have pulso morsus. That is a Corlissian power."

"Actually, it's a Corlissian power and an Avid power."

"What?"

"Here's a little family history that none of us were ever taught by our parents or Hotch. Avids are descendants of Talyr and Corliss. Yes, we are. Unlike our half-brothers, half-sisters, and cousins we actually liked our power. We became outcasts because of that one little thing. Our families abandoned us and shunned us. So, we formed our own race. We didn't associate ourselves with Corlissians or Talyrians, instead we decided to take them out for their treatment toward us."

"So, you're going to take me out because I'm a Corlissian?" I asked.

"No. I like you entirely too much to do anything like that. Plus, you're a very valuable asset. The race that has you backing it is going to be the side that wins this centuries long war."

"But we've fought alongside you since we were kids. How in the hell do you just blend in?"

"Because I'm like you all. Why would you suspect someone who has pulso morsus of not being a Corlissian? It was easy. The only problem was that my eyes don't glow blue, or green, or in your case, purple. I just had to make sure that when I used my power, I wasn't looking at anyone. That was really only tricky at practice."

"But your parents…I mean your mom is a pyromancer."

"They are not my real parents. I was orphaned and the Avids who were raising me decided I could be used elsewhere, to spy on Corlissians. So, they switched me out with the Malik's newborn son. Technically, my last name is Carden, but I like Malik better."

I felt tears start to slide down my face. "You were my best friend," I muttered.

"I'm still your best friend, Emily," he smiled.

"What are you doing here?" I asked taking a step back from him.

He let out a little breath. "That brings me to our last topic of discussion. See, I know you will never willingly join with the Avids, so it is my duty to bring you to our side."

"And how do you plan on doing that?" I asked taking another step away from him.

"Well, I thought I'd start out asking you. Emily, is there any chance that you would willingly join the Avids?"

"No!" I said wiping the tears away with my fingertips.

"Yeah, I figured that would be your answer. So, now I'm going to use brute force."

"Bring it on, bitch."

Sam and I circled the couch. We were like two guys in a boxing ring about to punch the shit out of each other. Sam dove at me and I sidestepped him. He slammed into one of the dining room chairs. He stood up and as soon as he did, I had pulso metus dancing around my fingertips. I threw it at him, but it didn't do a damn thing.

"Fuck," I breathed.

He pulled his shirt up to reveal several new tattoos covering his chest. There were Latin words and runes I was very familiar with. I could only use pyromancy on him.

He smiled deviously. "Yes, my love, I am protected from your evil little powers." Then he took another dive at me, but I was closer to him this time and he took me down hard onto the wood floor.

I managed to get my right knee up and shove it into his crotch. He made a gagging noise and rolled off me. As I was getting up, he reached out and grabbed my ankle and flipped me over so I was on my stomach. I could feel his warm breath right next to my ear.

"You're a better fighter than I thought you were," he whispered. I brought my elbow back to hit him, but he caught it. "But I'm still better than you are."

He flipped me over so he could face me. He had his legs pinning my legs and his hands were clamped over my wrists.

"I'm going to ask you one last time, will you come with me?"

"You're going have drag me out of here in a body bag," I spat.

"Oh, I don't want you dead, Em. But I guess unconscious will have to do."

He took one of his hands off my wrist. He cocked his fist back to punch me in the face, but I was quicker. I snapped my hand forward and connected the heel of my hand to his nose. The shock on his face was quickly followed by blood running down his chin.

I scooted out from under him and nailed him in the face a second time with my boot. I scrambled to my feet. He stood up slowly. He was smiling with blood covering the bottom part of his face and staining his teeth red. He wiped the back of his hand across his nose and mouth and looked down at it.

"Okay, I clearly need to go with my final course of action," he muttered. He dug into his pocket and pulled out a syringe. He popped the top off and strode toward me. I backed quickly away, but was halted when my back slammed into the wall.

I reached my hands around and pulled both my daggers out. He was standing right in front of me.

"What is that?" I breathed keeping my eyes on the syringe in his hands.

"Something that will make you see things my way."

He closed the distance between us and I rammed one of my daggers into his stomach. His eyes were huge. He took a step back and looked down at the hilt sticking out of him. He looked back up at me like, "Why did you just do that?"

He stumbled for a moment and then went down on his knees. He wavered for a moment and started to tumble to the side. Before he went over though, he brought that syringe up and stuck it in my left thigh. I quickly pulled it out and threw it on the ground. I had no idea what was in it or how much he had injected in me.

I kneeled over him. He was still breathing. He was just staring blankly at the wall. "Sam?" I whispered. He blinked slowly and turned his head.

"I can't think of a better way to go than at your hands. If you don't shove that dagger in my heart, I will come after you again and again," he breathed. He rolled over so he was lying on his back. "Do it, Emily."

I brought the dagger up by my ear and I felt the hot sting of tears running down my face. This was not really happening to me. This was all some really fucked up dream I was having. My whole life was just one fucked up dream.

Sam palmed the dagger that was sticking out of his stomach. Before he could pull it out though, I brought mine down and nailed him directly in the heart. I heard his final breath leave his lungs. I reached forward and closed his eyes so they weren't staring at the ceiling.

Then I fell backward onto my butt. My hands were shaking violently and my breath was coming in short little gasps. I had killed Brothers and Nexes before. I never had any problem with that. It never caused me to lose sleep. I had never met an Avid though. And here was one lying in front of me who just so happened to have been my best friend for nearly fourteen years.

I wiped my nose with the back of my hand and stood up. I glanced in the mirror to see that there was some blood on me, but I knew it wasn't my own. I didn't have any damage, save for the needle prick in my leg that I couldn't even feel.

I went to the kitchen and pulled out a note pad and pen from one of the drawers. I scribbled a quick note and left it on the counter where someone would see it.

I walked back over to where Sam lay on the floor and pulled both my daggers out of him. I wiped the blades on his shirt and slid them back into their holsters. I stared at him for a moment. I wanted to remember every detail about him; that titanium ring in his bottom lip, the plugs in his ears, the tattoos on his right bicep. I knew that he had a lime green tongue ring in too. He always flicked it against the back of his teeth when he was thinking. His cigarette pack was barely peeking out of his shirt pocket.

I sucked in a breath and stood up. I walked back to the kitchen and grabbed my bag. I left the house and didn't bother locking the door behind me. If anyone did decide to break in, I didn't think they'd stay for long when the saw the dead guy lying in the living room.

I got in the Audi and tossed my bag into the passenger seat. I turned the car around and drove down the drive.

I was on the highway out of Autumn Falls when the tears started streaming down my face again. I just couldn't stop thinking about how he deceived everyone. I thought Lian was the King of Lying, but Sam had him beat by a long shot.

For seventeen years we all knew him as Sam Malik. He was the easy-going, laid-back guy of our group. He never pissed anyone off and everyone wanted to be his friend. I had never heard anyone say a bad thing about him.

But it was all a front. He had sat patiently by earning our trust and becoming one of us so he could eventually bring us all down.

It was sick and fucked up, but this was my reality now. Every part of this war was starting to come to a head. It had cost me too many relationships with friends and family. I was tired of it. I wanted it all to be over with. I wanted to sleep through a night without being woke up by the fear of a Brother standing over my bed or being called out at strange hours to take out a host of Nexes.

Yes, I was going to the stronghold to get my aunt back, but I was going to do a hell of a lot of damage on my way out. I wanted to cripple our biggest threat in any way I could. I wanted them to be weak and for attacks on them to come easily. I wanted the Talyrians to fall.

Chapter 20

Lian

Sunday was a typical day for me. Wake up, go to training, shower, change clothes, eat, and hang out with Zoë. It was a routine that I was now very familiar with. But it was a little different on this day.

I glanced down at my watch. It was 10:18 p.m. I was pacing the living room again. I had a travel bag packed and sitting on the leather couch. I was just waiting on Tovan to come get me. I didn't know what he considered Sunday night, but I kind of hoped to be on the road by now.

There was a knock on my door. I quickly walked over there and yanked the door open. Zoë was standing there. "Well, someone is dressed awfully nice. Planning on wooing Emily with your fancy new wardrobe?" she asked before walking passed me and into my room.

"Emily is not so materialistic that she chooses guys based on their clothing," I said. I glanced down the hall both ways to see if Tovan was coming. The hall was empty.

"Don't worry, he'll be here shortly. He had a lot to get done to make this go off smoothly. It takes time and careful planning. He said he'll come get you Sunday night and he will," Zoë stated sitting on the leather couch and flipping on the TV. "I swear there is nothing good on Sunday nights right now," she muttered scrolling through the guide.

We started watching some movie that was halfway over. We were trying to guess how it would end after only seeing part of the show. Before we saw the conclusion, there was another knock on my door. This one was a lot softer than Zoë's knocks were.

I opened the door to Tovan standing there glancing at his watch. "We need to go now if this is gonna work."

I nodded my head and grabbed my bag off the couch. "Bye, Zoë," I said leaving her sitting there. She gave me a head nod and went back to watching the show.

I followed Tovan down the hall. He was walking really fast. It wasn't hard to keep up with him or anything. He continually checked his watch.

We ran down the stairwell on the east side of the stronghold. I had been down this one once before when I was following Zoë down to the dungeons. And once again I found myself in the dungeons. Tovan though took some turns down halls that Zoë and I didn't go down.

I noticed that there were little marks on the corners of the halls he was taking. He had probably made those himself so he could map his way around down here. The dungeons were a confusing maze just as the stronghold above it was. This place was made to get lost in.

We walked for a long time with Tovan keeping his quick pace in front of me. I would see his watch light up frequently. Sometimes he wouldn't say anything and other times he would mutter about being late. I was starting to imagine him as the White Rabbit from Alice in Wonderland.

Finally, we came to a door. There was something written on it, but it was black and I couldn't read it. I could barely see Tovan turn around.

"Okay, I need you to stay right behind me. This is the tricky part. If we get through this, then we're all good. All right?"

I nodded my head. He cracked the door open just enough for us to squeeze through. I was able to quickly read what the door said: GUARDS QUARTERS.

So, we were where the guards hung out on their off time. I didn't know how many guards would be down here or if anyone of them would stop us. Then again, maybe they were in on getting people out and in the stronghold.

I stayed right behind Tovan like he told me to. I kept my head down so that if we did pass anyone, I would not make eye contact with them.

I heard Tovan sigh and then someone began talking. "Hey, aren't you that Marlow boy?"

I brought my head up and looked at Tovan. He glanced at me then back at the guard who was asking me the question. It was the same guard who stopped me from going out the front doors the other day.

"Yes, he's my best friend, Lukas. I was just showing him around. He's going to be a very high-ranking Talyrian before long. He wants to know this stronghold's every nook and cranny," Tovan stated.

"Don't call me Lukas. You know I hate that. And I think I should make a call to the King to see if this an approved visit," Lukas said.

"Yeah, you go call the King about someone being down here. I'm sure he has nothing else going on at the moment," Tovan said rolling his eyes.

"Then I'll call his dad!"

"My father is the one who suggested I do this," I chimed in. "Go ahead and call him," I stated.

Lukas licked his lips and his eyes were fluttering around the room. "Maybe later," he whispered. He then took off walking briskly.

Tovan shook his head. "That guy gets on my last fucking nerve. He's going to be the one who blows this for me. I should take him out before he gets the chance. A little shove off the roof would do the trick." He looked at his watch again. "Shit, come on!"

We took off at a jog and thankfully we did not pass any other guards. We walked down a long narrow hall that had water lightly covering the floor. There were florescent lights spaced at wide distances on the right side of the wall. It was barely enough to see very far in front of you.

We came to another door that Tovan didn't hesitate to open. There was a small concrete pad and a set of stairs. Tovan jogged up them and we were outside. The guard stand that Tovan worked at was to our left. This was his entry into the stronghold.

"Okay, the Lexus is around the corner and the keys are in the glove box. When you get back on Wednesday, just leave the car there. Make sure you come here after 4 p.m. There will be someone else working before that and then you're screwed. I'll get you back in the stronghold. Okay?"

I nodded my head. "Seriously, thank you for this."

"It's not a problem. Like I said, I'm just glad we're friends again."

I took off at a jog down the dark gravel drive. And just like Tovan said there was the car waiting for me. I couldn't really make out what color or model it was in the dark. I got behind the wheel and set my bag in the seat next to me. It took me a few minutes to figure everything out. I should have asked for a basic car, not one that looked like the inside of a spaceship.

I finally got the engine turned over and the headlights on. Then I was on the road headed south to Autumn Falls.

I had to make a few stops along the way for gas and food, but I still made good time. I finally got to see that the car I was driving was a midnight blue Lexus LFA. I didn't know who Tovan knew to get a car like that, but he must have had some damn good connections.

I came in along the same stretch of road that I walked into town on several months ago. That seemed like someone else's life, not mine.

I slowed down when I drove by the drop off that looked down over the beach. That was the first time I saw Emily. I was instantly drawn to her even from that far away.

I glanced at the clock in the car and saw that it was just after three. I'd made damn good time. I was driving eighty the whole way though. I figured the Corlissians would be at practice for another hour or so, but maybe their trainer gave them the day off or something. Sometimes Emily skipped practice too. It wasn't like she needed more training.

I went by the Domus where my old apartment was. I got out of the car and headed up to the second floor. All my clothes and books were still scattered around. The bed was still unmade; exactly how I left it last Friday morning before school. Absolutely nothing had changed.

I grabbed some of the clothes I wanted and exited the building and got in the car. I then drove over to Emily's house. There wasn't a single car in the driveway. I figured that Kate's car would be there, but maybe someone was using it since Kate didn't need it at the moment.

I walked up the front path and up the stairs. I cupped my hands around my eyes and leaned against the big picture window that was in the living room. What I saw shocked me. What I could see of the living room was destroyed. There was glass all over the floors, the couches and chairs had been sliced open, pillow guts were everywhere, and pictures with shattered frames were lying in random places.

I stepped back and looked at the door. I could see that it had been kicked in. The place wasn't even locked up. No one had bothered to put a new lock on it. I guess when everything in the place is broken who's going to steal anything?

I knew Emily was at the lake house the times she had talked to me. I thought she had just been there chilling, but I was guessing that's where her family was living. I decided to head out to the lake house. Maybe she was there.

I turned around and I was immediately shoved up against the house. No one had touched me though. Then I felt a pressure on my throat that started to lift me off the ground.

Coming up the stairs was Thea with her head tilted and a smile on her face. Behind her were Mason and Drew.

Thea lifted me up a little further until I was just on my tippy toes. The trio walked up the stairs and Thea and Drew stared at me like they wanted to kill me. Mason was turned around looking at the Lexus.

"You have a lot of nerve coming here, Killian," Drew spat.

I couldn't say anything since Thea was using her psychokinesis to practically choke me out. She tilted her head to the other side and narrowed her eyes. She was looking at me like I was an insect under a microscope.

"So, where is my sister?" Drew asked. I pointed at my throat to indicate that I couldn't talk. "Thea, loosen your grip," Drew ordered.

I was lowered back down so my feet were on the porch. The pressure left my throat and was placed on my upper arms instead. She wasn't about to let me go.

"Now, where is my sister?" Drew asked again with more force in his voice.

"Which one?" I asked rubbing at my throat.

Drew sighed. "Which one do you think, dumbass?" he snapped.

"I just got here. I was coming to beg Emily not to go to the stronghold. I knew she was going to come, but I can't let her near that place," I said.

"Why would she go to the stronghold?" Drew asked.

I saw Thea glance at Emily's brother and bite her bottom lip. She knew, but Drew didn't.

"He found Kate at the stronghold. He called Emily Friday night at the party and told her," Thea said.

Drew's head snapped in Thea's direction. "You mean this whole weekend she knew where Kate was and she didn't bother to tell her own siblings?" I watched as his face grew increasingly redder.

"I guess. I thought she would tell you," Thea muttered.

"So, we know she left, but we just don't know when," he said.

Mason finally tore his eyes off the car and turned around. "Man Killian, I am liking your new style. You got a bad ass car and you are dressing better than I am," Mason said. He walked forward and opened my suit jacket and peered inside. "Yeah, this is quality shit you're wearing, bro."

"Mason! Don't 'bro' him. He's a Talyrian!" Thea snapped.

"Oh right!" he said taking a step back. "Still I have to give props to his stylishness," he muttered.

Thea shook her head. Just then a white Mercedes squealed to a stop right in the middle of the road. I saw Toby jump out and run up to the porch. He was red faced and looked like he'd seen a ghost.

"She killed Sam. His body is in the middle of the fucking living room with two stab wounds. There is blood everywhere, but she's long gone. She left this though," Toby said handing Drew a piece of paper.

Drew read aloud, "Yes I killed Sam, but he told me he was an Avid and he was trying to get to me come with him. We had a fight, which is why the house is a wreck, and I stabbed him in the stomach. He told me to kill him because if I didn't, he'd keep coming after me, so I stabbed him in the heart. He stuck me in the leg with a syringe. I don't know what was in it though. I'm going to the stronghold because Kate is there. I'll see you guys in a few days. ~ Emily."

Drew wadded up the paper and threw it against the house. Then he stalked off the porch and started pacing up and down the sidewalk.

"What should we do?" Toby asked.

"Maybe we should just wait. I mean this is Emily we are talking about. If anyone can get in that building without being noticed and get out with another person, it's her," Mason said.

"I have to agree with Mason on this one. There is no point in all of us going up there. We might actually blow her cover. I say we wait it out a few days. If she's not back, then we do something," Thea stated.

Toby looked up and furrowed his brows when he saw me standing there. "What the hell is he doing here?" he asked.

"He was coming to stop Emily from going to the stronghold," Thea said. "What are you going to do if I let you go?" she asked me.

"Not move. There are three pyromancers here and I don't want to get roasted," I said.

"I think we should let him go. If he was going to stop Emily, then maybe he can help Em get out of the stronghold," Toby suggested. I really liked that suggestion actually. It involved no harm coming to me.

Drew walked back up the stairs. "How in the hell do we not know anyone else is in our group is a fucking Avid? Hell, Micah could be one for all we know!"

"Micah is not an Avid. Look at his parents!" Mason said shaking his head.

"That tells me nothing. I thought Sam looked like his parents. Fucking Avids creeping in to Corlissian ranks. What's next? Nexes siding with Talyrians!"

"I'm letting him go so he can help Emily," Thea said looking at Drew.

Drew waved his hand in the air. "I don't care what you do. I just want my sister back," he mumbled.

Thea sighed. "Will you go up to the stronghold and help her?" Thea asked.

"Of course!" I felt her grip on me go away. I cautiously walked across the porch and down the steps.

Thea fell in line beside me as I walked down the sidewalk toward the curb where the Lexus was parked.

"You actually love her, don't you?" she asked once I stopped by the driver's side door. She looked up at me and used to her hand to shield her eyes from the sun.

"I don't see the point in answering that question. You're going to hate me whether I love her or not," I said.

"Don't be a turd and just answer my question!"

I furrowed my brows. I hadn't been a called a turd since I was in elementary school. Thea was using some old put-down terms. "Yes, I do love Emily. No, I don't think there is any chance of us getting back together. I'm helping her because it's the right thing to do."

I opened the car door so I could get up to the stronghold as soon as possible. I knew this would throw Tovan off since I wasn't supposed to be back until Wednesday. I would be back Tuesday now.

Thea grabbed my arm before I got in the car. "What do you think Sam stuck her with?" she asked.

"I don't know. Maybe it was just something that would make her pass out. I don't know what kind of shit Avids use," I said. "But when I do see her, I'll make sure she's all right."

"I cannot believe he was an Avid. He'd been our best friend since we started school. All that time he was lying to us about who he was. That's really fucked up shit, Killian," Thea said. I saw tears in her eyes.

"I'm sure Emily's having a harder time dealing with it, Thea. She is the one who had to kill him after all."

Thea nodded her head and gave me a tiny smile. "Go. And please make sure nothing happens to her. I don't want to lose another friend," Thea said.

"I will." I dropped into the car and took off. I hoped I could keep that promise to Thea. I didn't know how many hours ago Emily had left. Hell, I could have passed her on the road and not even known it.

I knew I would be too late to stop her from getting into the stronghold, but I could at least help her and Kate get out. It would be tricky, but it would be easier than them climbing fences. Also, I was concerned because I didn't know what Sam had injected in her. I was hoping that it was something that would make her drowsy. But like I told Thea I didn't know what the Avids had. They were a pretty secretive group as a whole.

Once I was out of Autumn Falls and on the open road, I grabbed my cell phone out of the cup holder and called Zoë.

"Wasn't expecting to hear from you so soon. How's everything going?" she asked.

"Badly. Very badly. I need to get in touch with Tovan. Can you get him to call me as soon as possible?"

"Yeah, of course. What's going on, Killian?" she asked. I could hear the worry in her voice.

"Emily already left and she's probably way ahead of me. She could be at the stronghold by now. One of her best friends was an Avid and she killed him before she left town. Oh, and he injected her with something. I think that's all. I'm on my way back. Now, get Tovan!"

"Okay."

I hit the gas and the Lexus responded by shoving me back deeper into the seat. I sped along the four-lane road for a while and only passed a handful of cars. I knew that there was a good chance that a cop could pull me over and I already had a plan in my head if that happened. I would hit the accelerator even harder and I would dare him to catch me. I would dare him even further to get into the stronghold. I was sure that would make all the Talyrians happy…let the local police know where we all live!

My cell phone rang and I picked it up. "Yup?"

"What's up, Killian?" Tovan asked.

"I'm coming back now. Will you be able to get me back inside in the morning?" I asked.

"Aww shit! What happened?" he asked.

"It's a lot to explain right now. Is it gonna be a problem?"

"Umm, I need to make some calls. I'll call you back."

I tossed the cell in the seat next to me. I didn't let off the accelerator until the gaslight came on. I stopped off at the nearest exit and gassed the car up for hopefully the last time. I walked inside to pay.

There was a guy working behind the counter who looked a little older than me. I figured I'd ask him if he'd seen Emily. It was a long shot that she even stopped here, but it wouldn't hurt to ask.

"Hey, did a girl stop in here recently? She would have had brown hair with purple streaks and gray eyes?" I asked.

"Mmm hum," he muttered with a toothpick dangling between his lips. "She was driving that A5 and she was wearing this leather get up. Man did she know how to wear that. Girl had quite the body. She your girl?" he asked.

"She was," I muttered.

"You're a fool. I wouldn't let something that fine get away from me. You trying to get her back?"

"Something like that."

"Well, she's about eight hours ahead of you. She could be across the border by now. Better run that nice car you have into the ground to get to her."

"Yeah. I'm trying."

I jogged out to the car and burnt out of the station. As soon as I had the speedometer up to 150 MPH did my cell ring again. I picked it up.

I didn't even have to say anything for Tovan to start talking. "I had to change shifts with a couple of guys, but I got you covered. Just leave the Lexus at the end of the drive and I'll get you inside. Now, since I know you're in a car and have nothing to do but drive you can talk. Why are you on your way back?"

"So what did Zoë tell you?" I asked.

Tovan laughed. "A lot. She said that there is this Corlissian girl you've got a thing for and her aunt was kidnapped and she's the lady you and Zoë were looking for. And now she is planning on coming up here to get her aunt back."

"Okay. Well, I went to talk Emily, that's her name, into not coming up here and well she had already left. There is a really good chance that she is currently breaking into the stronghold as we speak actually."

"Are you fucking serious?" Tovan asked.

"Yeah, and if anyone can do it and not get caught it's her. And let me warn you, Tove, if you come in contact with her just let her pass. She is very lethal."

"Duly noted, my friend. All right, just gimme a call when you get here. And if I see a fine ass Corlissian girl I will run the ot...FUCK!"

I could hear some screeching, high-pitched noise in the background. "What the fuck is that?"

"That would be the stronghold's alarm. I think your girlfriend is here and everyone knows it too. I gotta go, Killian."

The line went dead. The cell slipped out of my grasp and fell between the seat and the console. I slammed my palm against the steering wheel repeatedly. This is the one thing that I thought wouldn't happen. I hadn't even factored in Emily tripping an alarm. I figured she would sneak across the three lines of defense and climb up to the roof or something.

I drove through the night and into the morning. I didn't even stop to get anything to keep me awake. The fact that Emily was probably captured and being held in the dungeons was enough to keep my eyes wide open.

Around four in the morning I sped through the town of Lake Edisto, the place I was raised, and called Tovan, after dislocating my arm to fish my cell out from under the seat.

"I don't know what's going on, Killian. I don't know if she was caught or not. I've been trying to find something out, but no one is talking."

"Don't worry about it, Tove. Hey, I'm almost up to the stronghold."

"Okay. Yeah, I'm out here already. You're good," he said. He sounded out of breath like he'd been doing laps around the stronghold for hours.

I finally slowed the Lexus down when I rounded that last corner that the stronghold's drive was on. I brought the car to a stop and grabbed my bag and my cell. I ran up to the guard's booth that Tovan was standing out front of.

Tovan turned and jogged down the stairs and opened the door at the bottom. "The entire stronghold is going absolutely crazy right now. Everyone wants to know what's going on, but the King hasn't said anything yet. We're hearing word that he's going to gather everyone in the main hall," Tovan told me as we walked briskly down the long hall.

"What's he gonna tell them? That a 17-year-old Corlissian girl almost broke into the stronghold? Yeah, that will boost their morale."

There were no guards in the quarters when we walked through. Tovan held the door open. "Listen, I've gotta get back up there. Just follow the white marks on the walls and they will lead you back to the stair well. I'll see you later." He patted me on the back and bounded back through the quarters.

I let the door slam behind me and used the sparse lighting to guide me back to where the stairs were. This was going to be the last time I ever came into the dungeons again. I was sick of this dank place.

Chapter 21
Emily

I honestly had no idea where the Talyrian stronghold was. There had been a lot of speculation about its exact location for years. The thing was no Corlissians could find it. They knew it was in a general area, to the east of Lake Edisto, but somehow that massive building was under cover.

I had to stop frequently to check the map. My plan was just to drive to Lake Edisto and then go east. Just because every other Corlissian couldn't find the stronghold from land or air didn't mean I wouldn't. They wanted to find it so they could attack; I just wanted my aunt back.

The day dragged on and I was thankful that I didn't know where the stronghold was. That kept my mind off the one thing I didn't want to think about, the fact that a guy who I thought was my best friend was lying dead in my family's lake house.

I stopped at a gas station to fill up my car. I was hoping it would be the last stop I'd have to make. I grabbed the folded-up map off the passenger seat and took it inside with me.

I paid for the gas then spread the map out. "Can you tell me how far it is from here to Lake Edisto?" I asked the guy behind the counter. He was wearing a flannel shirt over a dark gray T-shirt and a baseball cap on backward with a toothpick pinched between his teeth. His eyes roamed up and down my body. That tended to happen when you wore all leather.

He didn't even look at the map. "'Bout an hour and half, maybe two hours depending on how fast you drive." He glanced out the window. "But I see you got that nice car out there and it looks like it's built for speed."

"Right. Well, thank you for your time and have a nice evening," I said picking the map up.

"Now what's your hurry?" he asked. "You got a job up in Lake Edisto or something?"

"For fuck's sake! I. AM. NOT. A. STRIPPER. And I'm seventeen you creep. Go find some girl your own age!" I stalked out the gas station and got in my car. I shoved my foot into the gas pedal and burned the tires.

As much as I couldn't stand Mr. Gas Station Weirdo, he was correct on the time it would take to reach Lake Edisto. I slowed down as I passed through the town. It was similar to Autumn Falls. All the houses were brick, some were medium sized, but most were huge. From my vantage point on the road I did not see any run-down homes. I did see a school building, random offices, and restaurants. The only difference between Lake Edisto and Autumn Falls was that my town was on the beach.

Even as I exited the town limits, I did not pick up speed. There were no cars behind me and even if there were, they could have gone around me. I didn't know exactly what I was looking for; a beautiful, wide, well-paved drive with gates that had a giant T on them, or some nondescript, beat up lane that looked like the place that led to where horror movies happened.

I passed a concrete drive and a black top drive, but I could see both the houses, that those lead to. Then I passed a crappy looking gravel drive with potholes in it. There was rainwater pooled at the bottom of those potholes. I couldn't see the house that the drive led to since there was a bend to the lane. I drove a little further and I saw a fence sprawling quite a distance down from the lane. I just knew that a fence that long was hiding something quite large behind it.

A mile down from the gravel drive I pulled my car into a small little gravel area that was at the side of the road. I grabbed my bag and got out of the car. I tossed it on top of the trunk and made sure no cars or nosy people were around. Then I started stashing daggers and throwing stars all over my body. I popped the trunk and threw the bag in and slammed it closed. I slid my car key into a small pocket on the side of my jacket. I made sure my cell was off and I slid it into another pocket.

I jogged down the ditch at the side of the road and I was quickly hidden in the tree line. I kept a careful eye out for trip lines and cameras in the trees. There was nothing. I came up to the chain link fence. I hovered a distance away from it trying to see if it was electrified. I doubted it was.

I heard a rustling to my right. I ducked down behind a tree and peered around only to see a squirrel scampering in the leaves. He ran up to the fence and sniffed it, then scuttled up and over it.

If it didn't zap a squirrel, it wasn't going to do anything to me. I hopped over it and glanced down its length. I didn't see anyone around. I didn't think this would be the only line of defense the stronghold would have. I had a gut feeling that their security grew more aggressive the closer to the stronghold I got.

I kept my movements slow and precise. I hid behind trees and kept a watch above me for any cameras and on the ground for wires. Again, there was nothing. I kind of started to wonder if this was the stronghold I was sneaking up on. Maybe it was a farm or something with a really long fence.

Then I saw the brick wall with one person moving on it. I leaned against a tree and watched his movements through the trees. I watched how many steps he took and when he turned around and went the other way. He was very precise and he must have been counting his steps in his head. Forty steps to the right, forty steps to the left, then back again.

I didn't want to kill anyone, least of all the first Talyrian I came upon, but then he wouldn't hesitate to kill me. I pulled two throwing stars from their holster on my leg. I army crawled closer to the wall. I counted the guard's steps that was right above me. As soon as he hit thirty-eight, I stood up and winged the star at him. It hit him directly in the left shoulder.

He stopped and looked down at the tips of the star that were imbedded in his shoulder. He touched the star and then looked down the right side of the wall, then the left, then down at the ground. I stepped forward and I saw him pulling a dagger from his belt. He aimed and threw it at me. I yanked my head to the right and it went whizzing by me.

I fired the second throwing star and it hit him in the center of his chest. He stumbled a little and he disappeared. I glanced down the wall and using the offset of the bricks climbed up the bastard.

I crouched down when I was at the top. I didn't see any guards that were close to me. I looked down the other side and saw the guard lying at the bottom in an unnatural position.

I swung my body over the edge of the wall and climbed down that side. I bent down next to the guard and checked for a pulse. Nothing.

I leaned my back against the wall and took in where I was. There were more trees in front of me and through them I could see another wall. That wall was twice as high as the one behind me. And I could see a lot more movement on that one. The guards were tighter together and not as spread out.

I thought for a moment how to take down a number of them without drawing too much attention. There were at least eight guards I would need to move out of the way to get over the wall.

I checked the trees and the ground for cameras and wires again before I stood up and moved through the trees. I cracked my knuckles as I walked slowly toward the behemoth wall.

"*Dolor*," I breathed. With my leather jacket on I could only see the red when it ran through my fingers. "*Dolor*," I said again and it obediently spilled out around me. I shoved my hands behind my back and I could feel it staying hidden behind me. It knew exactly what I wanted it to do.

I stayed hidden in the tree line and when the guards were as close together as they would get, I shoved my hands forward. The red tendrils shot forward and attacked every person that was in my sights. I could hear their screams of pain as I ran forward and climbed up the wall.

It was still attacking them when I reached the top. I hopped to the other side and whispered, "*Intereo*," as I climbed down. Their screams stopped. I knew someone would have heard them, so I needed to get to the stronghold quickly. I was praying that this was it. I didn't know how many lines of defense the stronghold needed.

I hauled through the trees and there in front of me stood the massive building. The sheer size of it made me stop. I had heard about this building my entire life and how big it was. I had heard tales of it being set up in a manner that even if someone did get into it, they would get lost inside. I had been told so many things about the Talyrian stronghold, but seeing it in real life didn't do any of those tales' justice. I couldn't believe that anything that big didn't just sink in the ground. I swear the thing stretched a solid mile. I was standing near one corner of it and I couldn't see the other end.

I snapped out of my trance and ran to the end. I leaned against the side of it in between a set of windows. I pulled two daggers out and palmed them tightly. I took a deep breath and just as I was exhaling when I heard what sounded like a tornado siren going off. Then I heard the high-pitched alarm going off inside the building behind me.

I guess the Talyrians knew I was here. I turned around and looked up at how high the stronghold was. I counted the windows and let out a sigh. There were eight stories and nine to the roof. I had climbed enough shit today I didn't want to climb any more. I didn't have a choice since there wasn't a door with a big sign over it reading: Corlissian Invaders Enter Here! These Talyrians just weren't hospitable at all!

I holstered my daggers when I heard a noise coming from the back of the stronghold. It sounded like something slamming shut. I was sure that meant guards were coming outside. I took a few steps back and ran up and jumped. I managed to get my fingertips on the edge of one of the windowsills. I started to pull myself up when I heard someone yell, "Hey! You! Stop!" Yeah, that wasn't going to happen.

I felt someone grip my ankles and yank. I glanced down to see two guards below me. They each had both their hands on my ankles. With one hand gripping the top of the window I reached down and pulled a dagger out. It was an awkward position I was in. I couldn't get a good angle to throw a dagger down with the building pressed right up against me. Still I fired it down and managed for it to hit the hands of the guard who had a hold of my left ankle. His hands snapped free.

I pulled myself up as much as I could and then shoved off the window. I twisted my body around and the other guard's hands snapped free of my ankle. I landed about ten feet away from the building in a crouch.

The guards were standing there staring at me. They exchanged a quick glance with one another.

"It's just a girl," the one whose hand was bloody stated.

"She is still a Corlissian," the other replied.

I rose up and cracked my neck from side to side. "Which one of you boys wants to be screaming in pain first?" I asked with a smile.

They looked at each other again. "Is this girl serious?" Bloody Hand asked.

"Of course I am. And I will take the both of you on without using a single power," I replied with that smile still fixed on my face.

"Okay, the Corlissians are fucking twisted," the other guard said.

"Oh, no they're not. It's just me who is."

They both took a few steps forward. I saw the one without the bloody hand wiggle his fingers. I knew he was an aquamancer. And I no idea what power the other one had. He opted to pull weapons out of his belt.

I grabbed two more daggers. I twirled them both in between my fingers. The guard's mouths popped open and they watched transfixed as the daggers spun through my fingers without doing any damage. I was so glad my dad taught me how to do that.

I tossed the dagger that was in my right hand up in the air while still twirling the other one. I grabbed the dagger by its tip and quickly sent it soaring toward the guard with the daggers in his hands. I hit him in the stomach and heard him let out and "ooopphhhffff." He stumbled back until he hit the stronghold. He yanked the dagger out and tossed it on the ground.

The other guard sent a flourish of water spraying toward me. I tucked and rolled out of its way. It was kind of fun just toying with these guys, but I needed to stop jacking around and get my ass inside.

I put another dagger in my free hand and stalked forward. I felt a pain rip through my leg. I glanced down and expected to see a weapon sticking out of my thigh, but there wasn't anything. Then I remember that Sam had stabbed me with that fucking syringe.

The guards came toward me quickly. I took a step back and kicked the one who was closest to me in the knee and heard the bone snap. He tried to shoot another blast of water at me, but the pain from his leg prevented him from doing anything.

The guard with the daggers grabbed onto my arm, but I threw my free arm around and elbowed him in the face. Then I kicked the guard on the ground in the face too.

The pain in my leg reared its ugly head again. I bent over and that's when the guard jumped on my back and pinned me to the ground. I felt a fist blast me in the side of the head before I blacked out.

Chapter 22

Lian

It seemed to take me forever to make it to that damn stairwell. I only took six wrong turns. I let out a major sigh of relief when I saw that door. Tovan had left it propped open and there was light streaming out of the crack.

I hauled ass up those stairs and down the halls until I turned the corner of the hall my room was on. Zoë was pacing from my door to hers. Her eyes lit up when she saw me.

"What is going on?" she asked.

"Emily's here. I don't know anything passed that. Get in your room and stay there. Understand?" She nodded her head and did as I asked.

I ran in my room. I threw my bag in the bottom of my closet and yanked my clothes off in a hurry. I took a quick shower and shaved. I turned the TV on and sat in front of it with nothing but my boxers on. I wanted it to seem like I hadn't been doing anything illegal today.

There was a knock on my door. I knew there would be. I just didn't know who it would be.

"It's open," I yelled. I was leaning forward with my elbows on my knees. There was some game on that I was pretending to be very interested in. I didn't know shit about sports.

The door opened and I glanced to see my father standing there. "Killian, why are you not dressed?" he asked.

"I just got out of the shower. I was about to. What's going on anyways?" I asked.

"Someone attempted to break into the stronghold. The King wants to see you immediately. Get dressed and go to his office." Then he left my room.

I shut the TV off and grabbed my cell phone. I called Zoë since I didn't want to go into the hall in my boxers with my father nearby.

"Really? You're that lazy that you're calling me from across the hall?"

"Yeah. I need you to help me pick something out. I've gotta go meet with his Royal Pain in My Ass-ness."

Zoë giggle. "I like that. I'll be right there."

She walked in the door and headed straight for my closet. She pursed her lips and tilted her head from side to side. She reached in and pulled out one of the nicer suits I had. It was black with charcoal lapels. The pants were black with a charcoal stripe running up the outside seam. She grabbed a charcoal vest, a black oxford, and a black and charcoal striped tie. Then she tossed a black fedora on top of the clothes she's piled up on my bed.

"I'm not wearing that."

"Eh, thought I'd try," she muttered as she put it back in my closet. "You're welcome, by the way," she said loudly as she walked out of my room.

"Thank you!"

I quickly put the clothes on and took a glance at myself in the mirror. I had to admit I looked pretty damn good. Then I headed down to the first floor. I didn't want to be a sweaty mess when I reached the bottom floor, so I took the elevator.

I had a feeling that the King wanted to know exactly what I knew about Emily. I still planned to play stupid with him though. I had made one promise to her and that was not to tell anyone what I knew about her. That was a promise I was going to keep.

I walked down the marble halls passed the main hall and around to where the King's and other council members offices were. That blood red rug ran from where I stood clear to the door that led to the main hall.

The door to the King's office was open, so I knocked on the doorframe. Aldous had black-rimmed glasses on that made him look years younger. He looked up and squinted. He took his glasses off and laid them on his desk.

"Ah, Killian. Come in!"

I walked in and sat in the same seat I occupied my first day back. It had only been a little over a week.

"My father said you wanted to see me."

"Yes. There is something I need for you to do for me. There is an occupant down in the dungeons. I need for you to go downstairs and tell the guards to bring that person up to the main hall. Can you do that?" he asked.

"Umm, will the guards know who you mean?"

He smiled at me. "They most certainly will. I think you will know too. There is a door that you can use to take you downstairs to the left of the hall."

He put his glasses back on and resumed whatever I had interrupted. I knew that our conversation was over. I left his office and made my way to the end of the hall. There to the left was an old wooden door that matched nothing of the grandeur that surrounded it. I opened it and there were old concrete steps leading down. Looked like I was going to the dungeons…again.

I slowly descended the narrow spiral staircase. There was a rope anchored to the inside wall that acted as a makeshift handrail. The stairs were slick with moisture and seeing as how I didn't want to break my neck, I gripped the rope tightly in my left hand.

The stairs seemed to go on forever. I breathed a sigh of relief when my feet finally hit the solid floor of the dungeon. This part of the dungeon was well lit by modern lights. Not like the other part that was lit intermittently by janky ass lights that worked whenever they felt like it.

There was a long, narrow hall that stretched out in front of me. After a distance, the hall widened. There were a few cells on one side of the hall and in a small alcove was an L shaped desk. No one was behind that desk though. That was highly unusual.

I turned my head to left to see if there were any prisoners in the cells. I sucked in a breath when I saw her. Emily. Her head was hanging down and I couldn't tell if she was unconscious or she was just staring at the floor. I noticed that there were leather gloves on her hands and around each wrist was a metal cuff that was attached to a chain that was bolted to the floor.

I moved toward the bars and my foot scraped against the floor. Her head popped up. For the briefest of moments her eyes looked dead, but that was quickly replaced when she realized it was me. There was hate and loathing and all-around disgust. Her eyes started glowing violet at just the mere sight of me. That killed any hope I had of a happy reunion.

"Emily," I whispered. I wrapped my hands around the bars. "I cannot tell you how…" I started when the sound of someone dragging their feet stopped me. One of the guards rounded the corner. I looked back at Emily whose glowing purple eyes were on the guard and a smile was on her face.

I looked back at the guard whose eyes met mine. He shook his head. He was walking with quite a limp. He had two black eyes and was holding a bloody cloth under his nose. He gently leaned against the corner of his desk.

He brought the cloth away from his nose. It was a mess and twisted at a weird angle. His bottom lip was swollen.

"Be careful around that one. She may have all the outward appearance of an angel, but she is a killer," he stated. He put the cloth back under his nose.

"She did that to you?" I asked even though I already knew the answer.

He nodded his head. "Broke my leg too," he mumbled. "I would be up in the hospital, but Jenkins had to go up first 'cause he was worse than I was if you can imagine that."

I turned to face Emily again. That smile was still on her face as she stared at the guard. "That wasn't very nice of you."

"I will do even worse to you," she whispered.

"I think I could hold my own against you," I said.

Her eyes narrowed. She took a few steps toward me until she was inches from the bars. Her arms were stretched out behind her being pulled taut by the chain. "You've been training for what, a week? I have been training to kill your kind since I came into this world. I would love to see you try and fight me for even a minute," she hissed.

"Emily, taunt me as much as you want, but I will not fight you…ever. And no, that does not make me a coward. It makes me a guy who will not hit a girl."

She rolled her violet eyes at me and took a step back so her arms were hanging at her sides.

"Why do you have her chained up?" I asked the guard who was moving around to sit in the desk chair. He propped his leg up on another chair and let out a sigh.

"Do you know how dangerous she is? She did this to me with her bare hands. She didn't use whatever her power is. We put those gloves on her so she can't use her power. I don't want to imagine what she can do with that."

"The King wants her brought up to the main hall. Now." I looked at Emily again. Her eyes were back to that lovely dark gray. I gave her a wink and shoved off the bars. She kissed her lips at me and smiled devilishly.

I was a fucking masochist. The fact that this girl threatened to kill me and I still wanted her. I was sick in the head. Those feelings that I thought were strong for her only intensified when I saw her. She was still as beautiful as ever. Her hair was hardly out of place and she had that leather get up on that was too hot. There was only a small scratch on the right side of her head.

Compared to the damage she'd done to one guard; it was impressive that was the only wound she incurred after passing through three lines of defense.

I took my time walking back up those slick spiral stairs. They were worse going back up and I was wearing shoes that had zero tread on them. I wished I could wear my boots, but nope I had to dress the part of a good little highborn.

I reached the top of the stairs and slammed the wooden door behind me. I leaned against it and scrubbed my hands up and down my face. I didn't know what was wrong with me. I got what I wanted. I wanted Emily here. And now she was here, but she was chained up in the dungeons.

I was planning to come back here and help her get out of the stronghold with her aunt. I knew that after that I would probably never hear from her or see her ever again. It would have killed me, but it would have been better than what was happening.

I heard a lot of noise coming from the main foyer. I walked down the hall to see what looked like every Talyrian streaming into the main hall. That's where the King wanted Emily brought. I wave of panic ripped through me. What in the hell was he going to do? The first thing that ran through my mind was a public execution, a morale booster and a show of what happens when our enemies try to break into the stronghold.

I wanted to race downstairs and get her out of that cell and out of this building. I would go with her too. If I was found helping our enemy, I would have to run.

A hand clamped onto my shoulder and I jumped. My father was standing there with a smile on his face. "Everything okay, son?" he asked.

"Umm, yeah," I muttered. No, everything was a fucking mess. I felt sick. This was all my fault. If I had left Autumn Falls when I discovered that Emily was a Corlissian, then none of this would be happening now. I should have just left her alone.

"Come on. The King wants everyone in the main hall. I'm not even sure what's going on." There was excitement in my father's voice. I don't ever remember hearing him sound like that.

Father led the two of us into the hall. We met up with Mom and Zoë who were standing close to where the two thrones were.

A woman with black hair and pale skin was sitting in the smaller throne. I was assuming she was the Queen, but I hadn't seen her since I'd been here.

There was a frown on her face. You'd think the highest-ranking female of the Talyrians would be a little happier.

I nudged Zoë with my elbow to get her attention. "Is that the Queen?" I whispered.

Zoë nodded her head. "It's rare to see her," she replied.

"Why does she look pissed?"

"She's not pissed, Killian. She's depressed. She and the King have been trying to have a kid for years and they can't. They say the King blames her for them not having a proper heir to the throne." Zoë leaned in closer to me. "Did you see Emily?" she asked.

I nodded my head. The worry in her eyes probably matched mine. I didn't know what was going to happen to Emily. I didn't know if I could save her. I couldn't see how I would be able to. If I made any move to save her, I would be put to death just for attempting to help our enemy. But I'd be damned if I let anything happen to the girl I loved.

Chapter 23
Emily

I came too when I felt a chain clamp around my wrist. I glanced down and it took my eyes a while to focus. I clearly had a concussion and I was in some dank ass basement. It smelled like mold and the floors were slick from there obviously being a fucking leak.

Once my eyes adjusted, I saw that I was in a cell. My hands had leather gloves over them and thick metal cuffs were clamped around both my wrists. I snorted at the gloves. They weren't going to do anything. Yes, they would prevent me from using normal pyromancy, but *incendia* would burn right through them. And it would stop me from using normal pulso morsus, but I didn't use normal pulso morsus or pulso metus.

I figured I'd let the guards have their false sense of security around me. It was cute that they thought these bars and gloves would protect them from me.

The guard whose leg I broke lumbered off and the other guard headed upstairs. He was going to get healed first since I knifed him in the gut. I thought the other guy should go first, but what did I know. It wasn't like I was a healer or anything.

I sighed and let my head hang. I was staring at the wet floor and trying to figure out where I was. I was assuming I was in the dungeons of the stronghold. I didn't know what would happen to me. I knew one thing for sure; I was not going down without one hell of a fight. I would set this place on fire before they took me down.

I heard a scrape on the floor and I popped my head up. I figured it was one of the guards, but it was Lian standing there. He was wearing a suit and even though I wanted to choke him I had to admit that he looked damn fine. Not that I would tell him that.

I knew that my eyes were glowing. I could see that this upset Lian. What did he expect? I wasn't going to throw my arms around him and confess that I had missed him. If my arms were around him, I wouldn't be hugging him that was for sure.

"Emily," he said as he wrapped his hands around the bars that separated us. "I cannot tell you how…" he stopped when the guard came limping around the corner. I smiled at how badly I had fucked him up. I was so damn proud of myself and I didn't even use a single power to do it.

I watched as he leaned against the edge of the desk and brought a blood covered cloth away from his face. You could really see all the damage the bottom of my boot did. His nose was broken and his bottom lip was fat. He had two black eyes too. He was so pretty!

"Be careful around that one. She may have all the outward appearance of an angel, but she is a killer," he said to Lian. I really didn't think I had the appearance of an angel, but thanks for the compliment.

"She did that to you?" Lian asked him. I was guessing he was playing stupid. He of all people knew how much damage I could inflict on someone with my bare hands.

"Broke my leg too," he grunted. "I would be up in the hospital, but Jenkins had to go up first because he was worse than I was if you can imagine that."

I was still smiling when Lian faced me again. "That wasn't very nice of you."

"I will do even worse to you," I replied.

"I think I could hold my own against you," he said in all seriousness.

I narrowed my eyes at him and walked forward. Those chains stretched my arms out behind me. I thought about burning through them just to scare the fuck out of Lian and the guard, but I refrained.

"You've been training for what, a week? I have been training to kill your kind since I came into this world. I would love to see you try and fight me for even a minute."

"Emily, taunt me as much as you want, but I will not fight you…ever. And no, that does not make me a coward. It makes me a guy who will not hit a girl."

I rolled my eyes at him and took a few steps back so my arms weren't at an awkward angle.

"Why do you have her chained up?" Lian asked the guard. Like he didn't know. He was really playing stupid.

The guard scooted around and sat down behind the desk and propped his broken leg up. "Do you know how dangerous she is? She did this to me with her bare hands. She didn't use whatever her power is. We put those gloves on her so she can't use her power. I don't want to imagine what she can do with that."

"The King wants her brought up to the main hall. Now," Lian stated. He winked at me as he pushed himself away from the bars. I blew him a kiss.

I swear we were the most messed up people in the world. Even in the positions we were in we were still toying with one another. There was something seriously wrong with the two of us. That in and of itself is why we were not meant to be together.

The guard struggled to pull himself up. The poor guy had just sat down too. He really needed to see a healer. Instead he was being ordered to haul me upstairs to meet their leader.

He limped over and unlocked the cell and came closer to me. He unlocked the cuffs and led me out of the cell. He shoved me forward and told me to sit in one of the chairs.

"You know the King is going to make an example of you," he said.

"Sounds like fun," I muttered.

"You won't be saying that when you're lying dead in the main hall."

"Well, I won't be saying anything if I'm dead. That is a side effect of dying."

"You have an attitude problem."

"Yeah, that is a side effect of your people killing my parents."

His mouth slowly parted. "Both of them?" he whispered.

I nodded my head. "Aren't you supposed to be taking me upstairs?" I asked.

"I'm waiting for Jenkins to come back," he said leaning against his desk. "We both need to take you up."

"Then when are you gonna get healed?" I asked.

He shrugged his shoulders. "Later, I guess."

"You need to get that leg reset. I could fix your nose for you."

He glared at me. "You're a healer?" he asked skeptically.

"Yup."

"Healers don't usually fight like you do."

"Oh, so you fight Corlissian healers regularly?"

"Well…no, but…can you really fix my nose?"

I took the glove off my right hand and stood up. I held my hand inches from his face and whispered, "*Sanare.*" I could have used one of my other powers on him and killed him. The thing was killing him would do me no good. I had no idea how to get out of where I was. He would at least take me upstairs and I had a better chance of escape. Plus, if I established a bit of trust with this guy he might come in handy later.

His nose stopped bleeding and the crack in his lip sealed shut. "I, uh, I need to snap your nose back in place," I said. He sighed and nodded his head. "Do you want to bite on a piece of wood or something?" I asked.

"No. Just do it."

"All right." I placed my hands on either side of his nose. "Breath in," I ordered. He did. "Now out." Just as he was exhaling, I shoved my right hand in and heard his nose crack.

He let out a scream. I jumped back from him. "That really fucking hurt," he growled.

"Stand up and I'll heal it now."

He did as I told him. I held my hand over his nose and watched it turned from a dark blue to a soft pink. I stood back and checked out my work.

"I would try and heal that leg, but I think it's best if you get that done by professionals."

He wiggled his nose up and down. "Hell, you did you a good job on my nose."

The other guard came back a few minutes later. "We're ordered to take her up to the main hall."

"Yeah, I heard all about it from the healers," Jenkins said. "All right little missy, time to meet our King."

Jenkins led the way. I was expecting us to go the same way Lian had gone, but we headed the opposite way. The other guard was behind me. I slowed my pace so I was walking beside him. I held my arm out to him and he smiled and accepted it.

"What's your name?" I asked.

"Wyatt. And yours?"

"Emily."

"It's nice to meet you, Emily. And don't worry yourself. Our King isn't the kind who has people killed. He probably just wants to meet the Corlissian who managed to get passed every line of defense. It's quite impressive what you did."

"Come on, you two!" Jenkins barked at us. "We don't want to keep his Royal Highness waiting."

"That guy is an ass," I muttered.

"Oh, I know. He's been my partner for two years and I've hated every second of it. I thought he might grow on me, but he never did. How's your head?" he asked.

"It's okay. I've had worse injuries."

"You know, with most people I would think they were joking, but I have feeling you're not lying. How many fights have to been in?" he asked.

Jenkins was standing in front of us holding a door open. I could see a flight of stairs.

"Umm, about five in the past couple months," I said as we went upstairs. Wyatt's pace slowed considerably on the stairs. He was putting most of his weight on the handrail, but he still kept a grip on my arm.

Jenkins scurried passed us and opened the door that was one flight up. Once we were through the door Jenkins grabbed my arm and yanked me forward. We walked down a long hall with marble floors. I glanced back to see Wyatt hobbling along behind us.

Jenkins rounded a corner and passed through a set of double doors that were wide open. The room was filled with people standing around all sides of the massive room. Some rose up on their toes to get a glimpse of me. Fucking Talyrians.

Jenkins grip on my arm tightened as we walked further into the hall. I kept my eyes fixed on the hardwood floor in front of me. I took a few deep breaths to calm myself down. I needed to have a clear mind if I was going to get myself out of this situation. Hell, if I talked myself out of fighting Midnight Brothers in the Perlinian Hotel I could talk myself out of this easily.

I glanced up quickly and saw some pale woman wearing black sitting on one of the thrones. The other throne was unoccupied. When we were near the thrones, Jenkins yanked me to a stop. Then he shoved me forward so I ended up on the floor. That dude was a serious jackass and he was going to be the first person I killed.

I felt that pain in my thigh again. I swear it was spreading. I felt a little feverish too. Then again that could be because I was in a massive room surrounded by nearly every fucking Talyrian.

I didn't try and sit up nor did I look around. I didn't want to see all those faces of the Talyrians waiting to see what would happen to me.

I heard the sound of shoes coming near me. It was the only sound in the room. A pair of shiny black shoes came into my field of vision. They stopped. I lifted my head slightly to a pair of dark gray pinstriped pants. My eyes traveled up further to a dark blue dress shirt with a dark gray pinstriped vest on over it. It seemed that all Talyrians men were well dressed, with the exception of their guards.

I lifted my head up so I could see this guy's face. I mean he was the King of all the Talyrians after all. I wanted to get a good view of the guy I was probably going to have to kill to get out of here.

I figured that whatever Sam stabbed me with was finally getting to my head because I was clearly hallucinating. There was no way that the face I was seeing was the real face of the King.

The King knelt down so he was closer to me. The face didn't change even as he got closer. A smile spread onto his face. "Hello, Emily," he whispered in that familiar voice. It hadn't changed at all.

"Dad?" I croaked.

CPSIA information can be obtained
at www.ICGtesting.com
Printed in the USA
BVHW050407311222
655320BV00004B/219